IN THE SINISTER HEART OF CHINATOWN,
LIFE COMES

AND GREED A ... **E**

SO-AVX-323

BEN CARTWRIGHT—He built the Ponderosa with nothing but sweat, grit, and stolid determination. But now with the fate of the vast Nevada ranchlands in jeopardy, Ben travels to San Francisco . . . where he becomes locked in a bidding war for precious timber rights . . . and where one of his sons draws him into a showdown in Chinatown's most dangerous den.

HOSS CARTWRIGHT—In San Francisco to rescue the kidnapped niece of the Cartwright clan's faithful cook, Hop Sing, he follows a crooked trail through seedy Chinatown . . . only to end up squaring off against the powerful underworld kingpin with a stranglehold on the city.

ALDINA CUTHBERT—A passionate crusader for women's rights, she is determined to save innocent young girls from lives of brutal degradation on the dangerous streets of Chinatown. But to break the far-reaching slave trade, she will need the help of Hoss Cartwright.

CHAN TAN TAN—The berobed Oriental's smooth, soft-spoken ways shroud his evil and murderous nature. The king of the Chinese underworld, he isn't about to let a foolhardy western rancher bring down his empire . . . and he's gambling on Hoss Cartwright's one weakness: his basic human decency.

DAVID THORNTON KENDALL III—He has inherited legal control of the vast Cartwright holdings, and he isn't going to give it up without a fight. Ambitious and smart, the green young lawyer will stoop to anything to cover up a terrible mistake . . . a mistake that could cost Ben Cartwright the future of the Ponderosa.

The Bonanza™ Series
Ask your bookseller for the books you have missed

THE PIONEER SPIRIT
THE PONDEROSA EMPIRE
THE HIGH-STEEL HAZARD
JOURNEY OF THE HORSE

JOURNEY OF
THE HORSE

STEPHEN CALDER

BANTAM BOOKS
NEW YORK • TORONTO • LONDON • SYDNEY • AUKLAND

JOURNEY OF THE HORSE
A Bantam Domain Book / June 1993

ISBN 0-553-29044-4

Published simultaneously in the United States and Canada

PRINTED IN THE UNITED STATES OF AMERICA

RAD   0 9 8 7 6 5 4 3 2 1

For Pa,
who first took me to Nevada and Bonanza country

CHAPTER 1

Pulling his watch from the pocket of his broadcloth trousers, Ben Cartwright snapped open the battered steel case and stared at the spidery hands. The Waltham was a dependable watch, almost as dependable as his son Adam. But now it was half past six and there was no sign of Adam or sons Hoss and Joseph. All were due to return home for dinner at seven, but Adam was returning from Virginia City, with the mail.

Ben clicked the watch cover shut and slipped the timepiece back inside his trousers pocket. He stared at the map of the Ponderosa on the wall behind his desk, considering how much easier it had been to carve the great ranch out of the wilderness than it was to keep it going, the pressures of the times eroding at the boundaries from all sides. Maybe the letter he hoped Adam might bring would remove one of those threats, the pressure to start clearcutting timber on Ponderosa land bordering Lake Tahoe.

The silver mines of the Comstock Lode had never produced more than they had this year, but for every ton of silver the miners brought up from the ground, they took down a forest of timber into the hot and damp bowels of the earth. On the Comstock Lode veins of silver were the biggest ever found by man, some as much as sixty-five feet wide. Without square-set timbering, the igneous syenite laced with these great veins would collapse under its

1

own weight once the silver ore was removed. Ben had seen the timbered skeletons beneath the earth, had bought timber for Cartwright Enterprises' own Bristlecone mine and knew of the mines' voracious appetite for wood.

Because the timber convenient to Virginia City had already been felled, the Ponderosa's wooded slopes were coveted by many. The letter from San Francisco might ease Ben's worries, if only his bid was highest. Across the border in California's High Sierras, the federal government was selling leases for timber. With one of those leases, Ben figured he could reduce the pressures on the Ponderosa and make an honest dollar in the process. After all, a dozen Virginia and Truckee Railroad trains a day carried timber into Virginia City to shore up the mines, and firewood to fuel the smelters. Respected San Francisco lawyer David Thornton Kendall, Jr., who handled all Cartwright legal business in California, had submitted a $75,000 Cartwright bid for timber rights on 50,000 acres of high country forests.

If Kendall's letter or telegram arrived tonight with good news, Ben planned to celebrate by breaking out a bottle of California desert wine. Ben could smell the aroma of Hop Sing's cooking from the kitchen, and could hear his discordant singing. He much preferred Hop Sing's cooking to his warbling. Of all the things Hop Sing could do well, singing was not one of them. A clatter of pots and pans accompanied his solo for a moment, followed by a crash of utensils. Hop Sing followed with a smattering of Chinese, then resumed his song.

Ben paced around the stocky redwood desk where he conducted the Ponderosa's business, his fingers clenching into fists as he walked. At fifty-eight, Ben Cartwright still stood straight, his 190-pound, muscled torso the match of many men half his age. His silver hair, still full and thick, was combed back and topped his head like the majestic crown of a snow-covered mountain. His eyes were the color of fine mahogany beneath his black eyebrows, which were the last remnants of the fine black hair of his youth. His complexion was tanned and rugged, his face finely chiseled, with a broad nose and sharp cheekbones. The experience of many years and many places was etched in the crow's-feet tugging at the corners of his eyes. He had traveled the world as a sailor and crossed this continent afterward, holding his own against the elements and other men. But for all he had done and all he had seen, only his three sons meant more to him than the Ponderosa.

Outside, Ben heard the sound of a trotting horse. Adam? He slid around the desk, its papers neatly stacked in precise order of importance, and stepped quickly to the window, parting the curtain with his thick fingers. Dismounting from his black and white pinto was his youngest son, Joseph—Little Joe to everyone else. Joseph's face split into a wide smile as he jumped from the saddle and tossed the reins around the hitching post. Jogging toward the house, he looked back over his shoulder, then disappeared from Ben's view. Almost simultaneously, Ben heard the squeak of the thick wooden door opening on thirsty hinges. He would have to ask Hop Sing to oil them.

Ben walked away from his desk and entered the hallway in time to see Little Joe flinging his flat-brim felt hat at the table by the door, rather than hanging it on one of the four hat hooks. Ben just shook his head. At nineteen, Little Joe had a free spirit, much like his mother had had, though he still lacked her maturity. The smallest and handsomest of his three sons, Little Joe had a quick smile punctuated by the dimple in his chin. Laughing as he took off his gun belt, he dropped it on the table by his hat, then slapped at the dust of his denim jacket.

"Ahem," Ben cleared his throat. "How many times must I tell you to do that outside or in back?"

Little Joe spun around, the impish grin draining away from his face like water from a leak, his gold-flecked hazel eyes widening with surprise. "Didn't realize you were here, Pa."

"So I gathered, Joseph," Ben replied. "Have you seen any sign of Adam?"

Little Joe shrugged. "I passed the railroad siding. His chestnut was in the corral."

One of the advantages of being a stockholder in the Virginia and Truckee Railroad was having a siding where

Ponderosa hands could load stock or where he and his sons could catch a train to Carson City and from there to Virginia City or north to Reno. Ben took a deep breath as Little Joe brushed another layer of trail dust onto the rug by the door. "Where's Hoss, didn't you two work cattle together?"

Before Little Joe could answer, Ben heard the sound of a galloping horse and a yell.

Little Joe jumped to the door and cracked it open, peeking outside. Instantly, he shoved the door closed and latched it. "Excuse me, Pa," he whispered. With that, he dashed from the door and bounded up the stairs, two steps at a time.

No sooner had Little Joe disappeared than the door seemed struck by a storm, pounding the thick wood. Ben moved quickly and unlatched the door. As it groaned open, Hoss howled in like windblown debris.

"Where's that runty little brother of mine?" he demanded.

Ben shook his head again. "What this time?"

Hoss stepped around his father, his blue eyes taking in every possible hiding place in the parlor, the dining room, and the office. "Ran upstairs, didn't he, Pa?"

Ben nodded.

Hoss pounded his palm with his fist. "That runt untied the cinch on my saddle. You know what happened when I tried to mount?"

Covering his mouth with his hand, Ben moved too late to disguise his amusement.

Hoss shoved his balled fists on his hips and stared at his father, his teeth gritted between narrow lips, his ice-blue eyes wide with exasperation, his prominent chin jutting forward. "Dad-blame-it, Pa, Little Joe's hell with the hide off, always playing the polecat, only difference is you just can't smell him coming." At 240 pounds, Hoss could put a lot of weight behind his words, but more frustration than anger heated his utterances against his little brother.

Smiling, Ben nodded at his middle son. "There's still a lot of boy in Joseph."

Hoss scowled. "Runt of the litter!" Then Hoss spun

around on his heels and strode out the door, slamming it in his wake.

Ben flinched. Hoss never seemed to pass through a door without banging it shut, even when he was perfectly happy, which was most of the time. He didn't realize his own strength, mainly because he had a gentle touch about him. Ben chuckled again. The mountains must have shaken when Hoss tumbled to earth.

Outside, Ben could hear Hoss slapping his hat against his clothes, brushing his frustrations away like the dust from his pants.

The stairs creaked and Ben twisted around in time to see a flash of Little Joe's face at the corner. "Okay, Joseph, fun's over," he called. Little Joe reappeared around the corner, then came slowly down the steps, looking around the room for Hoss.

"One of these days Hoss'll outsmart you, make you regret this mischief," Ben said.

Little Joe laughed. "Ah, Pa, he's not that smart."

"And you're not big enough to take your medicine from him."

Little Joe cocked his head at his father and stretched as tall as he could without standing on his toes. "Why, I'm five feet nine and a quarter inches tall. And still growing."

Ben covered a smile with his hand and just shook his head. Behind him the front door squeaked open. Without looking back, Ben spoke emphatically. "I don't want you bringing your pranks inside, Hoss."

"You've got the wrong Cartwright," came the reply.

Ben spun around to face his eldest son. "Adam! Any mail?"

Adam held up a canvas mailbag with v&TRR stenciled on the side. Offering it to his father, Adam spoke quietly. "I don't think you'll find what you're after."

Taking the bag, Ben spread its leather-lined opening and shoved his hand inside as he moved toward the desk. "How do you know, Adam?"

His eldest son's black eyes stared over a patrician nose. "Lawyer Kendall in San Francisco." Adam removed his hat and hung it from the second brass hook by the door. His hands fell to his waist and he unbuckled his holster, wrapping his cartridge belt precisely around his Colt .45, single-action Army revolver, and placing it on the table.

Ben pulled about four dozen letters from the bag, then dumped a couple more onto the desk, scattering them like a kid opening a sack of marbles. Bending over the desk, he began to leaf through them.

"I handled all the Bristlecone correspondence in Virginia City, Pa," Adam said as he ran his fingers through his black hair, then wriggled them back through his widow's peak. He scrutinized Little Joe and shook his head. "What'd you do to Hoss this time?"

"Uncinched his saddle," Little Joe answered, his brow furrowed. "What about Kendall and San Francisco?"

Adam ignored the question and strode to the desk beside his father. "Unless I overlooked it, Kendall's reply is not there."

As Ben checked the letters, he sorted them into three piles by their importance. The last letter he held a moment between his fingers, studying the Chinese hieroglyphics. "Hop Sing's," he muttered, then dropped the letter with the Celestial handwriting onto the corner of the desk. He straightened a moment, then put his hands on his hips. "I don't understand it," he said to Adam. "Thornton's always been so prompt responding. He should know something by now."

"What?" Little Joe said, stepping to the desk beside Adam. "What's this all about?"

"Joseph," Ben said, his gaze boring into Little Joe's like twin brown augers, "go get cleaned up for dinner."

Little Joe turned to Adam for support. Receiving none, he nodded curtly at his father, said, "Yes, sir," and slipped away, passing by the dining table and into the kitchen, headed for the back door to avoid Hoss. As soon as Little Joe entered the kitchen, Hop Sing's voice lifted in frustration that his culinary kingdom had been invaded.

Ben slumped down in his chair, propped his elbows on the desk between stacks of unopened mail and rested his forehead in the palm of his hands. "You don't think Kendall's turned this over to Davey to handle, do you?"

"Perhaps," Adam said, sitting on the corner of the desk. "This isn't that complicated a matter is it? Important, yes, but complicated? I'm carrying a bigger load of responsibility for Cartwright Enterprises, why shouldn't Kendall allow the same for his own son?"

Ben studied Adam a moment. "You've always had a higher regard for Davey than I have."

Adam nodded. "I know him better. He's no longer Davey, Pa, now he's David."

"He's not the man his father is, Adam."

"Neither am I, Pa. Nor Hoss, nor Little Joe."

Ben lifted his head, pursing his lips and stroking his chin between the thumb and finger of his writing hand. "Some fathers aren't the measure of their sons."

At the sound of Hop Sing working around the dinner table, Adam stood up from the corner of the desk. "Give Kendall a couple more days. You know how slow the government can be."

"Two days, then I'll telegraph San Francisco." Ben pushed himself up from the leather seat and accompanied Adam to the dining room. "Smells good, Hop Sing," he said. He checked his watch; it was precisely seven o'clock.

Hop Sing clasped his hands together in front of his chin and nodded once at Ben before disappearing back into the kitchen, quickly reemerging with a bowl of plum sauce and a platter of roasted squab with almond stuffing. Dishes of boiled carrots, stewed tomatoes, and boiled cabbage appeared on the table with each of Hop Sing's subsequent trips.

As Ben and Adam stood in the dining room, the front door swung open, admitting Hoss, then slammed shut. At Ben's hard stare, Hoss grinned sheepishly, acknowledging he had closed the door too exuberantly. As the Cartwright men took their positions at the table, Hop Sing emerged from the kitchen, Little Joe trailing him to the table. Hoss scowled and Little Joe answered with a chuckle.

"Mind your manners," Ben commanded, taking his

seat at the head of the table. "No wine tonight," he told Hop Sing, who retreated into the kitchen with the unopened bottle.

Adam moved into his chair at the foot of the table, his back straight, his expression serious.

Hoss and Little Joe approached their chairs from opposite sides of the table. Hoss plopped into his, grabbed his napkin and tucked it in his collar. His father grimaced. Little Joe eased tentatively into his chair across from Hoss, suspicious of his huge brother, particularly when Hoss offered him his widest gap-toothed smile.

Clearing his throat, Ben got Hoss's and Little Joe's attention, then offered thanks. As soon as he was done, Hoss grabbed the platter of squab and claimed two of the browned birds for himself. Immediately, he picked up the bowl of plum sauce and dumped a couple spoonfuls on the succulent birds.

Hop Sing came from the kitchen again, carrying freshly baked bread and a pot of hot coffee. As he filled Ben's cup, Hoss took the basket of bread and, ignoring the knife by his plate, tore off a chunk, then passed the basket to Adam.

"Good meal, Hop Sing," Hoss said after savoring his first bite of squab and cabbage. "Pass the pepper, Adam."

Hop Sing scowled for an instant, not liking Hoss's desire to season his supper beyond what he thought appropriate. After filling everyone's coffee cup, Hop Sing bowed to the head of the table. "Anything more, Mr. Ben?"

"No thank you, Hop Sing," he replied. The cook nodded, then stepped toward the kitchen, stopping the instant Ben held up his hand. "I forgot your letter."

Hop Sing watched with displeasure as Hoss continued to dash more seasoning on his squab from the crystal pepper shaker.

"Joseph," Ben said, "would you get the letter off the corner of my desk for Hop Sing?"

Little Joe nodded. "Sure, Pa."

As his son stood up, Ben gave instructions to Hop Sing. "Tomorrow, oil the door hinges, they're squeaking.

And sweep the entry, one of my sons tracked in some dust," he added as Little Joe passed by.

Hoss, seeing Joe's back to him and his father occupied with giving Hop Sing directions, unscrewed the lid to the pepper. With his fork he reached across the table, lifted Little Joe's squab, and dumped a mound of pepper beneath it. He shook his fork, and the squab slid back onto Little Joe's plate, hiding the mound of black pepper.

"Where's the letter?" Little Joe called from his father's desk.

Ben looked from Hop Sing to Hoss, pausing a moment, sensing something was wrong. "On the corner of the desk. You'll know it when you see it."

"Oh, here it is!" Little Joe returned to the table, holding the letter toward the window as if the light could interpret the Chinese for him. As he reached the table, he handed the letter to his father, who stared at the parchment, amazed that a letter could come from China, as this one apparently had, and find Hop Sing on the Ponderosa in western Nevada.

Hop Sing placed the coffeepot on the table, then looked from plate to plate, his gaze stopping at Hoss's.

Hoss held up his fork, pointing it at the cook. "Best squab you've ever roasted. Flavor must be from good seasoning."

Ben offered Hop Sing his letter.

After studying the letter for an instant between Ben's fingers, Hop Sing snatched it up and tore open the end, pulling out the single sheet of paper. His eyes scanned it furiously.

Little Joe, glancing at Hop Sing, forked a bit of squab and sopped it in the sauce at the base of the roasted bird. Hoss snickered as Little Joe lifted a pepper-covered bite to his mouth, his teeth closing around the food, his fork emerging empty. He twisted his lips as if considering the subtle flavorings. Then he yelled, "What the—" spitting the bite into his napkin. "Hop Sing, what did you do to this bird?"

Hop Sing stood opposite Ben, bewildered, glancing up from his letter to the table, not understanding what had happened, alternately staring at Little Joe's plate and the letter.

Unable to stand it anymore, Hoss cut loose with a thunderous laugh, pounding the table but once before drawing an unamused stare from his father.

Little Joe shook his fork at Hoss. "You did it," he said, then scooted the roasted squab across his plate with the fork, leaving behind a trail of pepper. Before he could say anything else, he was interrupted by Hop Sing.

"Hop Sing cook meals, slave all day, only one Hop Sing," the cook said. "Hop Sing sweep floor, oil hinges. Hop Sing mad, leave Ponderosa."

Before anyone could apologize, Hop Sing grabbed the coffeepot and disappeared into the kitchen. His departure was punctuated by the clang of the coffeepot being slammed atop the stove.

Ben stared hard at Hoss and Little Joe.

CHAPTER 2

C ome morning, Hoss dressed quietly and slipped from his bedroom into the upstairs hallway, the wooden floor creaking under his weight. Carrying his boots, he shut the door softly and hoped he had arisen before his father. Passing his father's bedroom, he paused, looking for a thread of light seeping from under the door. There was none. That was good. He could sneak downstairs, grab a handful of something to eat, and escape outside. Nothing made up for mistakes better in Ben Cartwright's books than hard work. Perhaps he could make amends that way for offending Hop Sing.

The stairs groaned under his weight. Escape seemed so close that Hoss smiled, until he saw the glow of light coming from the dining table. Reaching the foot of the stairs, Hoss gulped at the sound of his father's voice.

"Going somewhere, Eric Haas Cartwright?"

Hoss's shoulders slumped. "Chores need doing." He dropped his boots by the stairs and looked at his father, who sat at the head of a table still cluttered with dinner dishes. Running his hands through his thinning brown hair, Hoss gritted his teeth and approached the table. Little Joe was responsible for this!

"Have a seat, Hoss," Ben commanded. "Hop Sing's been mad, but never like this. He's asked for his money, and he's never done that before." Ben pointed to two bulg-

11

ing woolen blankets tied at the top with twine. "Hop Sing's belongings. He's quitting."

Hoss drooped into his chair. "Pa, if this ain't the dadburndest bunch of foolishness. Little Joe's always into mischief and I can't get anything on him without creating a bushel of trouble. Maybe Hop Sing's bluffing, you think?"

Ben shook his head. "You've offended him, even if it was a prank. He's proud of the meals he cooks, as good as anyplace, including the Washoe Club in Virginia City."

"But Pa, it just ain't fair. Joe uncinching my saddle and me busting my tail and everyone thinking it's funny. Me, I put pepper on Little Joe's plate and now we'll starve when Hop Sing leaves."

"Some of us'll last longer than others," Ben said, nodding at Hoss's girth.

"Life's still not fair, Pa."

"Nobody said it was, Hoss. I want you to apologize to Hop Sing and convince him to stay."

Hoss sighed. "Can't Little Joe help? He started all this."

Ben's eyes narrowed. "No!"

"Dad-blame-it," Hoss answered, and pushed himself away from the table. "I might just as well get it over with."

Hoss picked up a handful of dishes and marched around the table into the kitchen, expecting to see Hop Sing behind the stove, busily fixing breakfast. But the kitchen was dark and cool. Hoss could never remember a time when he had walked into the kitchen when it wasn't warmer than the rest of the house, testament to Hop Sing's dedication. And there was always something hot that he could eat to tide him over until the next meal. Not this morning, however. No kitchen warmth, no breakfast aroma, no Hop Sing!

Unloading dishes on the kitchen counter, Hoss fumbled for matches to light a lamp. A match flame spread from his fingers into a ball of light as he lit the burner on a kerosene lamp. Hop Sing's room was just off the hallway that led to the back door. Hoss strode to his door, knocking softly at first, then harder as he awaited a response.

"Hop Sing busy," the Celestial said. "Hop Sing not change mind, leave today."

"Dad-blame-it, Hop Sing, I didn't mean no harm," Hoss pleaded. "I was just getting even with Little Joe." Hop Sing could be stubborn, almost mulish when his mind was set. Hoss tried bribery. "I'll chop your firewood for a month," he offered, knowing Hop Sing detested that chore most of all.

"You chop wood, Hop Sing go anyway."

Hoss gritted his teeth. Little Joe started this mess, and now he was getting all the grief. He spun around on his bootless feet and retraced his steps to the kitchen. He'd do dishes this morning; he'd cook breakfast; anything to get Hop Sing to change his mind! Hoss pushed open the kitchen door, stepped to the dining table and grabbed a load of dishes. He felt his father's cold stare, then heard giggling from the stairs.

There stood Little Joe, his hand muffling only a fraction of his amusement. Little Joe toed at Hoss's boot. "Barefoot and doing dishes." Little Joe snickered, but the laugh died on his lips at the sound of his father's voice.

"Joseph," Ben commanded, "you started this with your pranks. Since Hop Sing has quit, you can handle the dishes and cooking."

Little Joe sputtered and stepped with disbelief toward the table. "Hop Sing quit?"

Hoss lowered the dishes to the table. With an exaggerated sweep of his arm, he pointed toward Joe then back to the dishes. "They're all yours, little brother!"

"But Pa, Hoss insulted Hop Sing, not me. What's he gotta do?"

Ben stood up from the table. "Convince Hop Sing to stay."

Little Joe grumbled beneath his breath.

"Pardon me, Joseph?" Ben stood with eyes squarely focused on Little Joe's. "We'll have no insolent behavior in this house, Joseph Cartwright."

Hoss cocked his head at Little Joe, but the swagger withered beneath his father's quick gaze.

"Nor from you, Eric Haas Cartwright."

Hoss nodded, then Little Joe. Through the window behind their father, Hoss could see the landscape gradually shedding the layers of darkness, giving way to the pastels of a new day.

Little Joe bent over the table and gathered knives and forks like he was plucking a bouquet of weeds. Hoss circled the table and headed for the stairs. Sitting down on the bottom step, he tugged his boots on and watched Little Joe. He thought about suggesting his little brother put on an apron, then reconsidered when he saw his father watching him, as if he could read his mind. Little Joe pushed his way through the kitchen door, carrying another load of dishes.

When the door opened again, out marched Hop Sing, wearing a coarse blue cotton blouse and baggy trousers. His head was crowned with a broad-brimmed hat of split bamboo, hiding his hair except the pigtail, or queue, which reached just beyond his waist. In his hand he carried a bamboo pole he had brought from China.

Ben shook his head. "Hop Sing, you're welcome to stay here."

The Celestial bowed his head to Ben. "Hop Sing go. Never do good work. Door squeak, need oil. Rug by door always dirty, no matter how much Hop Sing sweep. Only one Hop Sing. Too much work."

Ben shot a hard glance at Little Joe, who retreated to the kitchen door.

Hoss unfolded himself from the stair step and stretched to his full six feet, four inches. "I'll chop firewood for a month."

Hop Sing nodded, drawing a brief smile from Hoss until he spoke. "Hop Sing must go. Long walk to San Francisco."

Hoss's jaw dropped. "I didn't mean to upset you so."

"I'll apologize, too, Hop Sing. The Ponderosa needs you," Little Joe said meekly.

Nodding again, Hop Sing moved to the two woolen

blankets tied at the top like bags of giant marbles. He slid the bamboo pole under a couple of loops of twine strangling one bag, then picked up the second bag and attached it to the other end of the pole. Then he bent down and picked up the pole at the center, balancing it over his shoulder. He took a couple steps toward the door, turning carefully so his load missed the furniture. "Hop Sing hope best for Mr. Ben Cartwright and Ponderosa." Then he angled for the door.

Ben looked at Hoss. "Get the door for him, then come here."

"Yes sir," Hoss answered. Moving around a couple of chairs, he unlatched the door, then swung it open as Hop Sing passed wordlessly outside. "You can stay, Hop Sing." Hoss watched the bamboo hat bob a couple times, Hop Sing's queue moving with him. Walk to California? Hoss could not believe his joke was resulting in this. Why, Hop Sing might just as well swim to China once he reached San Francisco as walk that far from the Ponderosa. Hoss couldn't remember ever feeling more helpless. Meekly, he closed the door.

When he shuffled back to his father, he saw Ben standing there, his muscled arms folded across his chest. "Boys," he said, "you've got your work cut out for you. Joseph, as I said before, your job is to do all the cooking and kitchen chores."

"Aw, Pa—" Little Joe started. He stopped when Ben answered his words with a cold stare.

"Hoss, you're job is still to convince Hop Sing to return."

"Dad-blame-it, Pa, I'm not a good talker. I tried my best and he left anyway. I'll do the kitchen chores, if you'll let Little Joe talk him into coming back."

"Okay by me, Pa," Little Joe chimed in, a smile appearing on his face as he looked at the dirty dishes remaining on the table.

Ben shook his head. "Not by me. Now I suggest you both get on with your assigned tasks."

"Yes, Pa," Hoss answered.

Little Joe nodded.

Ben nodded back, then started for the stairs, pausing on the second step and turning around.

"Hoss, hitch up the buckboard and bring Hop Sing back after he's had a chance to walk off some of his anger. Don't come back here without him!"

This time Hoss nodded. Ben headed to the top of the stairs, disappearing from view.

When he was certain his father was not coming back down, Little Joe chuckled again. "If you can't convince Hop Sing to return, I don't guess we'll be seeing you on the Ponderosa anymore, brother."

Hoss's brow furrowed and his lips parted. He stood speechless for a moment, then pointed his finger at Little Joe. "If you're gonna be doing the cooking, it won't be worth coming back. We'll starve, if you don't poison us first." Hoss moved toward the door, stopping a moment to jerk his hat off its peg and tug it down over his head. Behind him he heard Little Joe stepping out of the dining area to watch. Out of frustration, Hoss picked up his holster and unwrapped his gun belt from around the Smith & Wesson Russian .44-caliber revolver. He started to put it on.

"Gonna shoot him if you can't talk him back, Hoss?" Joe giggled, then disappeared around the corner into the kitchen.

Hoss growled in added frustration, took a step toward the kitchen, then caught himself. Why let Little Joe bring on more trouble? He slapped the gun belt and revolver back on the table and walked outside, the door slamming behind him. He winced, told himself he needed to be more careful about shutting that door so hard.

Hop Sing had disappeared somewhere down the road. Afoot, he wouldn't be hard to catch. Hoss took his time going to the barn, giving himself extra moments to think through his plea for Hop Sing's return.

Like everything on the Ponderosa, the barn was big and sturdy, built to last and to handle the varied and multiple needs of the ranch. Hoss unbarred the door and swung it open. The horses stirred in their stalls, expecting their morning feeding. "You fellas can go hungry for a while, like me," Hoss said, turning from the door toward the buckboard and heavy wagon.

He grabbed the buckboard's wooden shafts with his strong hands and pulled the wagon outside. "Dad-blame-it," he said as he dropped the shafts.

From the barn he could still hear the stamping of the horses, impatient for their morning feeding. Hoss strode back inside, taking a single strap harness from the tack room and carrying it to the stall where a dappled gray gelding was tossing its head, awaiting fodder instead of a harness. The gray stamped and blew. Slipping the harness over its back, Hoss pulled the leather tight against its barrel chest, then hooked the wide leather belly band beneath its stomach and connected the breeching strap around its rump. After hooking the martingale between the leather collar and the belly band, he slid the headpiece over the gray's head, hooking the straps and then pulling the reins back over the animal's rump.

Hoss had a gentle touch with animals, and the gray backed out of the stall at the twitch of his wrists on the reins. Clearing the stall, the gray turned instinctively toward the barn door, the leather harness creaking with each stride. The gelding moved instinctively toward the buckboard, and Hoss had little trouble backing it between the tongue shafts and attaching the harness to the wagon. "Easy boy," he said out of habit. He drooped the reins over the spring-mounted seat and checked the harness a final time before climbing in the buckboard, the seat settling under his weight. He jostled the reins, and the dappled gray danced forward to the music of creaking leather and a rattling buckboard. Glancing toward the house, Hoss saw Little Joe watching him from the kitchen window. Mockingly, Hoss tipped his hat at his little brother, figuring the sentence to wash and cook until Hop Sing's return would wound Little Joe's pride. Laughing, he shook the reins against the gray's rump, and the gelding broke into a trot.

The road from the ranch house meandered through the great ponderosa pines that had so captivated his father's imagination that he would name his great ranch after them. The cool air of late spring carried the pleasant vanilla scent common to the bark of the pines, invigorating Hoss. A Steller's jay shook its pointed feathery crown at the buckboard and lifted its deep blue wings, then squawked a warning to its forest companions. A pair of chipmunks darted across the road up ahead. Hoss took a deep breath, savoring the fresh morning air and nature's ever-changing canvas. Give him the countryside over any city anywhere, he figured, but right now, most of all, give him Hop Sing.

After rounding a bend, the dappled gray slowed instinctively and Hoss saw Hop Sing walking down the middle of the road, his belongings swaying from the bamboo pole balanced on his shoulder. Without looking back, Hop Sing moved to the side of the road to make way for the buckboard.

Hoss eased back gently on the reins and the dappled gray slowed even more. When the buckboard reached Hop Sing, Hoss said, "Long walk to San Francisco. Want a ride to the place you belong?"

Hop Sing kept moving, turning his head toward Hoss, his eyes dark and determined. "Hop Sing can't stop, San Francisco long way." His resolve was as steady as his stride.

Never had Hoss seen Hop Sing like this. He was only five feet, four inches, and maybe 125 pounds, but he seemed bigger than that now. In other times, Hoss figured he could have physically forced Hop Sing to obey. A foot taller and almost twice Hop Sing's weight, Hoss knew he could overpower the cook, but he wasn't sure he could match Hop Sing's determination, not today, anyway. Hoss took off his hat and held it over his chest. "I didn't mean no insult to your cooking, Hop Sing. Really! I was just trying to get even with Little Joe."

"Hop Sing not mad at you."

"Then ride with me."

Hop Sing stopped, the buckboard passing him by before Hoss could halt the dappled gray. Hop Sing walked up to the back of the buckboard, lifted his belongings off his shoulder and dropped them behind the seat. Then he pulled himself up into the buckboard, sliding into the narrow slot Hoss's broad girth left on the seat.

Smiling, Hoss slapped his hat back on his head and shook the reins against the rump of the dappled gray. Finally, he had convinced Hop Sing to return to the Ponderosa with him. After two hundred yards the buckboard approached a small clearing among the trees. There was enough room there for Hoss to turn the buckboard around without backing. As he angled the buckboard off the trail and began his wide circle, Hoss grinned broadly. He had already convinced Hop Sing to return to the Ponderosa, and he'd bet Little Joe wasn't even through doing his dishes. The smile withered on his face at the commotion of Hop Sing beside him.

The Celestial was jabbering in Chinese and gesticulating with his arms. He twisted around in the seat and threw his bags of belongings out. Then Hop Sing babbled more Chinese and jumped from the buckboard, landing solidly on his feet, his hat flying from his head, his queue bouncing like a convulsive snake behind him.

"Whoa, whoa," Hoss called, drawing back on the reins. "What is it now, Hop Sing? You're coming home." Remembering his father's directive not to return to the Ponderosa without the cook, Hoss jerked off his hat and scratched his head.

Hop Sing retrieved his own hat, pulled it snugly over his forehead, then picked up his belongings, balancing the bamboo pole over his shoulder. "Hop Sing go to Carson City," he said. "Take train to San Francisco."

"Okay, okay, Hop Sing, climb aboard, I'll take you to the train station." Hoss's shoulders slumped with frustration.

Hop Sing wearily stowed his belongings in the back of the buckboard and eyed Hoss suspiciously before climbing back onto the bench seat.

They drove wordlessly for a couple of miles, passing the railroad siding the Virginia and Truckee Railroad had built on the Ponderosa for Ben Cartwright and reaching the main road into Carson City. Along the way, Hoss kept wondering what he could do to change Hop Sing's mind. As the buckboard rounded a bend and Carson City appeared before them, he still had no plan. And time was running out.

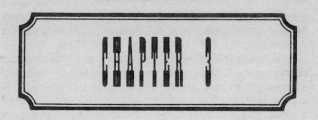

CHAPTER 3

The telegraph key clattered in the Carson City station, the circuit lever working up and down as the Morse message came in a letter at a time. Molly Ashe deciphered the communication from San Francisco in a handwriting as elegant as her long delicate fingers. As the only woman telegrapher on the Virginia and Truckee, she was as respected for her skills on the key as she was for her beauty. Even now as she took the message, two men stood on the platform outside the station window, admiring her blond hair, button nose, and her green eyes whenever they glanced up from the pencil and pad to the clock on the wall. Her delicate lips turned down at the corners as she finished taking the message. She hated receiving bad news, especially for a Virginia and Truckee stockholder. Folding the paper, she slipped it inside a yellow envelope and wrote Ben Cartwright's name on it. Then she stuck her pencil beneath the band of the green eyeshade she wore.

Glancing up from her desk, she saw two men quickly turn their heads. She smiled, amused at their attention, then stood up and straightened her bright green, ankle-length skirt. Adjusting the sleeve garters which made the arms of her full blouse appear like giant white flowers about to bloom, she slipped through the door to the passenger counter, where the crowd was gathering for the train to Reno. This train was the busiest of the morning because it connected with the Central Pacific express for San Francisco.

Ticket Agent Oliver Myers looked past the customer counting out money for the San Francisco fare and scowled at two men in the station corner, one whittling on a stick and the other sending a stream of tobacco juice at a corner spittoon, both dirtying the floor he had swept not an hour ago. Myers pushed the wire-rimmed glasses up on his nose and snorted. "Any baggage?" he asked the customer, who pointed to a trunk. Myers checked the man's payment, deposited it in the cash drawer and pulled out a coupon ticket. Stamping it with an inked marker, he handed the ticket to the passenger. "Next," he called, and another man stepped forward. Myers scowled as the two scruffy men who had been littering the back corner of the station sidled up to the line.

Molly Ashe stepped beside the ticket agent, who was half a head shorter than her. "Need any help, Oliver?"

"No," he said, frowning.

Molly had anticipated his refusal, being accustomed to his gruffness and his lordly manner when it came to his domain as station manager of the Carson City depot. Of the three largest stops on the Virginia and Truckee, this was the least prestigious, and that was vinegar to Myers's ego. Virginia City was the biggest jewel in the Virginia and Truckee crown simply because so much wealth came out of the mining metropolis and so many dignitaries traveled to the most influential city between St. Louis and San Francisco. Reno, to the north, was the stop on the transcontinental railway. All Carson City could boast of was being the capital of Nevada, making it a sometime stop for cigar-smoking politicians and the herd of influence-seeking whiskey dispensers who followed them for personal gain.

Myers had a close-cropped beard and big ears that on a larger man might have passed unnoticed. Barely five feet, four inches tall in the highest heels he could get on a pair of shoes without being ridiculed, he was a runt of a man, always out to prove himself the match of any other.

The bigger the man he dealt with, the more obnoxious he became. And it galled him particularly that Molly was not only taller than him, but also a better telegrapher.

Molly backed into the door of the telegraph room just as the baggage clerk darted out of the adjacent baggage room. Effortlessly, the muscular man picked up the trunk that had just been checked and carried it into the baggage room, dumping it on a cart. Molly checked the clock; fifteen minutes until the Reno train arrived.

The depot's doors swung open and a Chinese man entered carrying his belongings on a pole. She recalled having seen him somewhere, but for a moment could not place him. Then Hoss Cartwright came in, his arms outstretched, imploring the Chinese man about something, and Molly remembered the Celestial as Hop Sing, the Cartwright cook she had seen at a dance last fall at the Ponderosa. She smiled, and several in the station turned to watch, giggling that a man as big as Hoss was having trouble with a man Hop Sing's size.

Oliver Myers sniffed his nose at the sight of Hop Sing, then cleared his throat as if giving an imperial order for all to heed. The two men who had been fouling his corner with wood shavings and tobacco juice approached the window, demanding tickets to San Francisco. Myers twisted his face, adjusted his glasses, then met their request.

Molly retreated to her table, picking up the telegram for Ben Cartwright. Hoss could deliver it to the Ponderosa. She relished this opportunity to visit with Hoss. Of Ben Cartwright's three sons, Adam was too stern and bookish, Little Joe too frivolous and conceited for her tastes. Hoss, though, possessed a gentleness she found becoming and a shyness that intrigued her. She wondered if he might find her attractive.

With the telegram in her hand, she unlatched the counter gate and slipped away from her post by the telegraph. By his scowl, Oliver Myers signaled his displeasure at her mingling with the passengers and his impatience with the two men at the ticket window. Molly approached Hoss. "Mr. Cartwright," she said pleasantly.

For an instant Hoss failed to realize he was being addressed. When it did dawn on him, he jerked his hat off, holding it over his heart, and turned around. His smile was genuine, but his brow was furrowed with a moment of doubt.

"Molly Ashe," she replied. "We met at your dance last fall."

He nodded and put his hat back on his head. "You're the telegraph operator."

Molly smiled, pleased that he had remembered something about her. "I've something for you," she said, extending her hand.

Before she could explain, Hoss grabbed her hand with his big paw, crumpling the yellow envelope. He jerked his hand away when he realized what he had done, and the crumpled envelope fell to the floor. Molly bent quickly to retrieve it.

He apologized. "This isn't one of my better days."

Molly's smile seemed to put him at ease, until he realized Hop Sing was at the ticket counter. He scooted behind Hop Sing, motioning for Molly to follow.

"A telegram, Mr. Cartwright, from San Francisco for your father," she said.

"Call me Hoss! Pa's Mr. Cartwright," he said, taking the telegram from her and stuffing it in his vest pocket. "Thank you."

"Sure, Hoss," she said, disappointed that he seemed more interested in the cook than in her. Molly turned away, and saw the two rude men who had been plaguing Oliver Myers now studying Hop Sing. One wore overalls with a gun belt strapped around his waist, and the other was whittling a stick of wood with a knife much larger than the job required. When Hop Sing pulled out from under his blouse a pouch loaded with coins, the man with the knife nudged his partner, who licked his lips, exposing teeth dirtied from years of chewing tobacco. Then both men walked outside onto the platform.

Molly looked at the clock behind the counter. Two minutes until the train arrived. She heard the faint cry of the train whistle as she moved behind the counter.

"Can't do it," Oliver Myers told Hoss Cartwright.

"Are you deaf?" Hoss shot back. "You'll get your money. I need a ticket to San Francisco and I need it now."

"No cash, no ticket. Looks like you should carry a little money around, like your Chinese friend," Oliver Myers said, stretching to the full length of his five-foot-four frame, then fudging a bit by rising onto his tiptoes.

"Pa's a stockholder," Hoss shot back, "you know my word's good."

"Step aside, Cartwright, there's paying customers behind you," Myers said.

Hoss growled, but moved halfway out of the ticket window so an elderly couple could buy tickets. He noticed the couple's three bags on the slick wooden floor and placed them on the freight scales. Anything to expedite things.

Outside, the train whistle's shrill cry could be heard above the huffing of the locomotive.

Hoss knotted his fist and pounded his palm again and again. Hop Sing had left the station. Through the window, Hoss noticed two men badgering him. Hoss gritted his teeth and shook his head. The station's glass windows rattled as the steam whistle punctured the air and engine number 12, a 4-4-0 Baldwin Locomotive, chugged into the station, stopping with a loud hiss.

"Virginia and Truckee bound for Reno and all points in between, with connections to San Francisco and all points east and west," cried out Oliver Myers. "Last call for tickets."

Hoss twisted around in front of the ticket window, his legs spread, his arms apart with balled fists planted atop the counter. "One ticket to San Francisco," he demanded.

Myers ducked his head and looked between Hoss's arms and torso to see if anyone else was in line. "No money, no ticket," he said, quickly snapping a padlock on the cash drawer and scurrying away from the counter and into the baggage room.

Hoss pounded the counter with his fist until he saw Molly Ashe shaking her head. "I'm good for the money."

Stepping to the counter, Molly teased him. "You sure?"

Shrugging, Hoss moved for the door. "I'm getting on that train, ticket or not, and no dozen men can throw me off."

Molly laughed. "Hold your horses, Hoss. I'll get you a ticket, but don't go out there while Oliver Myers is prancing around."

A handful of men and women were emerging from the train as ticketed passengers lined up to board. Through the window, Hoss saw Hop Sing sandwiched between the two men who had been pestering him.

Behind the counter, Molly worked swiftly, pulling the appropriate tickets out of the ticket drawer and slapping them with the ink stamp. "Wait until the train starts pulling away, then run out and jump on. Myers'll have me telegraph the next station to pull you off, but I'll garble the message."

"Obliged, ma'am," Hoss said, reaching for the ticket.

"Call me Molly, and give me that telegram in your vest pocket."

"Huh, what telegram?" Hoss replied, sticking his fingers into the pocket slit and pulling out a crumpled envelope. "Oh!"

"It's some bad news for your father, I gather. We'll need to get it out to the Ponderosa," she said, taking the envelope from him.

From outside came the conductor's cry. "All aboard."

Hoss started for the door, then turned around, scratching his chin. "One more thing, ma'am. Can you have my buckboard and horse returned to the ranch? It's the dappled gray animal."

"Sure, Hoss," she answered, "if one day you'll return a favor."

Hoss nodded as a couple arriving passengers walked through the door. "All aboard," came the cry again, then the conductor looked along the platform. Seeing no one else moving for the train, he waved his arm at the engineer, who answered with two long blasts of his whistle.

Instantly, the drive wheels of the locomotive began to

churn, pawing at the rails like an iron bull, snorting steam and spewing cinders, breathing in great gasps. As the train lurched forward, the couplings between the cars clanked, the locomotive's power taking hold and jerking the train toward Reno. Inch by inch the train advanced.

Hoss charged out the door for the train, jumping over a valise and dodging the baggage clerk wrestling a trunk into the station.

"Stop!" yelled Oliver Myers, racing out the baggage room door and shaking his fist at Hoss. "Molly, wire Reno there's a deadhead on board."

The train was gathering speed when Hoss caught the handhold on the last swaying car and jumped onto the steps, then climbed up to the floor of the car. Leaning out over the back railing as the car cleared the platform, he took off his hat and waved it at Molly behind the window at her telegraph desk.

Thinking the gesture a taunt, Oliver Myers shook his fist at Hoss before storming into the station, his curses lost in the noise of the locomotive.

Hoss caught his breath, then opened the car door and stepped inside. The car was two-thirds full, with the new passengers settling into their padded seats and adjusting their valises and belongings. The sixteen high-backed seats on either side of the aisle were paired off facing each other. The two darkened kerosene lamps over the aisle swayed to the gentle rocking motions of the car, the oil-cloth ceilings painted with tapestries and geometric designs. In the middle of the car a baby squealed.

A couple of men laughed loudly at the far end of the car. That was where Hoss spotted Hop Sing, the cook's back to him. The two men who had been badgering Hop Sing on the platform had taken up positions to continue their bedevilment. One sat beside Hop Sing, the other occupied the seat behind. The two laughed when the one in back knocked off Hop Sing's hat. As Hop Sing bent to retrieve it, this same one caught his queue and tugged him upright. Despite the pain, Hop Sing gave no cry or made no effort to strike back. Hoss stiffened, his anger building.

Wrapping the queue around his hand, Hop Sing's tormentor pulled his knife. Hoss moved down the aisle as the bully jerked Hop Sing's head sharply, then slid the sharp edge of the knife under the braided hair. Only when he felt the honed steel against his hair did Hop Sing gasp, and Hoss knew why. By Chinese beliefs, a man who lost his queue would not be received in heaven.

With giant strides Hoss was instantly beside the bully, his hand clamping around the bully's fingers on the grip of the knife. Hoss squeezed, pulling the knife away from Hop Sing's head and crushing the man's fingers. The bully cried out.

"Let go of his hair," Hoss said, his voice menacing. "Now!"

The bully obliged, just as his partner in overalls realized what was going on.

"Let him go," the man demanded, moving for his pistol.

The man with the knife screamed as Hoss smashed his hand into the seat. The knife fell free and the man grabbed at his misshaped fingers. With a smooth motion, Hoss spun about and crashed his fist into the jaw of the gunman. Surprised, the gunman gulped and swallowed tobacco juice, coughing and lurching forward. Hoss caught his wrist as his revolver cleared its holster, and jerked the gun away. He lifted the revolver above his shoulders, then sent the gun barrel crashing into the man's skull, the man crumpling to the floor like a sack of flour. When the other man reached with his good hand for the knife on the seat beside him, Hoss swung the gun barrel into the side of his head, and he joined his partner on the floor.

Hoss lowered the revolver, then picked up the knife and looked around the passenger car. Every passenger stared with wide eyes, until a woman in an adjacent seat clapped her hands. Several others joined in, just as the conductor barged through the door.

"What's going on here?" he said, eyeing Hoss suspiciously. The conductor knelt over the man in overalls.

"They were troubling my friend," Hoss explained, "so I gave them a headache."

"That's right, conductor," said the woman who had

started the clapping. "They were threatening to cut the Chinaman's pigtail."

The conductor growled. "Troublemakers. One on every train." He motioned for Hoss to help him drag the two to the back of the car.

Hoss stepped over the man with the crushed fingers and opened the window wide enough to toss the knife and revolver outside. Then he picked up the knife wielder and carried him to the back as he would a doll, while the conductor struggled to drag the other one along the floor. Hoss dumped his groaning load onto an empty seat before striding back to help the conductor deposit the other bully by his friend.

"Be on your toes when they come to," the conductor suggested as Hoss strode back to the front and sat down opposite Hop Sing.

The cook spoke to Hoss. "Hop Sing glad you came."

With a sigh, Hoss looked Hop Sing hard in the eyes. "Then let's go home and quit this foolishnéss. I'll apologize a thousand times if we can just go back to the Ponderosa."

Hop Sing's shoulders drooped. "Hop Sing cannot do now."

"I was mad at Little Joe."

Shaking his head, Hop Sing spoke. "Hop Sing not leave because of that."

Hoss was exasperated. "Then dad-blame-it, what in tarnation did you leave for?"

Hop Sing slid his hand inside his blue blouse and pulled out the letter he had received last night. "Letter come, Hop Sing must go!"

Hoss took the letter, but could no more read its contents than he could ever seem to get the best of Little Joe.

"Letter from China. Sister need help."

"In China?" Hoss asked, bewilderment clouding his face.

"San Francisco."

"But why, Hop Sing, why?"

"Sister has daughter, young daughter, thirteen.

Daughter stolen, to San Francisco sent. Hop Sing must save her."

"Stolen?" Hoss asked. "For what?"

"Stolen by men for men."

Hoss shook his head in disbelief. "Your own people took her to ... to sleep with?"

Hop Sing nodded.

"Then all this foolishness about you leaving had nothing to do with me peppering Little Joe's supper?"

Again Hop Sing nodded. "You can go home now."

Hoss leaned back in his seat. "Pa said not to return without you. And we've got a little girl to find in San Francisco."

CHAPTER 4

The vanilla scent of Ponderosa bark permeated the pleasant evening air. Ben Cartwright sat on the porch, studying the gray columns of the *San Francisco Chronicle* that had come with yesterday's mail. Occasionally he glanced down the trail, awaiting Hoss's return. Had it been Joseph he had sent after Hop Sing, he would have fretted, because Joseph was still full of the youthful vigor and vinegar that could get him in trouble. Hoss had been assigned a task, and he would complete it no matter how long it took. Joseph, by contrast, would find plenty of opportunity to be sidetracked.

A flash of yellow caught Ben's eye and he watched a western tanager dart from the sky at an insect, then alight on the branch of a pine tree at the corner of the sturdy ranch house. The bird bobbed its red head for a moment as it pulled its black wings against itself. Ben cocked his ear to listen as the bird began its call, its song pattern resembling a robin's cry, only hoarser. "Pit-r-ick," the tanager sang, "pit-r-ick." From behind the house another tanager answered, and the bird fluttered away in search of its companion.

Ben rustled the paper as he turned pages, studying the legal notices for any mention of the government awarding timber leases. The agate print was tiny and Ben squinted to read it. He knew that he probably needed reading

31

glasses, but was still proud that at age fifty-eight his sight was good enough to spot a tanager on the wing. He attributed his sharp eyes to his years as a sailor and first mate, riding the world's oceans to exotic ports. At times he wondered how different his life would have been had he not given up the seven seas. He had to admit that some saltwater still flowed in his veins and he missed the gentle swaying of a hardwood deck beneath his feet, the spray of sea mist in his face, the swish of a slick hull cutting through the water, the snap of canvas catching the wind, and the music of creaking ropes.

From down the trail Ben heard another kind of music, the rattle of a wagon pulling up the incline toward the Ponderosa. Ben smoothed the wrinkles out of the paper and bent it precisely along the folds until it appeared untouched by human hands. It was late, but Hoss was finally returning home. Ben stood up, placing the paper on the log bench and stretching the kinks out of his shoulders. Nope, he thought, there were too many aches and creaks in his own vessel to ever give serious thought to sailing again.

The front door swung open and Joseph emerged, an apron around his waist, a dish towel over his shoulder, and a frown all over his face. Supper had not been one of the more memorable meals on the Ponderosa, the biscuits burned, the dried beans gritty from too little washing, and the thick slabs of steak burnt on the outside and almost raw in the middle. If Little Joe's future depended on his cooking, he would always be a poor man. "Sounds like Hop Sing's returning."

"And your brother," Ben replied, shaking his head.

"Hoss ain't as important as Hop Sing."

"Isn't as important," Ben corrected. "After eating your noblest efforts, I'd say Hop Sing's an asset to the Ponderosa."

When the buckboard cleared the trees and came into view, Ben leaned forward and stared down the trail. It was the Ponderosa buckboard, all right, there was his dappled gray pulling it, but the form on the seat was too small to be Hoss. Ben stepped off the porch, noting the unfamiliar horse trailing behind the wagon. The driver had a feminine form and was certainly not Hop Sing.

"Damn, no Hop Sing," Little Joe blurted out, then covered his mouth.

"Joseph, no cursing. It's an ungentlemanly habit."

Ben walked away from the house, dark thoughts entering his mind that perhaps something had happened to Hoss and Hop Sing. The driver offered a pert smile as she neared, allaying Ben's worst worries for a moment. He recognized the becoming woman, but could not place her until Little Joe joined him.

"It's Molly Ashe, the telegraph operator at the Carson City depot."

"Oh, yes," Ben replied, "best telegraph puncher in Nevada, some say."

"I say she ought to leave that to men, as pretty as she is."

"Now, Joseph," Ben responded, "that's odd of you to say, standing there with an apron around your waist."

"Oh, no," Little Joe muttered, jerking the towel off his shoulder then fumbling to untie the apron from behind him. The apron strings, though, became knotted, and Little Joe failed to undo them before the buckboard pulled up at the ranch house.

"Whoa," called Molly Ashe, nodding to Ben and smiling at Little Joe as she tied the reins.

Little Joe's face reddened as he slid the apron skirt behind him, pulling the knotted apron strings around to his belt buckle. He clasped his hands over his waist, disguising the apron strings as best he could.

"Evening, Miss Ashe," Ben said, extending his hand to assist her from the buckboard. "I hope it's not trouble that brings you here."

"No, no," she said as Ben helped her step from the buckboard onto a spoke of the wagon wheel and then to the ground. She dusted the skirt of her brown riding habit and tugged the leather riding gloves which protected her talented fingers. "Hoss is fine and I expect you'll hear from him when he reaches San Francisco."

"What?" Ben said.

Little Joe grimaced. "San Francisco? You should've let me go after Hop Sing, Pa."

Ben shook his head. "San Francisco, is it?" he said. Then he remembered his manners and offered her his arm. "Won't you come in?"

Molly declined the offer with a wave. "I can't stay. Late as it is, I need to get as far along as I can before darkness sets in."

"You'll never make it by nightfall," Ben said. "You're welcome to stay the night at the Ponderosa, if you'll just tell us more."

Shaking her head, Molly looked from Ben to Little Joe. "I've got to be at work at six in the morning. I'd prefer to ride back tonight. I promised Hoss I'd see your buckboard and horse home."

Little Joe stepped forward. "I'd be glad to ride with you to Carson City."

Molly smiled at Little Joe. "I'd hate to keep you from your dishes."

Little Joe grimaced, embarrassment etched in his face.

Ben laughed. "Now, please, tell us about Hoss."

"Followed your cook into the station. Hop Sing bought a ticket to San Francisco and Hoss said he needed a ticket but didn't have any money on him, so I gave him one, knowing a Cartwright's word was good for the money."

"It is," Ben said, "and I'll notify our banker tomorrow to reimburse you."

"Hoss got on the train, and that's all I know."

Little Joe crossed his arms, exposing the knotted apron strings at his waist. "Why'd Hoss do that?"

Ben smiled. "You know I told him not to return to the Ponderosa without Hop Sing." He scratched his chin while he pondered the situation. "Maybe there's something more to Hop Sing's departure. He wasn't the same after Hoss ruined your squab." Ben's brow furrowed. "Or after he received that letter. Maybe it was bad news."

Little Joe's head drooped. "Only bad news I know is

Hoss is heading for San Francisco and I'm here doing woman's work."

Molly laughed. "And I'm doing man's work. I guess it evens out, Little Joe."

Ben smiled again, but Little Joe saw no humor in her remarks.

"I must be going," Molly said, "but there's one other thing." She reached into the pocket of her high-necked blouse and pulled out a yellow envelope. "Telegram arrived this morning, just before Hoss came into the station."

Ben took it from her. "From San Francisco?"

Molly nodded.

"I've been waiting for this."

"It's not good news."

For a moment Ben wondered how she'd know whether it was good news or bad. Few folks outside of the family and his lawyer, David Thornton Kendall, Jr., knew about his bid for timber rights. "Thank you for bringing the telegram and returning the wagon."

"If only you'd brought Hop Sing back," Little Joe interjected.

Molly smiled. "Then, he could show you how to tie an apron without knotting it." Giggling, she marched around the buckboard and untied her bay mare. Lifting the reins over the mare's neck, she slipped her boot into the stirrup, a patch of pale white skin visible on her calf above her riding boots as she climbed into the saddle.

Little Joe watched approvingly. "I'll return the favor next time I'm in Carson City," he said.

Gently tugging on the reins, the mare danced around to face Ben and Little Joe. "Ah," she answered politely, "but it's Hoss, not you, that owes me a favor. Good evening, gentlemen." She touched her boots to the mare's flank and the bay turned and cantered back down the trail.

Little Joe nodded. "She cuts a fine figure. Think I ought to follow her, just to be sure she doesn't have any problems."

"You've dishes to do," Ben answered, turning around and walking back toward the house. Passing the bench where he had been sitting, he picked up the paper to finish later. Little Joe, twisting his apron back around straight, passed him. Ben held up the yellow envelope with his name on it and admired Molly Ashe's delicate handwriting. She had more spunk than Joseph could deal with, Ben thought. Further, by her comments, she seemed more interested in Hoss.

"Joseph," Ben called, "would you take care of the buckboard?"

"Instead of the dishes?"

"In addition to," Ben answered. Little Joe offered a mock bow as his father went by and entered the house.

Adam sat on a long couch, going over an assaying report from the Bristlecone mine owned by Cartwright Enterprises in Virginia City. His solemn black eyes were narrow as he read the papers. Without looking up from the report, he said, "Was that Hoss and Hop Sing? I don't think I can stomach another of Little Joe's meals."

"Hoss is headed for San Francisco," Ben answered.

Now Adam looked up, and cocked his head. "San Francisco?" He stroked his five o'clock shadow. "Then Hop Sing was serious?"

Ben nodded. "Must've been, and there's likely more to this than just Hoss's prank on Joseph, but we can worry about that later." Ben held up the yellow envelope. "Telegram from San Francisco."

Tossing the assaying report on the cushion, Adam jumped up from the couch and followed Ben to his desk. Adam lit the desk lamp as Ben used a penknife to slit open the envelope and pull out the telegram. Carefully, he unfolded it beneath the lamp. "Molly Ashe said it wasn't good news."

"We must not have gotten the lease. Damn," Adam said.

Ben ignored Adam's comment and held the telegram up to the light, his lips mouthing the telegram's message. He gasped. "Oh my God, not this, anything but this."

Adam snatched the telegram from his father.

Ben ran his fingers through his silver hair, then shook his head in disbelief. "Terrible, terrible news," he said.

Adam read the telegraph aloud. " 'Father died yesterday. Funeral today. Problem with timber bid unresolved. Will settle issue and advise when appropriate. David Thornton Kendall the Third.' " Adam whistled. "That is bad news. What's unresolved with the timber bid?"

"The timber be damned," Ben answered with rising voice. Ben shook his head. Adam was too businesslike, too unemotional. Ever since he had let the Ponderosa's first blooded bull gore Jean-Pierre DeMarigny, the ranch's first foreman, Adam had been too stoic, too impenetrable for his own good. "Losing such a valued friend, such a trustworthy man as Thornton, that's the tragedy."

"You know what I mean, Pa. A lot of things are left unanswered by this telegram."

"I know, Adam." Ben spoke softly now, the shock of Thornton Kendall's death giving way to reasoned thought of its implications for the Ponderosa. "It was unlike Thornton not to keep me apprised of matters. Of course, he was giving over more of his practice to his son. I'm not comfortable with Davey handling this for us. He's just not the man his father was."

Adam leaned over the desk, resting his hands on the edges. "Ever think any of your friends might be saying that about your sons? None of us are the men our fathers were."

Ben tapped his fingers on the desk. "Davey had a mischievous streak about him as a kid, something I don't trust in a lawyer."

"And you tell me I'm always too serious about matters."

"You are."

Adam held up his hand. "That's beside the point. When I was around Davey in San Francisco, he was adventuresome but never malicious."

"That's still dangerous in a lawyer."

"You owe him the benefit of a doubt until he proves otherwise," Adam shot back.

Adam was right, as usual, and Ben knew it was futile to argue the point with him. Adam could be stubborn as a mule when he was right, a trait made tolerable by his reciprocal willingness to admit a mistake when he was wrong. Ben nodded, knowing his son would not have to admit to being wrong on this count. "If nothing else, I owe it to his father."

"No," Adam replied. "You owe it to him." Then Adam grinned. "After all, we may need a friend in San Francisco to send Hoss and Hop Sing back or get them out of trouble."

CHAPTER 5

With his elbow, Hop Sing nudged Hoss, who stirred slowly, then lifted his head from his slumber. Hoss pushed up the seven-inch brim of his Carlsbad cut hat, his ice-blue eyes taking in the landscape, which slowed down as the engineer gently applied the brakes of the train. Houses were scattered among the tall trees on either side of the track, like wooden ghosts in the gentle mist that cast a gray pall over the landscape. They had descended from the rugged Sierra Nevadas, whose muscled peaks were still ribbed with winter snows.

They were approaching Vallejo, where the railroad ended, at the northeast shore of San Francisco Bay. From there the ferry would take them to the foot of Market Street in San Francisco. The train fare included the ferry fee and a meal as well, but Hoss knew he would be in trouble as soon as he stepped off the ferry onto the wharf. He had never expected Hop Sing's trail to lead this far from the Ponderosa. Consequently, he was penniless and unarmed, two conditions he preferred to avoid in a city as expensive and as dangerous as San Francisco.

As the train approached the station, the mechanical gasps of the locomotive slowed like the breath of a dying dinosaur. The air was thick with the odor of burning cinders which sizzled in the mist. The locomotive's shrill whistle startled Hoss, fully waking him. He stretched his arms and looked around the passenger car, each seat full except for the one opposite him and Hop Sing.

The trip had been peaceful since they changed trains in Reno. They had taken the last seat on the last passenger car of the Central Pacific express and been ignored by everyone. Now, the locomotive's bell began to clang as the train reached the Central Pacific yard and inched up to the long platform at the Vallejo station. Hop Sing jumped up, bent over and grabbed his belongings, stowed under the seat. Hoss yawned.

"Vallejo with ferry connections for San Francisco. End of the line for the transcontinental run," the conductor called out as he walked the length of the car, then turned beside Hoss and Hop Sing, tugging on his ear and scowling at Hop Sing. "You two," he said softly, so only they could hear, "exit through the back door." He tugged at the sleeve of his blue double-breasted frock coat, then spun around and retreated to the front. "Leave by the forward door," he instructed the others.

The train shook to a stop, rattling the windows and jarring the passengers, who rose from their seats, stretching and gathering their belongings and children. Hoss stood and picked up one of Hop Sing's bundles, but Hop Sing signaled for him to put it down.

"Hop Sing carry. Hop Sing carry two bundles better than one," he said as he picked up his bamboo pole from the floor and hooked each bundle over an end. As other passengers shuffled slowly out the forward door, Hoss opened the tight-fitting rear door with a shove, moving aside to let Hop Sing squeeze by. The mist held a chill as Hoss followed Hop Sing onto the platform amid the crowd rushing off the train. A couple of men cursed as Hop Sing scurried by, the swaying blanket bundles brushing against them.

The station's double doors swung open and Hop Sing darted between a pair of Central Pacific baggage handlers. Behind the long ticket counter inside, the station agent yelled over the din at the new arrivals. "Coaches outside for the San Francisco ferry." Men in suits powdered with cinder ash and women dragging stubborn offspring scrambled outside for the coaches.

Hoss was cut off from Hop Sing for an instant by a baggage clerk wrestling a large trunk onto a baggage cart. As Hop Sing approached the exit, Hoss saw a large man bump him hard, too hard for it to have been accidental. The man scowled at Hop Sing, who nodded but kept moving. Emerging from the station, Hoss saw a half-dozen coaches, and behind them, three wagons for baggage. For a moment he lost Hop Sing, then spotted him at the last coach, shoving his belongings in the door. As Hop Sing stepped up, Hoss saw a man from inside shove him back, then saw Hop Sing's belongings come flying out of the coach.

With his hat tumbling off and his loose blouse spreading out from the push, Hop Sing let out a cry of surprise. He hit the ground with a thud, but bounced up and gathered his hat.

"We don't want any Chinamen on this coach," came the assailant's gruff voice. The man shook his fist out the door.

Hoss trotted toward the coach. "You," he shouted, pointing his finger at Hop Sing's attacker, "come here and pick this up."

Hop Sing stepped into Hoss's path, grabbing his arm. "Hop Sing no want trouble. Hop Sing must go to San Francisco. No trouble. Hop Sing pick his things up."

"You wanna fight over a damn Chinaman," the man in the coach sneered, "then you'll be fighting every white man in California."

Hoss, feeling Hop Sing's grip tight against his arm, studied the red-bearded bully, noting his slight frame, crooked nose, and beady eyes. As Hoss shook Hop Sing's hand from his arm and bent down to help pick up his possessions, he heard the bully's mocking laugh, a high-pitched cackle that galled him like salt on a wound. Hoss hoisted the bamboo shaft over his shoulder and turned his back on the coach, heading for the baggage wagons. The mocking laughter stung his every step. At the baggage wagon he tossed Hop Sing's belongings in the back. Hop

Sing climbed over the wagon's dropped tailgate into the back and perched himself atop his bundles.

Standing akimbo, Hoss shook his head at Hop Sing. "Come on," he commanded, "we'll get us a seat in one of the coaches."

Hop Sing crossed his arms over his chest and shook his head. "No, Hop Sing ride here." His adamant eyes told Hoss he would not be moved.

Hoss shrugged. "Mist may pick up. You'll get wet."

"Hop Sing been wet before. Always dry off."

Hoss glanced from Hop Sing back at the coach, then at the baggage wagon. He shrugged. "I like your company better than theirs." He climbed into the wagon.

One by one the carriages up ahead departed for the ferry landing, then a skinny clerk pushed a cart of luggage out of the station to the wagon. Working around Hoss and Hop Sing, he unloaded the bags. "You two'll have to go by coach or walk. Company rules, and your driver is a stickler for rules."

Balling his fist, Hoss pounded it against the wagon's side board. "Some of your passengers didn't want Hop Sing on the coach."

"Folks in these parts ain't too fond of Chinamen."

"Why not?" Hoss asked, his brow furrowing in disgust.

The clerk glanced over at Hop Sing, then back at Hoss. "They're different." He fairly spit the words, then turned back for the depot, meeting another man heading for the wagon. The clerk jerked his thumb back over his shoulder at the wagon, and the other man stared hard at Hoss and Hop Sing. He was a little fellow with a wad of tobacco straining the elasticity of his cheek. His eyes were as murky as his tobacco-stained teeth.

Approaching the wagon, he spit a stream of tobacco juice toward the mule team. "I don't haul passengers in the baggage wagon, especially no Chinamens and fat mens," he said, eyeing Hoss.

Hoss stood up to the full height of his six feet, four inches and nodded at the driver. "And I don't take insults from runty drivers." He jumped over the side of the wagon, sending the driver backtracking a few steps as he advanced in anger. The driver retreated, but Hoss was upon him. He knifed his hands under the driver's shoulders and jerked him up off the ground until the man's eyes were level with his own. "We've got paid tickets, and you're taking us to the ferry," he growled. "If we miss the ferry, we'll have time to do something about your insults."

The driver gulped and nodded.

Hoss shook him. "I'm hard of hearing when you don't speak. Do you understand?"

This time the driver nodded vigorously. "Yeah."

Turning toward the wagon, Hoss carried the driver like he would a newborn calf. Taking a deep breath, he heaved the man up onto the wagon seat. "All aboard," he said emphatically as he climbed in the seat beside the driver, who fumbled for the reins. Hoss glanced over his shoulder and winked at Hop Sing, who smiled for the first time Hoss could remember since leaving the Ponderosa.

"Giddyup!" The driver whistled and the wagon lurched ahead.

The road sloped down toward the bay about a half mile away. At the foot of the road was the ferry wharf where the coaches were already unloading and people were filing onto the boat and climbing the stairs to the covered upper deck. All sorts of wagons and carts were inching their way aboard the ferry, the deckhands gesticulating at the animals and directing the wagons into their places.

"This wagon move any faster?" Hoss demanded of the driver.

"Yeah," the driver responded, shaking the reins against the rumps of the mules, "but the ferry waits on the baggage wagons."

Hoss stared at the driver. "You better worry about keeping us 'Chinamens and fat mens' happy right now," he suggested.

The driver gulped, swallowing some of his tobacco juice and spewing some over the front of the wagon and on the mules. When Hoss swatted him firmly on the back, the driver choked again and showered the mules with tobacco juice. The driver scooted away from Hoss on the seat. "No more help," he sputtered.

Reaching the ferry wharf, the mules moved by rote down the wooden ramp and onto the cumbersome ferry. The boat was a cacophony of noise, horses nickering, chickens clucking nervously in cages stacked as high as the driver in one wagon, a couple of dogs barking, deckhands shouting, kids laughing, and the ferry's huffing engine thudding, its great reciprocating arm extending from below deck up through the vehicle deck, the passenger deck, and the roof by the pilothouse.

No sooner had the wagon pulled under the cover of the ferry than the mist turned to a gentle rain. The cool breeze blowing across the fog-shrouded bay caused Hoss to shiver. Quickly, their wagon was surrounded by others, like moving pieces in a giant puzzle. Several men climbed down, lighting smokes and talking with other ferry regulars. A few men put blinders on their animals. The driver beside Hoss sat motionless, even when some men called him.

Hoss's anger had worked its way down to his stomach, reminding him of the meals he had missed since leaving the Ponderosa yesterday. He elbowed the driver. "Where's the food for train passengers?"

The driver lifted his thumb toward the second deck. "Upstairs."

Hoss stood up, the whole wagon shifting under his weight. "Now I'm gonna go fetch me and Hop Sing some food. If I come back and find anyone has bothered my friend, I'll settle up with you. See how much more of that tobacco juice you can drink."

Wide-eyed, the driver nodded.

"Hop Sing," Hoss called, climbing down from the seat of the wagon, "give me your ticket and I'll bring you something to eat."

Hop Sing obliged quickly, and Hoss realized that after all the years that Hop Sing had brought food to him, this would be the first time he would return the favor. Taking the ticket, he squeezed between the wagons, circuitously heading for the stairway at the end of the ferry. In places it was a tight squeeze, but food beckoned from somewhere upstairs and nothing would deter him.

As he reached the stairway, the deckhands closed the gate on the ferry and the shore hands winched up the wagon ramp. Instantly, the thud of the engine became a persistent pounding and the reciprocating arm in the middle of the ship began to churn up and down. The ferry lurched ahead, then glided through the calm waters of San Francisco Bay.

At the top of the stairway Hoss paused for a moment, watching the gulls gliding around the ferry, diving in and out of each other's way in a perpetual search for something to eat. The ferry sounded its foghorn, startling him. Glancing over his shoulder, Hoss was surprised that the wharf had already disappeared in the fog.

Opening the door to the passenger compartment, he stepped quickly inside a large room warm with humanity and two glowing potbelly stoves in sand boxes at opposite ends of the compartment. He could smell coffee from the back, and worked in that direction. As he neared a table where three white-aproned attendants were depositing coffeepots, he noticed a red-bearded man with beady eyes gulp down a cup of coffee, then pour himself another from the steaming pots. It was the same man who had pushed Hop Sing off the coach. Hoss angled that way as the red-bearded fellow moved back toward the bench seats. Just as he came within two steps of the man, Hoss mocked a sneeze and bumped into the fellow's right arm.

"Ahhhhgggg," the man yelled as the scalding hot coffee spilled onto his hand. "Watch where you're going, fellow," he said.

"Sneezed," Hoss answered sheepishly, then adjusted his course for the lunch counter. He showed the attendant his two coupons and was given two tin plates and tin cups. He marched down the line, covering both plates with sliced roast beef, thick brown gravy, boiled potatoes, dried butter beans, and six slices of bread. At the end of the line he picked up forks and headed for the coffeepots, a plate in each hand, the coffee cups balanced on the edge of the plates. An attendant, seeing his plight, took the coffee cups and filled them, placing them gingerly back atop the plates. Hoss thanked him, then meandered through the crowd to the stairs and back down to the wagon where Hop Sing sat meekly. The driver was opening a tobacco pouch and reloading his jaw.

Though Hop Sing's expression was inscrutable, Hoss thought he saw a glimmer of relief in his eyes as he approached with the food. Maybe Hop Sing was just as hungry as he was. Hop Sing took the plate from Hoss and placed it in his lap, lifted the cup to his mouth and sipped the hot coffee. Hoss crawled into the wagon beside him, making a seat of a couple mail sacks. He forked a bite of potato and meat. With food in his mouth, he took the coffee cup from the plate and placed it on the crate at his elbow.

"Hop Sing need food, just not so plenty of it," he told Hoss.

Hoss smiled broadly and scraped a clear spot on his plate, offering it to Hop Sing, who shoved as much from his plate onto Hoss's as was possible without spilling any of it.

From behind him Hoss heard the driver's voice. "You'd take food from a Chinaman's plate?"

Hoss twisted around, a wide smile on his face. "At least I don't eat tobacco juice, fellow. Now mind your manners while I eat, or I may throw you overboard for fish bait."

As Hoss was sopping up the last of his plate, the pounding of the reciprocating engine eased, gradually becoming a thud. The ferry slowed. As if by magic, a shoreline appeared where there had been nothing but fog. Gradually the ferry landing at the foot of Market Street took shape. Hoss finished his coffee, took his dishes, and motioned for Hop Sing to give him his. Turning around, he dropped them with a clang on the seat by the driver.

"Take care of these for us, fellow. Us 'Chinamens and fat mens' have had enough of your hospitality. We'll walk from here."

The driver grunted, but said nothing intelligible.

Hoss stood up in the wagon and motioned for Hop

Sing to gather his belongings, then he climbed over the side and took the bamboo pole with the blanket bags on each end from Hop Sing. Hop Sing lifted his leg over the side board and took a foothold on a wheel spoke. Bringing his other leg over the side board, he hopped to the deck, landing gracefully beside Hoss. In one smooth motion he took the bamboo pole from Hoss and balanced it across his shoulders. Hoss pointed the way, and Hop Sing moved ahead of him, weaving through the wagons. Hoss was amazed at how easily Hop Sing maneuvered his load among the crowd without once hitting any person or thing. Even if it was an odd way of carrying things, it allowed a small man to manage a cumbersome load. They reached the front of the ferry about the time the ramp was being lowered, and were among the first passengers off. The rain had stopped and the fog was thinning, but they could see little of San Francisco.

They moved along the dock, then entered the ferry building with other departing passengers seeking the exit onto Market Street. "Well, Hop Sing, we're finally here," Hoss said as he pushed the door open and allowed Hop Sing to pass. The city they could see in the fog was going full tilt, motion everywhere, and they could hear the grating roar of wagon wheels against brick streets, the shouts of impatient men. Once again, it confirmed to Hoss how much more he preferred the quiet life of the outdoors and the hard work of the Ponderosa. A man had freedom on the ranch, he wasn't regimented by the city like these men and women.

Looking around, he took a deep breath, and noted the policeman at the end of the building staring at him. The officer, leaning against the ferry building, had been lecturing a newspaper boy, shaking his billy club in his nose, until he saw Hoss. Then he stopped.

Hoss shrugged. There was nothing he could have done.

The policeman motioned with his billy club for the paperboy to go on his way, then pushing away from the building, strode straight for Hoss. Hop Sing moved behind Hoss.

"You," the policeman called, pointing his billy club in Hoss's direction.

Hoss pointed to himself.

"No, the heathen," the policeman yelled, jogging up beside them.

Hop Sing stood silent, the bamboo pole resting on his shoulders, his earthly belongings suspended from both ends.

"Hey, heathen," the policeman called as he neared Hop Sing. "You're breaking the law."

Hoss shook his head. "What? He just got into town."

The policeman turned to Hoss. "Who are you, his lawyer?"

"He works for me in Nevada."

"This ain't Nevada, you know," the officer said, lifting his billy club to his shoulder. He tapped the bamboo pole. "This is illegal, carrying laundry this way. He'll have to get rid of the pole!"

Hoss took off his hat and held it over his chest. "What? That pole is illegal?"

"You heard me, fellow, and you can go to jail with him if we don't get this settled."

"But why?" Hoss implored, waving his arms in frustration.

"It's a city ordinance to discourage these heathens from coming to San Francisco. Give me the pole or we'll all go to city jail."

Hoss slapped his hat back on his head, not believing what he was hearing. "Hop Sing, we've got to give this to the police," he said, grabbing the pole with his hand.

Hop Sing lowered his belongings and untied the twine from each end. Hoss took the bamboo from him and gave it to the policeman, who broke it over his knee. Hop Sing threw one bag over his shoulder and reached for the other one before Hoss grabbed it.

Angered, Hoss stared hard at the policeman. "We legal now?"

The policeman nodded.

"Good," Hoss replied, "now maybe you can help us.

This man's niece was kidnapped and brought to San Francisco."

"Good luck," the officer answered, stepping away.

Hoss put his hand on the policeman's shoulder. "You don't understand. His niece was stolen from China, brought over here as a slave for who knows what purpose."

"Likely for whoring," the policeman answered without sympathy.

"But she's only thirteen," Hoss pleaded.

"It don't matter none. Police don't interfere in Chinese matters unless they fool with white folks."

"No help, then?"

"Boy, you're pretty smart to be as big and ugly as you are."

Gritting his teeth, Hoss turned away from the officer and pointed toward Market Street. Hop Sing headed that way, suddenly awkward with the load on his shoulder. Hoss was as angry at the policeman as anyone who had harassed Hop Sing along the way.

"Welcome to San Francisco," the policeman called in their wake.

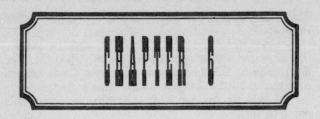

CHAPTER 6

L eaving the ferry building and the policeman behind, Hoss and Hop Sing ascended Market Street. Hoss led the way, Hop Sing always following a step behind, a custom that annoyed Hoss, particularly when he had something to say. The street teemed with humanity, a roiling river of people, the air restless with their movement and noise.

Among all the people in San Francisco, Hoss knew his father had many acquaintances. Broke and with no place to stay, he figured he could contact someone for help. Still, Hoss had never asked for a handout in his life, and it went against his grain to ask now, though he knew his situation would be temporary.

As he crossed Front Street, a turning beer wagon cut the corner too close to Hop Sing, its rear wheel missing him by inches and peppering his baggy trousers with puddle water. Hop Sing jumped for the walk as the driver looked back over his shoulder and laughed. Hoss yelled, but the beer wagon rolled on. Turning to Hop Sing, seeing his splattered trousers, Hoss asked, "You okay, Hop Sing?"

He nodded and plodded past Hoss, speaking as he went by. "Hop Sing must know. Where we go?"

Hoss took off his hat and scratched his head, scrunching up his face as he contemplated what to do. His companion continued walking, dodging the outstretched feet of a couple young bullies. The bullies laughed and strolled shoulder to shoulder on down the sidewalk, cocky as twin roosters. Hoss replaced his hat and adjusted his course, aiming to march between them. When he loomed over them, they split for him to pass. With his next stride, Hoss swung his right boot into the path of one, who tumbled to the sidewalk, showering the air with his curses. His friend laughed and slapped his knee at his buddy's awkwardness.

In a few quick strides, Hoss caught up with Hop Sing.

"Hop Sing go to Chinatown, find girl."

"I know, I know," Hoss responded, switching shoulders with the bag of Hop Sing's belongings. "I thought we'd go to the police, but I don't figure they'd be of any help, not after your welcome at the wharf. Whatever we do, we'll need someplace to stay."

An idea struck Hoss. His father always stayed at the Palace Hotel, where he had a standing line of credit for rooms and meals. Hoss knew this would ease his financial problems. He could always telegraph his father and have money wired to San Francisco, but knew if he did that, his father might order him home, an order he would have to disobey until he found Hop Sing's niece.

"We'll go to the Palace Hotel," Hoss said. "It's the grandest hotel you've ever seen, Hop Sing. Just up the street."

Hop Sing shrugged. "Hop Sing never stay hotel."

Hoss laughed. "Today'll be a first, then. We'll share us a room."

They crossed Beale, then Fremont and First streets, before coming to Second. "Up ahead," Hoss said, pointing to a building that consumed an entire block. They passed the Grand Hotel and stood at the street corner, admiring the Palace, all seven stories of it.

They crossed New Montgomery Street and turned down the brick—not plank—walk, heading for the hotel's grand entrance. With its brick walls painted white, and with the bolt heads of the structural supports gilded with gold, the Palace looked more pristine from afar than up close. Grimy soot, a by-product of city life, had coated the walls with a dull gray veil. But even so, the building's facade was eye-catching with its vertical banks of bay windows lined up like dominoes around the building. Each room—there were reportedly eight hundred of them—was said to have a bay window. Without a doubt the Palace was the biggest hotel in the West and one of the largest in the world. Much of the wealth that had made this possible had come from speculation on silver mines in the Comstock Lode.

At the grand entrance, shiny black carriages which seemed immune to the grime of the streets awaited their entrance into the courtyard. Hoss and Hop Sing stopped at the entryway, Hoss admiring the matched pairs of horses pulling the carriages, Hop Sing standing in awe of such a fine building. Hop Sing balked when Hoss nudged him toward the pedestrian walk leading into the courtyard, so Hoss led the way, Hop Sing following meekly behind. They entered a central court almost 150 feet long by eighty feet wide, with a circular drive where carriages could deposit their passengers onto a marble-paved floor amid a forest of potted trees and plants. Above them, a great domed roof of opaque glass let in the natural light, intensifying the sparse light of the gray day outside.

"It's something, ain't it?" Hoss said to Hop Sing, who stared in wide-eyed amazement at the plush facility. "Inside's even better." Hoss opened the door that led into the lobby. "There's five hydraulic elevators with mirrored walls and the prettiest gas lamps you'll ever see."

The lobby was elegantly adorned with rich mahogany, East India teak, rosewood and ebony panels and trim, contrasting with the delicate peach-blossom-pink paint that covered the lesser woods and spaces on the walls, twenty-five feet high. And everywhere, the wall was decorated with landscapes of the Golden Gate at sunset or Lake Tahoe or Yosemite or clipper ships under full sail. The large room was generously furnished with rugs specially woven in France and with comfortable sofas and plush chairs of the finest leather upholstery. Hoss couldn't imagine a finer room anywhere for bankers, mining magnates, ranchers, railroad owners, lumbermen, steamship operators, or promoters to conduct their business.

But apparently this was not a room where an Asian could conduct his.

"Hey, chink," called a sofa-bound man resting his pudgy hands over his bloated belly, "the Palace don't take to your kind."

Hoss scowled and strode toward the mahogany registration desk with a wall of pigeonholes behind it. He felt the stares of dozens of men, and he wondered if they would have been watching had Hop Sing not followed in his footsteps. A desk clerk with an upturned nose stood behind the counter, cleaning his wire-rimmed spectacles and squinting as he approached. The clerk stood ramrod straight in his starched shirt and pressed suit, his lip curling in disdain as Hoss stepped up and plopped the bundle of Hop Sing's belongings on the counter near the guest register, a thick book with gold-edged pages in a fine leather binding. The clerk returned his glasses to his nose, then hooked the earpieces in place and stepped arrogantly up to the mahogany counter, wiping at a speck of dust that besmirched the shine.

Finally, after studying Hoss a moment and twisting his neck to see Hop Sing, the clerk cocked his head and pursed his lips as he examined the bundled blanket on the counter. "With what your valise must've set you back, I doubt you've the money left for a room, if that's what you're after."

"The name Cartwright mean anything to you, fellow?" Hoss asked. He wadded his hands into fists and shoved them across the countertop as he leaned toward the clerk.

Instinctively, the clerk took a step back. "Nope," he answer smugly, just beyond Hoss's reach.

"I'm Hoss Cartwright, my father's Ben Cartwright, and he's got a line of credit here for lodging," Hoss said.

"Lodging." The clerk smirked. "The Palace is not lodging, it's luxury, the finest hotel in the West, if not the whole United States of America. You want lodging, go someplace else. You're not getting a room here without paying in advance."

"That's what I'm telling you, my word's as good as my father's line of credit, if you'll just check under the name of Ben Cartwright in your records," Hoss answered. He was losing his patience.

"The name Ben Cartwright doesn't mean beans to me," the clerk answered, folding his arms across his chest.

Hoss shrugged, reached for the guest register and began to flip back through the pages. "He was here back in February, stayed in one of your best rooms."

The clerk advanced to the book and jerked it away from Hoss's fingers. "It's Palace business, not yours, who's signed this book."

His anger rising like storm waters, Hoss hit the counter with his fists and whispered through gritted teeth, "All I want is a room for me and my friend."

"No room for you and no Chinamen in the Palace, it's that simple," the clerk said smugly, turning the register back to the current page and stepping away from the counter.

Hoss let out a slow breath, like steam escaping through a pinhole, then he exploded, grabbing the guest register. He took half the pages in his right hand, half in his left, and began to pull them from the binding.

"Stop!" shouted the clerk. But it was too late.

The pages began to rip as Hoss severed them from the leather binding, dropping them in two disheveled clumps on the counter.

The clerk gasped and turned pale, as if he feared his neck might be the next target of Hoss's incredible strength. He lifted his hand toward Hoss, then had second thoughts and let it drop down to his waist. Some other clerks had emerged from the office behind the counter and stood wide-eyed and motionless, as if watching a dangerous animal about to charge.

Hoss jerked Hop Sing's bundle off the counter and spun around, Hop Sing jumping out of his way. "Come on,

Hop Sing, we'll find us a place to stay where the hired hands are friendly. City folks and city manners," he huffed in disgust.

They retreated across the lobby and out the doors into the carriage courtyard. Hoss knew it was foolish to think he could find a room in San Francisco without money in his pocket, but he would sleep on the street before he'd stay in a hotel that would deny Hop Sing a bed.

Outside, it had started to rain again. Hoss swore to himself as he ran across the street to an awning where several other men and women had huddled like sheep out of the rain, Hop Sing following. Where could he turn now? he wondered. What was that lawyer's name his father spoke so highly of, the one with a son who had read law under him? Davey? "Yeah, Davey," Hoss said to himself. Kendall, was that it? "David Thornton Kendall," he said aloud, nodding to himself, for a moment proud that he had remembered, then uncomfortable about having to ask for a handout. He would remember the name in case things got really desperate, but for now he'd see what he could do on his own, broke and unarmed. "Any ideas, Hop Sing?"

"Hop Sing have money, pay for room."

"Can't let you do that, Hop Sing," Hoss answered, staring from under the awning at the sky, looking for signs of a letup in the downpour.

"Why Hop Sing not buy? Mr. Hoss plan to buy room for Hop Sing in fancy hotel."

Hoss shrugged. "You could, but I've got more money than you do, you know that."

"Hop Sing know that on Ponderosa. Hop Sing know this not Ponderosa. Hop Sing have more in San Francisco."

Hoss stamped his feet and shook his head. He hated debates, particularly with someone who made better sense than he did. No point in arguing. "It's just not right, Hop Sing, me taking money you've worked so hard and so long for. You'll need it to find your niece."

"Hoss stubborn as a horse. Hop Sing understand where he get odd name."

"Dad-blame-it, Hop Sing, it's 'stubborn as a mule,' and quit arguing with me. If you've got an idea, spit it out."

Hop Sing pointed to the north. "Chinatown! Hop Sing take you to Chinatown."

CHAPTER 7

When the rain let up, Hop Sing led Hoss away from the Palace, crossing several streets, dodging the pools of water that had gathered in the low places and the mud where the paving stones had been broken by iron-rim wheels and horseshoes. The heavy air muffled the rumble as men and women scurried by and downtrodden horses pulled their heavy loads up the inclined streets. From time to time Hop Sing shifted the bag of belongings over his back, his step faltering occasionally, but his head steady and fixed toward Chinatown.

Gradually the stately stone and elegant iron buildings standing shoulder to shoulder along south Dupont gave way to more pedestrian buildings of less noble stature and purpose. The structures were older, their windows cracked and smudged, their painted trim peeling with age and their signs as faded as their prosperity. Chinese character markings grew more frequent on signs, and as these strange signs increased, so did the number of Chinese men, most dressed like Hop Sing in loose-fitting cotton blouses, all blue, and dark baggy pants. Instead of split bamboo hats, these men wore black felt hats which covered their shaved heads and leaked only the long queue that reached to the waist or lower.

It seemed Chinatown was predominately male, Hoss estimating he saw fifteen men for every woman. The women walked about in the same baggy clothing as the men, though of finer and more colorful materials, usually with a bright sash around the waist and a fan to hide their shy faces from the gaze of others. Their hair was tied in knots and bows and crowned with paper flowers. They were pretty women, what there were of them. Children were even scarcer, even in the heart of Chinatown. The men and women were a petite race, their almond eyes staring in disbelief at Hoss's hulking six feet, four inches and 240 pounds. They would watch for but a moment, then turn away, occasionally speaking among themselves in their native tongue. Though none even implied a threat against him, Hoss felt uneasy among so many people with their strange language and odd customs. For a while he smiled in response to their glances, but they only averted their eyes and kept on walking. As he marched through the heart of Chinatown, he realized that now Hop Sing's presence offered him protection instead of the other way around.

Chinatown was an assault on the senses. It reeked of too many people crowded together in too few buildings. In places, the streets were littered with everything from fish heads and shrimp hulls to empty brandy bottles and tea grounds. The smoke of countless washtub fires mingled with the aroma of freshly starched laundry. Asians teemed from every doorway, loft, garret, and porch, even in the mist, and the walk was crowded with squatters jabbering over tables of fruits, nuts, and cigars; squawking for customers to use their services as cobblers, tinners, and menders.

The buildings were grimy and black from cellar to garret, and yet the men looked healthy, their dark eyes animated. The buildings were laced together by interwoven clotheslines that angled across the alleys and stretched from rooftop to rooftop, from window to window. In spite of the mist, laundry hung from the clotheslines in several places, even over Dupont Street itself, where Hoss and Hop Sing walked.

And while the streets were crowded, every alley Hoss passed seemed to be packed with even more debris. In places, Hoss thought he saw men sleeping under staircases or in doorways, but he could never be certain because there were so many of them everywhere and their customs seemed so odd.

Hop Sing turned down one street, up another, along a third and then down yet another, until Hoss had lost all sense of direction. On one back street, Hoss walked by a door with a caged window. Behind it he saw the jaundiced smile of a young girl, probably not yet sixteen. "China girl nice! You come inside, please?" Hoss stepped quickly beyond her view and heard her plaintive voice trailing after him. "Your father, he just go out!" Hoss shuddered to think this was the fate that might await Hop Sing's niece.

In Hop Sing's wake, Hoss passed meat markets with the hacked carcasses of hogs and beeves hanging in the windows beside plucked ducks and wildcats skinned up to the neck. In barbershops, he saw the proprietors shaving the foreheads and scraping the ears of their patrons or oiling and braiding their queues.

Finally, Hop Sing went down a narrow alley, the odors thick and strange. At the end of the alley, he turned down a narrow passageway, motioning for Hoss to follow. It was a tight squeeze for Hoss's broad shoulders, and he turned sideways, dragging the bag with Hop Sing's belongings against the grimy wall behind him. The passageway ended twenty feet from the alley at a dirty door. Hop Sing rapped on the entrance. In the dimness, Hoss saw a peephole open up and a pin of light emerge from inside, then grow dark again. Hop Sing spoke with animation, gesturing wildly to the peephole, which clicked shut. Hoss heard the grate of metal against the door as an iron bar was lifted.

A latch snapped and instantly the door opened wide, a pair of arms emerging, grabbing Hop Sing by the shoulders and jerking him inside. Hoss dropped Hop Sing's belongings, but before he could save Hop Sing, the door slammed shut and the metal bar clinked into place.

"Hop Sing," Hoss yelled. "Hop Sing!" He pounded on the door, then put his shoulder into it, but the iron was stout enough to discourage intruders. Damn, Hoss thought, he had followed Hop Sing so far from the Ponderosa, only to lose him in a dark Chinatown alley. Surely this was the back entrance to a building, but Hoss was not sure he could find the front, and even if he did, could he find Hop Sing? In frustration, he kicked at the door, then leaned against it. "Hop Sing!" he yelled with all the power his strong lungs could muster. The sound echoed off the building walls.

Turning around, Hoss kicked at the bag of belongings and started for the head of the passageway. Before he reached the alley he heard the scraping noise against the door, then the latch. He spun around quickly as the door swung open. There stood Hop Sing, his hands clasped before his chest, a smile upon his lips.

"Hop Sing let you in now. Hop Sing must keep Mr. Hoss out until cousin say it okay."

"Dad-blame-it, Hop Sing, why didn't you let me know?"

Hop Sing bowed as Hoss walked back. "This place Hop Sing's cousin's. White men not allowed unless cousin okay. He okay you. Not like Palace Hotel, he is!"

Hoss shrugged, picked up Hop Sing's belongings and threw the bag to him. Hop Sing caught the bundle and laughed, moving out of the doorway so Hoss could enter.

The room was cramped, and a veil of smoke coming from a pot by the door gave the air a stifling aroma unlike any Hoss had ever breathed. Along both sides stood three sets of narrow bunk beds made of cheap wood and filled with a layer of straw for a mattress. A few lethargic Chinese men lay on two of the lower bunks, watching Hoss with disinterested eyes. Hoss looked about the room, noting the candle and jug of water on a table in the back corner and a bucket of urine by the door. Hoss would never have found another entrance because there was none.

"Hop Sing and Mr. Hoss sleep here tonight. No cost Hop Sing. No cost Mr. Hoss," Hop Sing said, shutting the iron door.

Hoss stared from Hop Sing to the straw beds, scratched his head, then stuck his hand in his pocket, hoping he might find some money inside so he could buy better accommodations. As a man without money, he had no other option that would put a roof over his head. Even though this was the dingiest room he could ever remember standing in, he gave in to his only real choice. "I'll take a lower bunk," he said.

Hop Sing laughed and translated Hoss's words for his cousin, who answered sharply. Then both men laughed.

Hoss grimaced, then held up his arms to show his confusion.

"Hop Sing's cousin say you must sleep on bottom bunk. No one want to sleep in bed under big man like you."

His grimace turning into a grin, Hoss laughed with them, then stuck his hand out toward Hop Sing's cousin, who shook it vigorously, then stopped and flattened his petite hand out in Hoss's paw, comparing the size.

"Cousin named Yee Foo and says you be guest," Hop Sing said, showing his pride that his people would put up Hoss for the night, in contrast to the Palace Hotel employees. "Yee Foo know much of Chinatown. Yee Foo help find girl."

Hoss retreated to the back bunk, studying the greasy straw and the slick wood of the crudely built bed. Taking off his hat and hanging it on the corner post, he twisted around, lowered his head and sat down on the hard bed. He couldn't sit up straight without bumping his head. Just by sitting he seemed to take up half the length of the bed, and he knew it wouldn't comfortably accommodate his massive frame. The bunks were more shelves than beds, and for pillows, the men had a block of wood or a tin can at the head of each bed.

Hop Sing and Yee Foo began an animated conversation, gesturing wildly and talking in high-pitched voices that seemed too loud at times for the discussion to be entirely pleasant. It was gibberish to Hoss and of less concern than the hunger gnawing at his stomach and the exhaustion sapping his muscles. He was tired and needed rest, even if it was a while until dark. In the adjacent corner, he spotted four trays identical to those beside the two lethargic men who rested on the opposite bunks. On each tray was a lamp of cut glass, a smoking pipe, an earthen-ware bowl with a tiny hole in the center, a container the size of a pill box, and a cup of water. Periodically, while Hop Sing and Yee Foo argued, the two reclining men would warm the pipe over the lamp and inhale slowly, contentedly. From the aroma and the washed-out look of the two on the bunks, Hoss figured this was an opium den. He had heard of these in Virginia City, but had never been in one.

From the passageway drifted a commotion that ended with a knock on the iron door. Yee Foo and Hop Sing stopped arguing. Pointing to the trays, Yee Foo apparently issued orders to Hop Sing, who scurried to the corner, picking up a tray, handing it to Hoss and taking another for his own.

"Yee Foo lets white men see opium room," Hop Sing said. "White men pay dollar to see." Then he scrambled into a top bunk and lit the lamp. "Act like sleep on bunk, Mr. Hoss."

Hoss put the tray at the corner of the wooden bunk and eased over onto the straw, which did little to soften the hardness of the wooden slats below. Yee Foo nodded at him, and Hoss closed his eyes and bent his legs so he could fit himself on the tiny bunk. Yee Foo unbarred then unlatched the iron door, and spoke in Chinese with another man. Hoss heard the jingle of coins being exchanged, then heard the disgust as at least six men and two women took turns looking in on the dingy scene.

"Heathens," one man said.

"And the white man," a woman answered. "What kind of white man would allow himself in such a den of iniquity?"

Probably the same kind that would stand in the door watching, Hoss thought, though he gave no indication he was awake. Finally the door was closed, the latch turned and the bar slid into place. When he felt the vibrations of Hop Sing's movement in the bed above, Hoss opened his eyes in time to see Hop Sing jump down and land spryly on his feet.

Hop Sing swatted at Hoss's hand hanging over the edge of the bed. "Now can get up."

Hoss waved his hand away. "What's the use now, unless you know where your niece is?"

Turning, Hop Sing stared malevolently at Yee Foo and spoke with a surprisingly sharp tongue, especially to someone who had offered his hospitality, even if the quarters were sordid. "Yee Foo say Hop Sing and Mr. Hoss go back to Ponderosa. Give up girl, she likely dead."

"What?" Hoss said, sitting up quickly and bumping the top bunk. He rubbed his head, grimacing as much at Yee Foo's reluctance to provide help as from the bruise atop his head. "It don't make sense."

Hop Sing shook his head. "Niece come last week, sold next day. Cousin may know, but no tell who buy. Yee Foo scared of mean men killing him for talking. No want to help."

Still rubbing his head, Hoss frowned. "I don't understand you people, Hop Sing. He won't lift a hand to help because he's scared of threats from a few people."

Bowing his head, Hop Sing nodded. "Yee Foo tell Hop Sing only new ship come tomorrow at wharf. Slave girls come then. Yee Foo say that, nothing more."

Hoss studied Yee Foo, who responded with a meek smile. "I just don't understand," Hoss repeated. "You can't be intimidated if you want to find a little girl. We're her only chance."

Hop Sing nodded. "Chinatown bad for girls, but what we do to find her?"

"We'll go to the wharf and watch them unload the ship. If there are girls, we'll follow them. If the police and your own family won't help, we'll have to do it ourselves."

CHAPTER 8

The room was dark when Hoss awoke with a throbbing headache and cramps in his legs. It must be day, he thought, though he could not be sure in the windowless room. The candle on the back table had burned out, and all he could hear was the somnolent breathing of others. The atmosphere was thick with the oppressive aroma of opium, and Hoss craved a breath of fresh air. He rubbed his eyes, then rolled toward the edge of the bunk, his aching leg muscles balking when he tried to get up. Straw stuck to his pants legs and shirt as he arose, his head striking the upper bunk.

"Dad-blame-it," he muttered, rubbing his head and pushing himself disgustedly away from the bunk, which vibrated in his wake. In the upper bunk Hop Sing moaned for a moment, then all was quiet except for the heavy breathing of the others. Awkwardly, Hoss fumbled for his boots and shoved his feet inside. He felt for his hat and found it on the bunk's corner post where he had left it. Standing on his tiptoes, he tried to stretch the soreness out of his legs, then swung his arms around to work the cramps from his shoulders. By memory, he stepped cautiously to where he thought the door was, his outstretched hand finally touching it. His fingers groped for the latch, unlocking it with a twist. With both hands he tugged the iron bar free and pulled the door open, stepped quickly into the alley and took deep breaths, enjoying the air. Even if it were tainted with the alley's rotting odors, it was surely easier on the head than the opium smoke. Hoss walked to the end of the passageway and emerged into the alley itself, taking a deep breath with each step. He saw a tomcat pounce on a rat then lift it triumphantly into the air, shaking it to death in the grip of its sharp teeth and strong jaw.

The outside air helped clear the muddle from Hoss's brain. It was mid-morning, much later than he usually slept, and he wondered if he had been that tired or if the opium had dragged him into a deeper sleep. Either way, the answer to that question did not seem nearly as important as finding some food to fill the void in his stomach. He envied the alley cat as it marched regally around the corner with breakfast hanging from its mouth.

Hoss strode to the end of the alley, looking out on the street, which was alive with Celestials in their baggy clothes, speaking in their indecipherable language and occasionally staring at him, in awe of his size and in disgust at his intrusion into their world. After a while Hoss retreated back down the alley and along the passageway into Yee Foo's opium den. Hop Sing had still not stirred. The open door allowed a murky shaft of light into the room, and Hoss counted an extra man in one of the bunks, one who had not been there when he fell asleep, a tray of the drug paraphernalia at his side.

Disgusted, Hoss moved to Hop Sing's bunk and grabbed the cook by his shoulder. "Hop Sing," he said, "get up and let's get out of here, find food, and get to the wharf before the ship arrives."

Hop Sing stirred groggily, rubbing his face and eyes. Reluctantly, he sat up, then blinked at the murky light seeping through the open doorway. He sat up, reorienting himself, then shook his head vigorously and scooted to the edge of the bed. Hoss grabbed his arm to help him down. "Hop Sing awake," he managed.

Hoss stepped around Hop Sing and into the passageway, where the air was better. Shortly, Hop Sing joined him outside. "Hop Sing fear today. Cousin say powerful men not like Hop Sing to come for niece. Slave girls make them big money. Powerful men kill Hop Sing."

"I'm in this with you, Hop Sing. Don't forget that."

"You white man. Chinese no kill white man, but Yee Foo say maybe so if Mr. Hoss find slave girl."

Hoss took his hat off and slapped it against his knee. "This ain't right, dad-blame-it, them selling girls. It's slavery, Hop Sing, slavery, and this country fought a Civil War over slavery."

"Not over Chinese girls slavery."

"Then maybe it's time we did." Hoss tugged his hat in place furiously. "It just ain't right, Hop Sing."

"Hop Sing find one girl, no more!" he said, turning and retreating into the opium den again. In the dim light, Hoss saw Hop Sing digging around in his belongings. He pulled out a couple of tobacco tins, one rattling with coins, and slipped them in his blouse. Emerging from the room, he softly shut the iron door.

"Your hat, Hop Sing," Hoss reminded him.

"Hop Sing get new hat and Hop Sing buy Mr. Hoss meal."

Hoss licked his lips. "Sounds like a good idea to me," he said, then followed Hop Sing into the alley and out onto the street.

Hoss looked around, trying to fix his bearings, as Hop Sing led the way, taking a circuitous route before winding up at a hat shop. After an animated conversation, Hop Sing purchased a black felt hat while Hoss waited at the door. From the hat shop, Hop Sing took another disjointed route through Chinatown, Hoss at times convinced he had passed a particular location previously. He wondered if Hop Sing were trying to confound him. Surely not. Hop Sing seemed genuinely frightened.

Hop Sing paused at a window covered with Chinese lettering, then turned inside, a bell jingling as he pushed the door. As he entered, Hoss could smell a fragrant aroma coming from behind a curtain at the back of the room. Breakfast! It was a narrow room, maybe eight feet wide and twenty feet long, with rough-hewn wooden tables and small stools cramped together. Wooden bowls and spoons were stacked in the middle of each table. As Hop Sing closed the door to the tinkle of the bell, the curtain in the back parted and a Chinese man with a hooked nose and a yellowed towel over his arm appeared. He smiled, motioning toward a table near the back curtain.

Hoss slid onto a stool beside Hop Sing, who gestured and spoke to the waiter. Nodding, the waiter disappeared behind the curtain, returning shortly with two cups of steaming aromatic liquid. Hoss cradled one of the clay cups between his hands and lifted it to his lips, enjoying the fragrance of the spiced tea and then its hot flavor as it coursed down his throat. When he sat the empty cup down, the waiter picked it up and returned moments later with a refill in one hand and a large pot in the other. Hoss leaned forward as the waiter deposited the pot and then his cup of tea on the table. The pot was filled with a thick meaty soup of rice and vegetables Hoss did not recognize. The waiter ladled out a bowl and placed it before Hoss, then did the same for Hop Sing. The aroma was tantalizing, and Hoss's stomach churned with anticipation as he grabbed his spoon and scooped up a bite. It was delicious and hot upon his tongue. He attacked the soup with vigor while Hop Sing watched him with amusement. The waiter brought a plate of crackers, and Hoss took a handful to enjoy with his soup. When he had cleaned his bowl, the waiter refilled it. After finishing that bowl, Hoss filled it again on his own.

"Mighty good, Hop Sing," Hoss said with a wave of his spoon. The waiter returned with another cup of tea.

"Tell him it's good, Hop Sing, and ask him what it is," Hoss commanded between bites.

Hop Sing and the waiter conversed for a moment before the waiter turned to Hoss.

"Mighty good." Hoss said. "Now, what is it?"

The waiter nodded. "Bow-wow," he replied.

Hoss gulped, a spoonful of the soup stopping just inches from his mouth, then sliding back down to the bowl. "Bow-wow?" he said, turning to Hop Sing. "Does he mean dog meat?"

Hop Sing nodded. "Still good?"

Hoss dropped the spoon in the bowl and turned away a moment.

"Mr. Hoss have Hop Sing fix things Hop Sing not always like, but Hop Sing eat."

"But dog, Hop Sing?" Hoss scooted his stool back from the table and stood up as the waiter and Hop Sing apparently shared a joke.

Hop Sing hurriedly finished his bowl of soup and drained his tea cup, then paid the waiter.

The meal settled uneasily in Hoss's stomach, and he was glad to escape to the street with Hop Sing.

"Hop Sing take Mr. Hoss to wharf, see ship come in, look for slave girls."

"Just no more dog soup, Hop Sing."

Hop Sing cut easily through the crowd, his small frame moving through the sea of Chinese pedestrians. Being bigger, Hoss had difficulty navigating the currents. Gradually the Chinese pedestrians thinned as Hoss and Hop Sing skirted the edge of the Barbary Coast, the hard and dangerous section of town where a man could find an hour of fun and a lifetime of trouble. The Barbary Coast seemed to reek of liquor and was filled with the refuse of humanity. Men sprawled in the gutters, recuperating from last night's brawls or drinking binges. The tinkling of an out-of-tune piano and the blaring of some off-key horn accompanied the loud giggle of a harlot in one of the numerous saloons and brothels. Hop Sing plowed ahead, looking neither left nor right but straight down the street. Hoss, meanwhile, took it all in, wondering what would drive man or woman to waste a life in the squalor of such immorality. A man shook his fist at Hop Sing, taunting him with an obscene epithet as he passed.

At an intersection, Hop Sing turned onto Pacific Street, which sloped down toward a wharf that jutted out into the bay. Just coming into view in the middle of the bay was a steamship, its twin stacks punctuating the air with commas of smoke. Hoss gauged they were ten blocks away from the bay and wondered for a moment if they could make it before the steamship docked.

"Is that our ship, Hop Sing?"

"Hop Sing say so," he answered.

"We'll be lucky to get there by the time she docks."

"Hop Sing not safe sooner."

Hoss scratched his elbow, knocking off a piece of straw that had stuck in his shirt from his mattress. "I'm with you, Hop Sing. Nothing to worry about."

"Many much to worry about," Hop Sing replied. "Mr. Hoss see."

As they neared the dock, Hop Sing's pace grew cautious. At one point Hop Sing lifted his new black felt hat and wrapped his queue up inside it.

They were still two blocks away when the steamship eased into the dock, its whistle piercing the air to announce its arrival from China. That was but part of the noise. A crowd of burly thugs and hooligans had gathered at the end of the dock, jeering and shouting, shaking their fists at the ship. They chanted, "The Chinese must go! The Chinese must go! The Chinese must go!" And as the arriving Chinese men lined up to disembark, other cries carried over the chant. "Yellow bastards, yellow bastards! Kill the pigtails!"

Now Hoss understood why Hop Sing had no desire to arrive early. Behind him, Hoss heard the shouts of more hooligans.

"We're late for China steamer day," one shouted, knocking Hop Sing's hat off as he ran by. Hop Sing's queue fell out and another hooligan grabbed at it as he passed.

They were gone before Hoss could react. "You stay near me, Hop Sing. This is an ugly crowd."

"No worry. Hop Sing stay close." He picked up his hat and tucked his queue back in place beneath it.

Hoss stopped at the corner across from the wharf. "We'll wait here," he said, leaning up against the side of a red-brick warehouse, screening Hop Sing from the gathering mob. Some welcome to America, Hoss thought, the anger welling in him.

Four freight wagons rumbled down the street and headed straight into the mob, which split to let them pass, then came back together again like water after a stone's splash. The wagons circled to a stop on the dock and waited as a line of Chinese men marched down the gangplank in single file. They advanced with quiet dignity, many wearing bamboo hats and balancing their possessions at the ends of bamboo poles. The new arrivals were herded into the first wagon until it was crammed with men and belongings.

The mob cursed the baffled Chinese men, then began to throw stones at them. Their targets sat in the wagon calmly watching the hooligans. One thug pulled a slingshot and fired a stone, striking one of the men in the wagon on the chin. He screamed and grabbed his face as fellow passengers looked helplessly from him to the gang. Some in the mob waved the handles of pickaxes, and a few brandished butcher knives for cutting off pigtails. One man with a knife even had three pigtails hanging from his belt like scalps. When the first wagon was loaded, the driver released the brakes and rattled the reins, the horses darting forward at a gallop.

Jeers arose from the crowd as the wagon rumbled by, the thugs pummeling it with rocks or pounding it with their clubs. One Chinese man lost his balance and fell from the wagon. The hooligans were upon him like a pack of wolves, beating him, rubbing mud in his face, tearing at his clothes. Bloodied and terrified, the Celestial scrambled free and bolted after the wagon. A pack of thugs, laughing and jeering at his predicament, gave chase.

The hooligans, passing liquor bottles among themselves, let up a cheer as the second wagon started their way. The Chinese men in this wagon hunkered low for protection. The driver whipped the horses, and the wagon shot forward into the crowd, scattering the thugs, who responded with a barrage of rocks and empty whiskey bottles. One troublemaker, his reflexes dulled by too much liquor, tripped and fell. The wagon's rear wheel rolled over his ankle. He screamed while his companions gave brief chase after the human cargo. The injured man, his foot limp at the end of his quivering leg, lay writhing in pain until a couple of the gang grabbed his arms and dragged him across the street near where Hoss and Hop Sing stood.

As they deposited him out of harm's way, one of the men glanced up and saw Hop Sing, who slipped back into Hoss's shadow.

The thug nudged his companion and pointed to Hop Sing. "Here's the goddamn yellow bastard who broke McShane's foot," he said to his ally. "Let's teach him a lesson and maybe he'll swim back to China."

"That's an idea," replied the other. "Let's toss him in the bay and see if he floats."

Both men were Irish, by their brogue. They swaggered toward Hop Sing, fists clenched, eyes brimming with hate. Hoss could smell liquor on their breath. He glanced from them to the pack of thugs jeering at the dock. Fortunately, the other hooligans were focused on the third wagon being loaded up. Likely they would not notice Hop Sing and Hoss, particularly if it were a quick fight between him and the two approaching ruffians.

"Come here, you yellow bastard," the first hoodlum called, waving his fist at Hop Sing.

Hoss stepped forward. "Now fellows, Hop Sing's my Chinaman. I can't let you bother him."

Both Irishmen laughed. "Country boy, why don't you head back to the farm?" said the nearer one. "We'll just borrow your Chinaman for a while and give him a bath."

"Yeah," taunted the other, "we'll clean him up for you."

Hoss gritted his teeth and smiled, a heavy breath coming like steam from the flared nostrils of his broad nose. Hop Sing backed into the brick wall and froze as the two Irishmen advanced.

"Out of our way," said one.

"Yeah," added the other, "or we'll call our friends over."

Hoss stepped aside and waved his hand toward Hop Sing. "He's yours, boys, just don't maim him."

"That's the spirit, country boy," the nearest one said as they advanced.

Hop Sing trembled against the wall, his eyes wide with disbelief. Hoss had abandoned him.

As the two men stepped past Hoss, he spun around with a cat's quickness, grabbed them by their necks and smashed their heads together. Caught by surprise, the two men were stunned, their reflexes dulled. For an instant they were motionless in Hoss's grip, then they seemed to realize their predicament and tried to fight back. Hoss's fingers tightened around their necks. They gasped at the pain and flailed their arms, but he controlled them as if they were puppets. He drew back his arms and brought their heads together with a clunk. Both men groaned and stood groggily on their feet. He crashed their heads together again as easily as if he were clapping his hands. The knees of both men turned to mush as Hoss shoved them toward their companion with the broken ankle. They tumbled atop him, drawing a cry of anguish from him.

Behind him, Hoss heard a great jeer, and he spun about, expecting to see the mob charging him. Instead he saw the gang focused on the third departing wagon. Relieved, he turned to Hop Sing. "You okay?"

"Hop Sing scared, greatly scared."

"Maybe we better leave."

Hop Sing folded his arms across his chest and shook his head. "Hop Sing no go until last wagon—wagon with girls—leaves."

The third wagon raced through the crowd and up Pacific Street, weaving among other vehicles and horses, quickly reaching safety.

Hoss heard groans nearby and turned to see one of the hooligans he had knocked out coming to. "We'll walk up the street a ways, Hop Sing, watch from there. When this crowd breaks up, they may trouble us, and I can't whip all of them."

Hop Sing nodded and they started back up Pacific Street, waiting two blocks from the wharf and watching the final wagon being loaded. This time it was different. Nobody marched into the wagon. Instead, what seemed like crates were being loaded in back. Though many of the thugs still remained, the mob had begun to disperse, mainly because it was taking more than half an hour to load the final wagon. At length, the wagon did dart away from the steamer and down the wharf to the street, where the hooligans pelted it with stones, but not nearly as vigorously as the first three wagons.

"That wagon, Hop Sing, let's stay ahead of it as long as we can," Hoss said, the two falling into step, Hoss glancing over his shoulder as the wagon worked its way through the traffic. When it finally caught up with them after two blocks, Hoss slowed up. He could not believe what he saw. The human cargo was young girls, each riding in a bamboo cage, like poultry going to market. The girls wore cotton tunics and trousers, and several had checkered handkerchiefs in their hair. Their dark eyes were wide with terror, humiliated at being paraded so indignantly through the city.

"It's inhuman, Hop Sing," Hoss sputtered, then realized his companion was well ahead of him, moving toward Chinatown. Hoss scurried to catch up.

By walking rapidly, they were able to stay near the wagon as it skirted the Barbary Coast and reached the outskirts of Chinatown. At Dupont Street the wagon turned into the heart of Chinatown, drawing the smiles of Celestial men. At a soot-blackened building with dingy windows and faded Chinese signboards hanging from the awnings, the wagon stopped and men emerged from behind green iron doors to unload the cargo. Hoss counted fifteen cages as he and Hop Sing hurriedly approached. Surely some San Francisco police had noticed this caged cargo, but they had done nothing about it. San Francisco was a more heartless town than he had ever realized.

They reached the building just as the wagon pulled away from the walk and disappeared around the corner. "What'll we do now, Hop Sing?" Hoss asked, his fists planted on his hips.

Hop Sing stood silently by the building, reading the signboards and a new one that had been hung on the green door. He dropped his gaze when two stern Chinese men came outside. Crossing their arms, they stared at Hoss.

Hop Sing grabbed Hoss's arm, tugging him down the

street. "Hop Sing return tomorrow with Mr. Hoss for auction."

"What," Hoss exclaimed, "they're selling girls like cattle?"

Hop Sing nodded. "Tomorrow."

CHAPTER 9

B en Cartwright looked down at the plate of scrambled eggs, burnt bacon, and scorched biscuits. Little Joe sat across the table from him, still wearing
his dirtied apron, powdered with flour. Holding his fork
gingerly, Ben toyed with the greasy eggs, then poked at
the burnt strips of bacon. He broke off the end of a crisp
bacon strip and buried it under a forkful of eggs. Warily,
he lifted the fork to his mouth and slowly chewed. The bacon crunched between his teeth. Ben grimaced.

Little Joe frowned. He missed Hop Sing.

Gingerly, Ben put his fork beside his plate as if the
food might attack if spooked. He studied the biscuit. The
golden brown he was accustomed to in Hop Sing's biscuits
must be somewhere beneath the scorch marks of these.
Breaking the biscuit in half, he looked at its innards. The
burnt outer shell surrounded a ball of sticky dough. Little
Joe had gotten the oven too hot for biscuits. Ben dropped
the biscuit upon his plate and reached for his coffee cup.

"Experience is the best teacher," Ben said, holding
the coffee cup before his lips. "That's what I always believed, Joseph. Until now!" Ben tilted the cup to his lips
and sipped the warm brown liquid. At least it was tolerable.

"But Pa," Little Joe pleaded, "this is woman's work,
not honorable work for a man."

"Joseph," Ben said sternly, "all work is honorable. Hop Sing is a man and it's not too good for him."

"But Hop Sing's a Chinaman."

Ben pointed his index finger at Little Joe. "Now, Joseph, I'll have no talk like that around the Ponderosa. Hop Sing is an honest man. His ways are different from ours, but he is a man to be valued over the shiftless and the dishonest of any race."

Little Joe ran his fingers through his curly brown hair, his frown narrowing the dimple in his chin. His hazel eyes, flecked with gold specks, were troubled. "I didn't mean that, Pa, about Hop Sing. I mean some folks are better at some things than others. I can do ranch work, break horses better than Hop Sing could."

Ben finished his coffee and then threw his napkin on the table. "You can, Joseph, but there are people in this world, people around these parts, people in Virginia City even, that would look down on you because you work horses. It's beneath them. Intolerance, Joseph, is a great sin among men."

"Intolerance and burnt biscuits?" Little Joe replied, his eyes lighting up at his father's smile.

Ben nodded. "And burnt biscuits." He pushed his chair back and stood up, jamming his hands in his pockets, pacing back and forth by the table. "My appetite's been poor the last few days, Joseph, and it's not just your cooking."

"Hoss?" Little Joe replied.

Again Ben nodded. "Hoss and the timber leases. No word from Hoss or Davey Kendall." Ben shook his head.

"Maybe he's taking his father's death hard," Little Joe answered as he stood up to clear the breakfast dishes.

Ben pondered the possibility. "Davey's silence confounds me. And Hoss, it's not like him to run off. He knows I've acquaintances in San Francisco who could get a message back."

"Maybe I ought to go after him," Little Joe offered, standing at the kitchen door with dirty dishes in his hand.

"No, Joseph, I'm less worried about him in San Francisco than you trying to find him there."

Little Joe stepped into the kitchen. "I'm as smart as Hoss."

"Yes, you are, Joseph, maybe smarter," Ben acknowledged, "but not as wise as Hoss. And Hoss isn't as hot-headed as you can be."

Little Joe approached the dining table with a coffeepot in his hand. "Hot-headed?" He poured coffee into Ben's cup, then his.

"It's your mother's Cajun blood," Ben said wistfully. "She was a striking woman, a good woman, son, but she did have a temper."

"Wish I remembered her," Little Joe answered, then waited. If his father had a soft spot, it was for his three wives, each of whom had died tragically. From past experience, Little Joe knew that his father's ironclad determination and his sense of right and wrong always softened when the subject of his wives came up. Having been married to three had not diminished his appreciation of any of them, but rather had strengthened his love for each. He had fully loved each in her own way. His father's mahogany eyes seemed to shine at the bittersweet memories. Little Joe had seen this expression before, and it always lifted his father's spirits. Ben finished the cup of coffee and planted it firmly back on the table.

"Joseph, I've a telegram to wire San Francisco," he announced. "Why don't we ride into Carson City, attend to that and take the train over to Virginia City."

Little Joe smiled to himself. It had worked again, but he might milk his father's expansive mood just a little more. "I've got dishes to wash, and supper'll need to be ready when you return."

Ben laughed. "I was thinking of staying the night in Virginia City and maybe even letting you find us a temporary cook."

Little Joe danced back into the kitchen, carrying the coffeepot. "I'll have the kitchen done in twenty minutes, and I'll be ready to go in ten more."

"Fine, Joseph, and I'll saddle the horses."

Both went about their chores quickly, and in three quarters of an hour they were on the trail. The ride to Carson City was always invigorating, to traverse Ponderosa's high land, breathe its fresh air, enjoy its beauty, drink the fresh waters from its rippling streams, spot its abundant wildlife. Despite the numerous ventures of Cartwright Enterprises in mining and railroading, Ben still enjoyed ranching the most. He had been a sailor, a chandler, a merchant, and had held other occupations too numerous to mention in his younger years, but ranching had always been his favorite. He had once heard that no man ever worked cattle for more than a day without falling in love with ranching.

Ben wished that Hoss was by his side as well. Little Joe was entertaining, always lighthearted—until his temper got the best of him—but Hoss knew nature and observed things that no one else would notice, like the varied configurations of pine needles on different pine trees, or the vegetation that would grow on the south side of a mountain in the sunlight, different from that on the north side in perpetual shade. Little Joe was too interested in having a good laugh to notice those things, and Adam always too preoccupied with business.

It was a pleasant ride this time of year from the Ponderosa ranch house to Carson City. Ben and Little Joe skirted the Virginia and Truckee Railroad, passed Washoe Lake to the east and rode along Eagle Valley. Carson City was the county seat of Ormsby County and the capital of Nevada, with its statehouse of fine-grained sandstone occupying the center square. Riding in from the north, Ben and Little Joe could make out the capitol in the center of town, the state orphan's home at the edge, and the state prison just over a mile east of town. The railroad track ran into town and was lost in the Virginia and Truckee yards amid the large car shop and roundhouse, foundry and machine shop, all neatly arranged and freshly painted with canary yellow and Gloucester green, same as the coaches on the line. The depot was nestled at the edge of the yards, convenient to the wide streets, sixty-six to eighty feet across, which made Carson City so easy to get around in.

"We'll stop at the depot and send a telegram," Ben said. "Allow you to visit with Molly Ashe awhile before we stable our horses and take the train on into Virginia City."

Little Joe shook his head. "She'll just tease me about doing dishes and then have nothing else to do with me."

Ben laughed. "And that makes you all the more interested in her, since she doesn't fall for all your charm."

Little Joe cocked his head and answered with a sheepish grin that accentuated his dimpled chin. "It's like you always say, Pa, you appreciate those things you have to work for the hardest."

They reached the depot between trains, when things were slow. Tying their horses, Ben and Little Joe stretched their muscles before climbing the steps to the depot. Ben pushed open the door.

Ticket Agent Oliver Myers, lounging behind the ticket counter reading the Carson City newspaper, looked up lazily from the latest news, snapping to attention when he realized a stockholder from the Virginia and Truckee had just entered. He rattled the paper shut, then knocked it to the floor behind the counter.

"Good day, Mr. Cartwright," he said, "and you too, Mr. Little Joe, I mean Little Joe." Myers grimaced at how foolish he sounded and at the giggle of Molly Ashe, standing behind him.

"Heard from Hoss, Mr. Cartwright?" Molly called to Ben.

"Not yet, ma'am."

"And Little Joe, you still doing dishes?" Molly giggled.

Myers laughed loudly, as he always did when the joke was on someone else.

Little Joe turned to his father. "I told you that's what she would remember, Pa. Not my gallant offer to accompany her back to Carson City."

Molly Ashe tossed her head, her blond hair bouncing like her smile. "You'd make some old boy a good wife," she answered. Behind her the telegraph clattered, and she ran to take a message.

"I was glad to help your son Hoss get on the train to

San Francisco the other day," Myers said. "I don't often allow that for a person who has no money."

"That's what I understand," Ben said coldly, knowing Myers was overplaying his role in covering Hoss's fare, but realizing not all things were worth making an issue of.

Little Joe settled onto a bench, clasped his hands behind his neck and leaned against the seat, staring at the ceiling. Myers was an arrogant fool who hated every man taller or wealthier than him. And the feeling was usually reciprocated. Little Joe begrudged him but one thing, the pleasure of working each day with Molly Ashe. "Hey, Oliver," Little Joe gigged Myers, "you look like you've grown an inch, or maybe you're standing on a crate."

Myers scowled but didn't reply, for fear his answer would offend Ben Cartwright, who after all was a company stockholder. Instead he turned to Ben. "How may I help you, Mr. Cartwright?"

"It's Molly I need to see," Ben said. "If you don't have anything else to do between trains, you can go on back to reading your newspaper." Ben twisted around and winked at Little Joe.

Myers picked up a broom from the corner and barged into the waiting room. Vigorously, he shoved the broom over the shiny floor, spending considerable time in Little Joe's vicinity, making him lift his legs for the broom to pass. Little Joe just grinned.

Shortly, Molly emerged from her telegraph office, sticking a pencil between her ear and the band of the green eyeshade she wore. Little Joe wondered how the garters she wore on her sleeves might look on her legs.

"A telegram?" she asked Ben, who leaned against the counter.

"Indeed, Molly, to San Francisco."

"Trying to find Hoss," she said, pulling the pencil from over her ear and grabbing a pad of paper from the counter.

"Don't know where to turn for that, right yet. This is legal business."

"Go ahead then, tell me your message."

Ben nodded. "To Attorney Davey Kendall, San

Francisco. No response last message. Report due on timber bid by tomorrow noon. If none, you're relieved of legal duties for Cartwright Enterprises. Wire Virginia City with response. Ben Cartwright."

"That all?" Molly asked.

"That'll do it," Ben replied.

Molly did a quick count on the telegram length, then told Ben the charge. He pulled coins out from his pocket and paid her.

"Tsk, tsk, tsk," Molly said, watching Myers push the broom around the room. "Oliver, you left the ticket counter without locking the cash drawer." Molly grinned slyly at Ben, who covered his grin with a closed fist.

Oliver's big ears reddened and he angrily shoved the broom at a pile of debris, then calmed down when he remembered Ben's presence.

"When's the next passenger train to Virginia City?" Ben asked as Molly handed him his change.

"Two-ten," Molly replied, turning back to her office to send off the message.

"Oliver," Ben called across the room, "we'll be back to catch the two-ten to Virginia City. Have us a pair of tickets ready."

Myers nodded. "Yes, sir."

Little Joe stood up, stretched and pointed at the floor. "You missed some," he teased, then followed Ben outside.

"We've got a couple hours, Joseph," Ben said. "Let's grab a bite of lunch and visit Silas Ward awhile before we stable our horses and catch the train."

They ate at a new eatery a block from the capitol building, then went over to Ward's Mercantile, the largest general store in Carson City and the major supplier for the Ponderosa.

Cane in hand, Ward greeted Ben and Little Joe warmly, pumping their hands vigorously. Ward was a portly man, balding on top and growing around the middle. He always wore a fresh apron, sparkling white and crisply starched, just as he always carried a cane to help offset the hitch in his gait, the result of a broken leg when a barrel of pickles fell on him some years back. As he explained it, he had exchanged a good leg for a good cane.

"Howdy, Ben," he said, "hear Hoss is in San Francisco. Darn shame too, because I've got a new batch of horehound candy he'd sure like. That boy's quite an eater."

"Indeed," Ben answered. "How's business?"

Little Joe crossed his arms over his chest and just shook his head. Silas Ward always offered horehound candy to Hoss for free, but never made the same offer to him, perplexing Little Joe to no end. In fact, Little Joe didn't particularly care for horehound candy. It was just the principle of the thing.

"Business could be worse," Ward said. "Could be better if the Ponderosa would settle its account."

Ben laughed and slapped Silas Ward on the back. "That's what we dropped by to do."

Ward pointed to the back desk with his cane, and hobbled in that direction, Ben following after him.

Little Joe moved away from the door over by the tin goods, figuring to rest on a stool there. But then, across the room, he spotted a young lady with auburn hair, looking at bolts of material and millinery goods. She had a fine figure clad in a gingham dress, and she moved delicately around the table stacked with material. Little Joe took off his hat and ran his fingers through his hair. He rocked on his boot heels and whistled softly the tune to "Lorena."

He ambled her way, watching her every move, though she was quite oblivious to him. Still whistling, he approached the table. She looked up, smiled briefly, then shyly turned her eyes away. She dug a bolt of cloth from under several others and unwrapped a few lengths of material, comparing it with a red cotton cloth she had spread out on the adjacent cutting table.

Picking up a bolt of blue silk, Little Joe held it before her. "Here's a nice one."

"Yes, sir, it is, but much too expensive for me," she said. "A cotton cloth is what I must buy."

"How about this one," Little Joe suggested, picking up another bolt of silk.

The young lady smiled and looked into Little Joe's eyes. "You seem to be greatly interested in cloth. Do you sew?"

"No," Little Joe grinned, "I wash dishes."

Giggling, the young lady waved her hand. "You're funning me."

Little Joe was about to ask her name when he heard his father's voice behind him.

"Joseph, we've got to stable our horses and catch that train."

"Just a minute, Pa," Little Joe replied, shoving his hand into his pants pocket. He pulled out a five-dollar gold piece and flipped it onto the cutting table. To the auburn-haired beauty, he said, "A pretty lady like you should have pretty cloth."

She took the coin between her delicate fingers and nodded her thanks to him. When Little Joe turned around, she held the coin to her mouth and bit it, determining that it was in fact genuine.

Witnessing Joe's gesture and her reaction, Ben just shook his head, slapping his son on the shoulder as they marched out. They rode their horses to a stable near the depot and left them there, walking the rest of the way to the station.

In the distance, they could see a cloud of black smoke marking the approach of the Virginia and Truckee locomotive. The station was crowded now, with a line at the ticket counter. Seeing them enter, Oliver Myers motioned for them to approach a closed window at the ticket counter. As Ben stepped up, Myers opened it and slid Ben two round-trip passes to Virginia City. Wordlessly, he then returned to the open window to work the line.

Ben and Little Joe stepped out on the platform, dodging the baggage clerk as he rolled a cart of luggage and freight out of the baggage room. Molly Ashe waved to them from her office.

"Nothing from San Francisco," she called through the window.

Ben thanked her and turned around as the locomotive chugged into the station. There was a flurry of activity while passengers climbed out and others boarded, Ben and Little Joe among them.

The trip to Virginia City was quick and pleasant. Upon arrival, they made their way to the offices of the Bristlecone mine. They found Adam there in his shirt-sleeves, poring over assaying reports.

"Any word from San Francisco?" Ben asked him.

"No, sir, not a thing from Davey Kendall, or Hoss either."

Ben shook his head and pinched the bridge of his nose.

oss leaned against the iron facade of a dingy meat market across Dupont Street from the auction house. Chinese men marched singly and in clumps to the green door and waited in a slow-moving line, several staring at Hoss, who felt as conspicuous as a naked man in church. Two stern men, also Chinese, admitted the congregants one by one through the iron door. These two seemed as interested in Hoss as they did in keeping tabs of the Celestials. With eyes narrowed, lips tight, and flesh drawn taut against their clenched jaws, the two returned Hoss's stare with suspicion.

The Chinese passing through the green door talked with great animation. Hoss had seen such festive fellowships at livestock auctions before, but never could he have imagined this type of auction. The anger still burned within him as strongly as it had yesterday. He'd had a fitful night's sleep because of it. There was still Hop Sing's niece to be found and saved, but what about these others, so many of them, the boats bringing more weekly and the police not caring?

Hop Sing stood patiently by a lamp post at the corner of the street. A final surge of Chinese men crowded before the soot-blackened building with its dingy windows and its Chinese signboards suspended from the awnings. Hoss estimated it was almost ten o'clock. As the line dwindled,

Hop Sing angled across the street for the door. Hoss pushed himself from the wall and ambled for the building, his path intersecting Hop Sing's. Hoss stepped in line behind Hop Sing and waited.

The two guards scowled at Hoss, then folded their arms. They nodded at the last of the Celestials preceding Hop Sing and let them pass inside, but as Hop Sing stepped up to the head of the line, they stepped between him and the door. Hop Sing spoke in Chinese, and the two men shook their heads, slowly and in unison. Hop Sing raised his voice, then stepped toward the sentries, gesticulating wildly. Firmly, each took a hand and shoved him back. He stumbled into Hoss, who pushed him aside.

"We want in. No trouble unless you don't let us inside. Then I'll tear this building down if that's what it takes."

The two guards looked at each other, then shrugged, mumbling something in Chinese.

"Let me in, dammit." Hoss took a step toward them, and in a flash one pulled a hatchet and the other a knife from under their loose blouses.

Hoss exhaled slowly, then lifted his hand to his head and removed his hat, figuring he'd throw it in one's face while disarming the second. "You little fellas ever fought a big man before?"

Hop Sing stepped between them. "Hop Sing say no fight."

Hoss shoved him aside, and Hop Sing stumbled into the half circle of Celestials who had gathered. "You fellas take a step toward me and the fight's on," Hoss said.

The two guards looked at each other, shrugged and then moved toward Hoss, saying something in Chinese.

Hoss flung his hat at the knife bearer's face, then lunged for the upraised arm of the hatchet man. Grabbing his wrist, Hoss pinched it like a vise until the hatchet fell to the walk; then, in one swift motion, he swung his booted foot into the groin of the flailing man.

"Oooof," the guard grunted, collapsing to the ground, his hands rubbing the fire between his legs.

"Mr. Hoss, watch out!"

Hoss spun around to see the knife-toting Asian lunge for him. He dodged the flashing blade and kicked the hatchet from beneath his feet. As the guard grinned like a cat facing a cornered mouse, Hoss backed into the building, gauging the man's reach, including the length of the knife. "Come on, little fella," he taunted, as the guard advanced a step toward him. "I'll leave you like your buddy."

The man grinned wickedly, screamed, then charged.

"That's it, little fella," Hoss cried, lifting his foot. His leg straightened out at the level of the man's belly, and the guard ran solidly into Hoss's boot. His face widened with pain, his mouth opening as the air gushed out in a scream. With the wall for support behind him, Hoss held his leg rigid as his assailant swung his knife, which passed four inches short of Hoss's stomach; as Hoss had judged, his leg was longer than the knifeman's reach and blade. Flexing his knee, Hoss shoved the guard back toward the street. Falling, he flung his knife into the crowd, the spectators scattering, then diving for the weapon.

The guard rolled over, then crawled to his hands and knees, gasping for breath. Hoss picked up the nearby hatchet and stepped to the lookout. Grabbing his queue, Hoss jerked his head up and held the hatchet at his braided hair. The crowd gasped as Hoss made a motion to cut it off. The man screamed. When Hoss let go, the bloodied man fell face first to the sidewalk.

There was stunned silence for a moment, as Hoss looked around for anybody else that wanted to take him on. The crowd stepped back. The creak of the door opening was all Hoss heard for a moment.

Then a single pair of hands began to clap. "Very good, very good, man big as horse."

Hoss spun around to see a well-to-do Celestial standing in the doorway. His hands were pale and delicate with a gold or diamond ring on each finger. He bowed to Hoss, his silk trousers and blouse shimmering with the movement. When he straightened, his almond-shaped eyes were sinister black stones from Hell, his dangerous smile exposing teeth capped in gold.

"Who are you?" Hoss sputtered.

"Hip Ye Tung," he replied with disdain as his hand pointed at the lookouts on the ground. "These men work for me. Join us for sale, thank you very much."

"Not without my pal," Hoss said, motioning toward Hop Sing, who stood obediently nearby.

"Ah, Hop Sing," said Hip Ye Tung.

Hoss spun around at Hip Ye Tung. "How'd you know that?"

Hip Ye Tung flashed his golden teeth again, then bowed in mockery. "Word travel quick of man big as horse, and of friend. Man big as horse not stay at Palace when Hop Sing cannot stay. Man big as horse with huge hands rip Palace book, thank you very much."

Bending over, Hoss picked his hat off the sidewalk and dusted its seven-inch crown, noticing a nick in the brim where the guard's knife had hit it. His hands clasped in front of him, Hop Sing joined Hoss.

"Many Chinamen hear of man big as horse who not stay at Palace, think man big as horse deserve hospitality in Chinatown. Besides," Hip Ye Tung laughed wildly, his teeth flashing with mockery, "your body'd be too big to hide from police." He motioned vigorously for Hoss and Hop Sing to follow him inside.

Hop Sing moved ahead, Hoss turning to look at the two downed guards. One rolled on the ground, whimpering from the throbbing pain in his groin. The other stirred from unconsciousness. Hoss smiled and marched past the green door as Hip Ye Tung closed it behind him.

The long hallway led to a closed door barely visible in the dimness. The floor creaked as Hop Sing and Hoss advanced, Hip Ye Tung following behind them. Hoss could make out a muffled din, but he could not place it until Hop Sing opened the door. The noise was coming from downstairs. Over Hop Sing's shoulder Hoss could see a stairway descending to another closed door.

"Go on, thank you very much," Hip Ye Tung said, patting Hoss on the back.

Hop Sing and Hoss moved down the stairs, Hip Ye Tung closing the door behind them all. The din grew louder. Reaching the door at the bottom, Hop Sing twisted the handle and flung it open, as if he feared something. A blast of noise and heat rushed over them. Their eyes, accustomed to the hallway's dimness, were blinded by the unexpected brightness coming out of the large room. Hoss squinted until his eyes gradually adjusted to the light. What he saw surprised him: a vast basement, maybe forty feet wide and sixty feet long, teeming with Chinese men inspecting frightened young girls at various locations about the room.

Hip Ye Tung ushered Hoss and Hop Sing in and shut the door behind them. The oppressive heat and the pungent smell of unwashed bodies attacked the senses. But for Hoss, that was easier to stomach than what he witnessed. Men casually walked around cages holding girls, examining the captives, punching and squeezing them as they would prized animals at a livestock auction; nodding their approval, scratching their chins, figuring up their bids. It made Hoss sick, but there was little he could do to stop this travesty. He could disrupt this pagan rite, but that might seal the fate of Hop Sing's niece.

"Up front," Hip Ye Tung said to Hoss and Hop Sing. "Seats I kept for you. Sale to begin." Clapping his hands over his head, Hip Ye Tung shouted words in Chinese, followed by a sudden rush of men toward favored bench seats. Some men moved in pairs to the cages and carried the living merchandise to the front of the room.

Hoss followed Hop Sing, taking a seat at the spot designated by Hip Ye Tung, who then climbed the steps up to the platform and held his arms up to quiet the murmuring crowd that awaited the bidding.

As Hip Ye Tung spoke in Chinese, Hoss estimated that 150 men were participating. He was the biggest man in the room, and the only white man. He gritted his teeth and waited as Hip Ye Tung apparently reminded the crowd of the ground rules. At his final words, the men erupted into applause and cheering. At that cue, two men opened a cage and released a girl. Holding her under her armpits, the two men carried her up the three steps to the platform, where Hip Ye Tung began to tear off her clothes. She squirmed to resist, but the strong-armed men who had carried her held her arms tightly. Her resistance turned into embarrassment as she was stripped and restrained from covering herself. Her naked body glistened with sweat and tears.

Hoss sighed at the indignity, then nudged Hop Sing. "What's your niece look like? Could that be her?"

"Years since Hop Sing see niece," Hop Sing seemed embarrassed. "Hop Sing know name, not face, of niece."

Hoss stared at the auction platform. How would they ever find Hop Sing's niece? Even if this girl wasn't Hop Sing's niece, she deserved better. All the girls deserved better.

Hoss wanted to charge the platform, free the girl and the others and escape from this Hell. Instead he averted his eyes, and noticed the man sitting beside him. He wore garb like the two guards Hoss had whipped outside. This one, too, was brandishing a gleaming hatchet. Hoss turned away and glanced over Hop Sing to see another man brandishing a hatchet. Their eyes met, and Hoss could feel the hate they emanated.

Up on the platform, Hip Ye Tung prodded and poked the girl, then invited another man up on stage, who inspected her more thoroughly, checking each leg and arm, her back and her chest. Turning to the crowd, he made a statement, and the men sat forward in their seats, anticipating the bidding.

"Doctor man," Hop Sing said for Hoss's benefit.

Then the bidding began in a flurry. Men all over the room were shouting, waving their hands, standing up or climbing atop the benches to make themselves taller and their bids more obvious. Hoss had seen bidding at livestock auctions, but never so animated as this. He shook his head in disgust and stared at his boots, so at least he would not be intruding on the girl's modesty. Shortly, the bidding died down and it was between two men, one just down the front row, the other a couple rows back. Finally, the man on the front row sat silent and the bidder in back shouted to celebrate his purchase.

Hoss leaned over to Hop Sing. "How much did she cost?"

"Twelve hundred and thirty dollars."

Hoss caught his breath, then snarled in disgust. "Bastards," he said, then counted the cages lined up beside the platform. Fourteen girls remained to be sold. Hoss leaned over, resting his elbows on his knees and staring at the basement's stone floor, looking up only occasionally to see how many girls still remained.

As the number of unsold girls dwindled, the excitement built even more in the voices of the men. Finally, when but two girls remained, a great cheer went out, rattling the room and shaking Hoss out of his emotional lethargy. He asked Hop Sing, "What's going on?"

"Best girl," Hop Sing answered, "sold always next to last. Worst girl last."

Hoss straightened up on the hard bench and stared at the young girl being escorted up the platform. She was beautiful, Hoss agreed, fourteen years old at most. Hip Ye Tung stripped her and tossed her clothes away. Despite the humiliation, the girl had a quiet pride that burned in her eyes and a defiance in the set of her jaw. The doctor inspected her, seeming to linger over her more than any of the previous girls, inciting the potential bidders with his deliberation. Finally he turned to the men and announced his findings. Instantly, the men cheered, quieting down only after they realized the bidding would not begin until they were silent. The tumult gave way to whispers, then Hip Ye Tung gave the signal and the basement room exploded with loud, spirited bidding. Hip Ye Tung's face brightened, bringing out the rich smile of his golden teeth. At last only one voice responded to Hip Ye Tung's, and the prettiest girl of the lot had been sold. Hoss couldn't bear to see the purchaser. He just slumped over on the bench and cradled his forehead in the palms of his hands.

"Sold she at twenty-seven hundred dollars," Hop Sing said.

Hoss looked to Hop Sing and shook his head. "Meanest thing I've ever seen," he replied, his fingers knotting into fists. Beside him, the hatchet man watched his every move. Hoss stood, but Hop Sing grabbed his arm.

"Stay, Mr. Hoss," Hop Sing implored.

Up on the platform two of Hip Ye Tung's men brought the final slave girl for sale. She was pale and seemed weak, her eyes listless and her resistance nil. She coughed as they undressed her and seemed to shiver, even in the room's oppressive heat. She did not cry, and needed help from the two men to stand up. From out in the crowd a couple of men hissed and others began to stand and head for the exit. One man tossed a tomato at her and it landed at her feet, splitting apart and splattering juice upon her bare flesh. She did not flinch. The doctor came up and inspected her, checking her muscle tone and shaking his head. Then he placed his head against her bare chest and listened to her breathing.

Hip Ye Tung tapped his foot on the platform until the doctor stood and marched over to him. He whispered something to Hip Ye Tung, then left the platform and joined many of the others who were leaving. Most of the front three rows had departed, these being the auction's best buyers. What remained were men wanting a girl cheap. Hip Ye Tung announced the doctor's findings to the audience. At his words, several more men stood up and joined the exodus from the basement.

"What did he say, Hop Sing?"

"Girl sickly, may get better, may get worse," Hop Sing replied. "Cheap buy."

Hoss could feel his face burning with anger. "Buy her, Hop Sing. I can't let this happen to her. I'll repay you, Hop Sing, just buy her."

The bidding started, Hop Sing cringing each time the bid went up, but the enthusiasm present during previous sales was missing. When the bidding slowed, Hop Sing stood up and yelled something at the platform. The hatchet men on either side of Hop Sing and Hoss looked at each other and grinned.

Hop Sing upped his bid three times, finally having the last word. Hip Ye Tung implored the remaining bidders to top Hop Sing's offer, but the men were streaming out now, ready to escape the basement's heat and to curse their bad luck for not leaving with a girl.

Hip Ye Tung pointed at Hop Sing and nodded, his sign of a final sale. Then he laughed and shook his head in disbelief. "Man big as horse like Chinese girl?"

Hoss ignored the insult. "How much, Hop Sing?" Hoss asked.

"Sixty-three dollars."

Hoss stood up and rubbed the cramps out of his arm muscles, then bent over to pick up the young girl's garments. The girl was escorted from the platform and shoved at Hoss's feet. She crumpled to the floor before Hoss could catch her. He quickly pulled the blouse over her shoulders and the baggy trousers over her thin legs.

Hop Sing walked around the platform and up the steps, pulling his money pouch from his baggy blouse and counting out sixty-three dollars in silver. He offered it to Hip Ye Tung, who spurned the payment and pointed to the girl. Hip Ye Tung spoke sharply at Hop Sing.

Hoss felt his frustration building, not being able to understand what was being said. Looking from Hip Ye Tung to Hop Sing, he waited for an explanation. "What'd he say, Hop Sing?"

"Hop Sing give money to girl," he answered, squatting down beside the sickly girl. He put the silver coins in her palm, then folded her fingers around them.

Her eyes flickered and then the coins leaked from her hand.

Hip Ye Tung bent and retrieved the silver. Licking his lips, he turned to Hoss to provide an explanation. "Hip Ye Tung not sell China girl. China girl sell self and give Hip Ye Tung fee for finding her home in new country. Thank you very much."

"Same difference," Hoss replied, sliding his arms under the girl and picking her up. He turned to Hop Sing. "Ask him about your niece so we can get out of here! What was her name?"

Hop Sing nodded first to Hoss. "Mai Ah Toy," he answered, then nodded to Hip Ye Tung.

"Ah," Hip Ye Tung said, nodding his approval. "Fine Chinese girl, sell last but one, one week ago."

Hoss was relieved. If she were sold next to last, that meant she was considered the best of the lot. At least as a high-priced girl, she likely received better care than the cheap ones. He was angry at himself for thinking of young girls like he would animals. "Who bought her?" Hoss studied Hip Ye Tung, who seemed to ponder the question as if he were weighing whether to answer with a lie.

"Lin Wo Pai buy fine Chinese girl. The doctor Lin Wo Pai."

Hoss looked for signs of a lie. "Why you tell me this?"

"One fine girl no worry to Hip Ye Tung, long as Hip Ye Tung can sell many more fine girls, make plenty money. Hip Ye Tung tell man big as horse, and tell Lin Wo Pai about man big as horse. I tell man big as horse so he not return to auction. White men no care what we do, police no care what we do with little girls, just old ladies care."

"Is Mai Ah Toy used by many men?" Hoss asked.

Hip Ye Tung shrugged. "Hip Ye Tung not know. She a bit young, maybe thirteen. Fourteen best age for girl to sleep with many men."

"Damn you, Hip Ye Tung," Hoss said.

"Thank you very much," Hip Ye Tung replied, then pointed his index finger at Hoss's nose, the rings glittering in the basement's light. "Hip Ye Tung tell man big as horse so he never come this auction again."

Hoss looked at the sick girl in his arms, then up at Hip Ye Tung. "If we don't find Mai Ah Toy, we'll be back."

"Man big as horse return here, he will die," Hip Ye Tung answered. He pointed to the door. "Leave now before patience escapes Hip Ye Tung."

Hoss spit on the floor and left.

CHAPTER 11

On the street the girl clung to Hoss as a baby would to its mother. All around him Celestials stared, some nodding with knowing smiles. Hoss glared back at them, standing frozen for a moment, wondering where best to turn for help. He must borrow more of Hop Sing's money for food, a room, and maybe medicine. He could not keep her in the opium den. He considered his options, but he had few. He ignored a shout over the clamor of the Chinese pedestrians.

A white woman approached him from across the street, her purse swinging in her hand. She yelled again, and Hoss realized she was talking to him. "Where'd you get that child?" she shouted, brandishing her purse like a weapon.

"What?" Hoss said. His eyes slowly focused on an enraged woman in her thirties. "In there," Hoss said, motioning with his head toward the auction house.

"You bought her?" Her green eyes flared in anger.

"Yes, ma'am," Hoss replied, "I plan to take her—"

Before he could finish, the woman swung her purse, aiming for his head but striking his shoulder. She drew back and swung again, striking his back as Hoss spun around to protect the girl. "You, you, you animal," she sputtered. "How dare you buy this child. You're as bad as the heathens. You vulgar oaf, give me that girl so I can protect her from your filth."

Hoss dodged her blows as Hop Sing stepped between them, fending the woman off and shouting English among bursts of Chinese. "Hop Sing buy sick girl for Mr. Hoss."

"What?" the woman yelled. Her purse sliced through the air toward Hop Sing, who danced around her blows, yelling Asian epithets.

"You vile men!" she shouted.

"Stop it, ma'am," Hoss called out, "you don't understand."

The woman paused, her hands on her hips, her purse in her hand. "I don't understand," she said softly, then exploded, "so explain it to me!" She attacked again with a swinging purse. "You smell like an opium fiend."

"Dad-blame-it, ma'am!" Hoss dodged the purse and shoved the girl toward Hop Sing. "Take her," he shouted as the woman pummeled him with the purse. Hoss yelled at one sharp blow and spun around to confront his attacker.

She feinted for his knees, then swung the purse over her head, aiming for his. The purse sliced through the air, her legs solidly braced for the direct blow she expected to land.

Hoss ducked. The purse struck his hat and knocked it aflutter like a wounded quail.

The unexpected miss surprised the woman, and she half spun around to maintain her balance. Hoss charged, grabbing her under her arms and hoisting her into the air. She screeched and blindly swung the purse at him. With his great strength, Hoss held her aloft, shaking her roughly until her brown hair tumbled in curls from the bun where it had been neatly pinned.

"Let me down!" she cried out. "Let me down, you animal!"

Hoss rattled her some more. "Dad-blame-it," he shouted back. "Think you can be quiet long enough to listen, you woman wildcat?"

"No," she shouted back, "not as long as you buy little girls."

"Woman, you don't know what I planned to do with that poor girl. Who the hell are you, anyway?"

"None of your business until you put me down," she said icily.

Hoss shook her again, rougher this time, the purse falling to the walk.

"Aldina Cuthbert," she replied wearily.

"Ma'am," Hoss said, "you think you can listen for a moment instead of jumping to so many confusions?"

"I'll try," she replied, "if you'll just let me down."

Hoss eased her to the walk as she muttered her displeasure at this forced compromise.

She pulled hairpins out of her collapsed brown hair, waving them at Hoss, as if to tell him she was not defenseless even if he was more powerful than her. Then she ran her fingers through her long hair, which cascaded below her shoulders. Holding the hairpins unladylike in her teeth, she tucked her shirtwaist into her green skirt which was gathered in back.

Hoss studied her, taking in her green eyes, aristocratic nose, slightly rouged high cheekbones, and full lips. When she wasn't swinging her purse, she had an attractive bent to her. She was obviously one of those headstrong women who could match any man in intellect but had never learned to channel her emotions. Slender and elegant, she stood just over five feet, six inches tall.

"Now, what are you doing in Chinatown?" Hoss asked.

"That's what I'd like to know from you," she said sarcastically.

Hoss felt his fingers wad into a fist on his right hand, and he pounded his left palm with it, trying to get her attention. He wasn't debating her all day over this. "Now what is it you're doing in Chinatown?"

"I come here every auction day to save these poor girls. You know what they do to these children?" She paused, then answered her own question. "You must, seeing as how you bought one."

"Now, ma'am," Hoss answered, "me and Hop Sing are in Chinatown looking for his niece. This was a sickly girl in the auction, the last one sold. We bought—I mean, I bought her, to see if I could find her medical attention."

Aldina Cuthbert looked stunned for a moment, as if she didn't know whether to believe him. Hoss shrugged.

"Bless you, sir," she apologized, "and forgive me, please. I see so many of these girls abused, I get zealous defending them." She stooped over and picked up Hoss's hat, dusting it off, pushing out the dent from her purse, and offering it to him.

Taking his hat, Hoss pulled it over his head, then suggested they get away from the auction house. Hop Sing sidled up to Hoss, passing the young girl into his arms, then picking up Aldina's purse.

Aldina Cuthbert hooked the strap of her purse over her wrist. "I'll carry her," she said to Hoss, taking the young girl into her arms and rocking her gently. "Poor baby," she cooed at the girl, "you feel hot, fevered."

As they walked away from Chinatown, Hoss introduced himself and explained how he had come to San Francisco to help Hop Sing find his kidnapped niece before she was sold into slavery and a life of prostitution. He explained they were likely too late to save her virtue, but perhaps they could find her and spirit her out of San Francisco in time to save her life.

"Hoss Cartwright." Aldina Cuthbert kept repeating the name. "Hoss Cartwright, where have I heard that name before?"

Hoss shrugged. "I'm not from around these parts. You ever been to Virginia City?"

"Hoss Cartwright . . ." Aldina mused for a moment, alternately glancing between Hoss and the young girl in her arms. "Oh," she tittered, "now I remember. The paper. One of the papers told of a man named Horse going to the Palace Hotel and ripping the guest register in half when they wouldn't give him free lodging. They said you had the strength to match a name like Horse."

"It's Hoss," he corrected.

"You know the papers." Aldina slipped her hand out from under the sick child, poking it in Hoss's direction. "I'd like to shake your hand, someone standing up for these people that way. Their culture's different, they need some education on things, like how they treat their young girls, but they're still people."

Hoss took her hand and shook it gently so as not to wake the girl now asleep in her arms. "You're a perplexing woman, first attacking me and now congratulating me. It beats all."

Aldina Cuthbert directed Hoss and Hop Sing down Dupont and then along a side street toward a block of modest residences clinging to the slopes of a steep hill. As she started up the hill, she grew winded from the load. Hoss took the child from Aldina, marveling that she had carried the girl as far as she had without complaint. Hoss studied the woman's slender frame, attributing it to a spiritual determination or dedication more than physical strength. That was the case with most crusaders, he thought. After witnessing the auction today, he figured San Francisco needed more women like her. A hundred women who put their mind to something could accomplish it quicker than a thousand men, he figured.

At the top of the hill, Aldina stopped at a narrow clapboard house clad in a coat of fresh white paint and trimmed with green gingerbread. It was a small but neatly kept house, with bay windows stacked one atop the other on the first and second floors. Aldina turned through the opening in the wrought-iron fence and strode up the steps to her home. Opening the door, she motioned for Hoss to enter. "Place her on the sofa," she commanded, then allowed Hop Sing to pass before she went in.

Gently, Hoss lowered the girl to the plush maroon cushions of the high-backed sofa. Aldina rushed into a back room, and by the clatter of pots and pans, Hoss knew she was in the kitchen.

Hoss followed her to the stove. "You need wood, ma'am?"

Nodding, she pointed to the back door. "By the stoop you'll find all you need."

Hoss went outside, grabbed an armload and returned to the kitchen, filling the wood box, save for a few medium-sized pieces he shoved atop the coals glowing in the stove. The coals took to licking the wood, and shortly the stove grew hot to the touch.

Aldina placed a kettle of water atop it and scurried about the kitchen as it boiled. Then she prepared a cup of warm tea and carried it into the parlor. Kneeling on the floor by the girl, Aldina lifted her head and slid the cup beneath her nose. The girl's eyes fluttered at the aroma and a smile washed the frown from her face. Her lips parted and she drank the tea greedily. "That's a good sign," Aldina said to Hoss.

When the girl finished, Aldina retreated to the kitchen, to find Hop Sing studying the stove. "Hop Sing cook. Hop Sing good cook. Ask Mr. Hoss," he said. "Hop Sing fix meal."

Aldina smiled. "Thank you, Hop Sing. There's rice in the cabinet and tins of tomatoes and peaches too. I think rice and soda crackers would be good for our little angel."

Hop Sing grinned widely, held his hands together and bowed toward Aldina. "Hop Sing work."

Aldina prepared another cup of tea and returned to the girl, lifting her head and sliding a cushion beneath it. She helped the girl drink the tea and then stroked her head and cheek. "Tea and food should help, Mr. Cartwright."

"Just Hoss, ma'am."

A frown clouded Aldina's attractive face as she nodded at Hoss. "How much did she cost, Hoss?"

Realizing he was still wearing his hat, Hoss jerked it off and rolled the brim between his fingers. "She being sickly, cost us sixty-three dollars."

"Damn," Aldina said, jerking her hand to her lips as her face reddened with embarrassment. "Pardon my crude language, Hoss."

"No bother, ma'am, it was an experience I'm not proud of. At least I could save the little one there." Hoss thought he saw the glistening of tears in Aldina's eyes. He sat down.

Aldina looked down at the sofa and gently stroked the girl's face. "They keep them in cages, girls her age and younger. They are forced to sleep with men, Chinese and white, for four or five years. By then they may still have their youth, but they are no longer children. Their looks are gone and likely they are diseased. Their owners turn them out on the street or keep them in back rooms until they die."

"Dad-blame-it, can't something be done?" Hoss asked, leaning forward in his chair. "We treat livestock better."

"Nobody cares, except me and a few others. Police won't do anything about it. The Chinese accept it. Most people don't believe it." Aldina caressed the child's face, soothing her sleep.

"Can you take her and keep her, ma'am?"

"Oh, yes, Hoss, that was my intention. She'll be the forty-seventh I've taken in. I'll find a school or boarding-house, or at worst, an orphanage. But the girl you are after, tell me more."

"Best I know," Hoss explained, "she's Hop Sing's niece, named Mai Ah Toy. Kidnapped and sold last week at the auction house to a Dr. Lin Wo Pai."

Aldina scowled. The sudden change in her expression caught Hoss off guard. "Doctor," she said, fairly spitting the word across the room, "he's a snake-oil salesman, a medicine man. It would be enough if his wicked ways had only taken in his own kind, but many fashionable San Franciscans go to him for his heathen cures. They make him rich, and he either gambles the money away or buys young girls for his personal use."

"You know about him, then you can show us his place."

"Sometimes it takes weeks to get an appointment, the rich demand so much of his time," Aldina said. "Every ailment, he says, is attributable to liver problems, and he concocts bizarre potions to pass as cures. But the rich are gullible; what he does to innocent girls like this one is despicable."

Hoss kept rolling the brim of his hat between his fingers. "I'd like to get my hands on the one who bought Hop Sing's niece."

Aldina frowned and bit her lip. "These men, they

know not to harm whites, and they don't unless their graft is threatened. I can agitate because they don't take women seriously. But you, you must be careful, you and Hop Sing. They will kill you if you disrupt their despicable activities."

"But I gotta try."

"You've got to be careful as well," she said, sniffing at the aroma coming from the kitchen. "Smells good, Hop Sing," she called, then turned to Hoss. "Can I ask you a question?"

He shrugged. "Yes, ma'am."

"Do you smoke opium? It's a vile habit, you know, and your clothes smell like they are saturated with opium smoke."

Hoss stood up and tossed his hat on a table. "No, ma'am. I got away from home with no money and can't buy a decent room."

Aldina cocked her head as if he were lying. Her green eyes narrowed. "Then why'd you seek a room at the Palace if you were broke?"

"My father stays there, has a standing agreement with them. When they wouldn't let Hop Sing in, I tore the register and left, no place else to turn. Hop Sing took me to stay with his cousin in an opium den. Worst two nights sleep of my life."

The smile returned to Aldina's face. "Then you and Hop Sing should stay here the night, much safer than in Chinatown, once word gets around who you are looking for. I've a spare room upstairs, you and Hop Sing both can stay."

"Obliged, ma'am."

Hop Sing came to the kitchen door. "Hop Sing need dishes help, then meal ready."

Aldina carried the girl to the table, asked Hoss to bring a pillow she could sit on, then motioned for him to take a place beside her. Aldina retrieved dishes and eating utensils as Hop Sing placed a pot of rice and a bowl of tomatoes on the table. She added a tin of soda crackers and provided cups of tea all around, then pointed for Hop Sing to take a seat. She disappeared in the parlor a moment and returned with a bible in her hands.

"I always read a scripture when I have guests," she explained. "From the seventh chapter of Proverbs, I read today." Then she started: " 'The merciful man doeth good to his own soul; but he that is cruel troubleth his own flesh. The wicked worketh a deceitful work; but to him that soweth righteousness shall be a sure reward.' " She closed the bible and went instantly into a prayer. "Thank you, Lord, for this meal and these righteous men, as they save your noble creatures such as this girl you have blessed this house with. Watch over and protect us all. Amen."

"Amen," said Hoss.

Aldina served the girl's plate, giving her abundant rice and crackers and a small serving of tomatoes. "We don't even know your name, child."

Hoss pointed at Hop Sing, "Ask her her name?"

Nodding, Hop Sing spoke quickly in Chinese.

Meekly, the girl answered, "Hin May." She stared at her plate, looked up at Hop Sing then back at her plate.

Aldina realized the problem, and picked up the fork by the plate, inserted it in Hin May's fragile hand, and gently showed her how to work it. Gradually Hin May learned, though her execution was not without spilled rice. Nonetheless, she was able to eat under Aldina's careful gaze.

By early afternoon they had finished their meal and Aldina had bathed Hin May and put her to bed. Hop Sing cleared the kitchen, drawing praise from Aldina when she returned downstairs.

"You two should go get your belongings. And Hoss, when you get back, you can bathe, and I'll want to wash your clothes."

Hoss lifted his hand to argue, but she would have none of it. When Hop Sing was done, he took off his apron and said he was ready to return to Chinatown. Taking his hat from the table in the parlor, Hoss and Hop Sing marched out of the house. Hoss had a better idea of Chinatown's layout this time and thought he could find his way to the opium den, but Hop Sing kept taking unexpected turns, until Hoss had to admit he was lost.

Finally they reached an alley that looked familiar, and Hop Sing turned down the garbage-strewn path that led from the street toward the narrow passageway in back. A big black dog was licking at the threshold. Hop Sing and Hoss held back to give the dog room to escape. "Get," Hoss yelled, throwing a stone at the dog. The stone banged off the door, and the dog darted from the passageway.

As Hoss and Hop Sing slipped to the door, a new and troubling odor bothered Hoss's nose. Hop Sing called in Chinese to be admitted. No answer. He called again. The peephole stayed closed. The door remained closed. Hoss leaned over Hop Sing and pounded on the door, which swung open from the impact. There was the smell of opium escaping and then the smell of something much more sinister. Death. Hoss pushed the door open, then gasped at what he saw.

There on the floor, in pools of blood, were Hop Sing's cousin and two of his customers, their bodies hacked to pieces. Hoss thought of the hatchet men, wondering if they had come for him and taken their anger out on the others.

Hop Sing spoke quickly in Chinese, almost chattering. Hoss lowered his head. He was not interested in seeing any more of the gruesome sight than was necessary; his eyes focused on a puddle of blood at the threshold. Hop Sing caught his breath, then stepped inside, tiptoeing around the bodies and moving back into the corner for his bundled possessions. He retreated quickly, then ran past Hoss out into the alley. Hoss pulled the door shut and followed.

They emerged onto the crowded street and moved swiftly and wordlessly away from the alley, away from Chinatown. Only on the outskirts of Chinatown did they slow, but even then they had nothing to say. Their eyes had seen too much for there to be anything to discuss.

Finally reaching Aldina's, they entered without knocking, startling Aldina, who was sitting on the sofa reading the bible.

"Hop Sing's cousin, two others murdered," Hoss blurted out.

Aldina sighed and dropped her head. "They're telling you to give up. You'll be next, if you keep seeking the girl."

CHAPTER 12

From the second-floor office of the Bristlecone mine, a major investment of Cartwright Enterprises, Ben Cartwright stared out the window at Virginia City. It was, said boisterous newspaper columnists, the richest city on the face of the earth, its mines surpassing even the mines of King Solomon in wealth. But for all its wealth, Virginia City was a homely spot, nestled halfway up the eastern slope of Mount Davidson, a rocky, treeless peak some 3500 feet tall. The town had been built like a jigsaw puzzle around the mining claims, and its contrasts were as varied as the wealth of its mines, more than thirty in all. Those who had struck it rich on silver lived in fine brick mansions with fixtures imported from Europe and fine tapestries brought from the Middle East. Those who had not, lived in tar-paper shacks with tin roofs and dirt floors and survived on hope and the free meals offered with purchase of a drink in dozens of saloons.

The hospital, the schools, the churches, the stores, the mansions, the shacks, and even the saloons were scattered about the mountainside between the giant hoisting works which looked like iron insects preying on the bowels of the earth. Great waste dumps of worthless minerals, pulled an iron bucket at a time from the earth, grew at the base of the mines like a pile of droppings from these mammoth bugs. And huge brick smokestacks punctured the sky, their trails of black smoke waving in the breeze like the giant antennae of those iron insects. The smoke from the stacks and from the locomotives of the Virginia and Truckee Railroad drew a grimy veil over such a rich lady as Virginia City. And the town rumbled, as if a perpetual storm were moving in, because of the stamping mills which crushed the ore to begin the extracting process that made some people richer but most people poorer. Mining was a worse gamble than a rigged poker hand.

Ben Cartwright stood watching Virginia City, but his thoughts were on San Francisco. There, Davey Kendall should be handling his timber bid. From there, Davey Kendall should have sent a telegram answering his pointed request for information. Ben dug his steel-case watch from the pocket of his broadcloth trousers. Five minutes until noon, Davey's deadline, and still no word from him.

Neither had Ben received communication from Hoss. He had faith Hoss could take care of himself and Hop Sing as was necessary, but he was not so confident of Davey Kendall. Slipping his watch back in his pocket, he stood with his feet wide apart, a habit of his sailing days when he had learned the secret to a seaman's balance. The freedom and the exhilaration of sailing were seldom matched by anything he had done since. But sailing was no life for a practical man, and if Ben was anything, he was indeed a practical man.

Turning from the window, he studied Adam's Bristle-cone office, neatly arranged, his desk clear of all papers except those stacked in two crisp piles. Even the two dozen pigeonholes in the rolltop desk were neatly arranged. Adam had a place for everything and everything in its place. He would have expected no less from Adam's precisely organized mind.

Outside the door, Ben heard the creak of the stairs and knew Adam was returning from the telegraph office. By Adam's pace, he knew it was either bad news or no news. The door handle twisted and the door slowly opened. Adam came through shaking his head. "Nothing," he said, hanging his hat and dropping a stack of assay reports on his desk.

Ben clenched his teeth in disgust. "That's what I expected."

Adam pulled a newspaper from under his arm and handed it to Ben. "Latest news from San Francisco. No mention of the timber leases. You reckon there's some chicanery with that bid?"

Ben jerked the paper from Adam's fingers. "Most likely it's Davey Kendall's incompetence. Surely nobody bid as high as we did on those leases," he answered emphatically. He pulled a chair to the window, where the light was stronger, and snapped the paper open.

Adam slid into his swivel chair and propped his feet up on his desk, then grabbed the stack of assay reports and began to peruse, frowning regularly. "We may not need timber for the Bristlecone unless these reports get better."

Lowering the paper, Ben could see the concern buried deep in Adam's eyes. "We don't get the timber leases, we may just as well sell the Bristlecone. You want that?"

"No," Adam shot back, "but we go deeper and deeper and the ore doesn't grade out any richer. This is costing us $275,000 a month."

Ben nodded. "The cost is steep, but the return can be even greater. You know the engineering and the business, I know the cost. And with all that, mining is still instinct. We'll stick with it if the timber leases come through. If not, then we'll decide." Ben studied Adam, knowing his oldest son needed encouragement from time to time. It was a side of Adam no one else ever saw. They could not get past the stoic demeanor, the dark, piercing eyes, his stern expression.

Finishing an assay report, Adam tossed it on the desk and picked up another from his lap. "Where's Little Joe?"

"Hiring us a cook until Hop Sing returns," Ben replied, lifting the paper back to eye level.

The two men sat silently for several minutes, Adam tossing unfavorable assay reports atop his otherwise neat desk, Ben reading every column of the paper. Suddenly, Ben leaned forward in his chair.

"Well, I'll be," he said, lowering the page until he could see Adam.

"I missed news on the timber leases?" Adam asked, dropping his feet from the desk to the floor with a thump.

Ben cleared his throat. "No, but just listen. 'During the brief history of the Palace Hotel, we at the *Chronicle* have come to expect an oddball mix of celebrities and outright characters enjoying its many modern conveniences, not to mention its exquisite luxuries. Each guest has signed the guest register in his own hand, in his own language, and seemed most satisfied at such an honor to add his name to the list of distinguished visitors who have graced our fair city.

" 'Now comes one man who, unsettled by the Palace's refusal to give him free lodging, rips the guest register in half with his bare hands. Identifying himself as one "Horse Cartwright," this brute seemed not to understand the hotel clerk's pleasant refusal of his offer to stay free at the world's biggest and most luxurious public hotel.' " Ben shook his head, then continued.

" 'Anyone who has ever queried the front desk at the Palace knows that hotel personnel are as congenial a lot as can be found in all of California, and likely in all of the United States, and they should in no way be blamed for the poor manners of penniless brutes who might wander in off the street for a glimpse of the decorum they are quite incapable of matching.

" 'While we admire the strength of this brute, we think he should more appropriately put it to work in some form of hard labor that would not tax his weak brain and perhaps someday might provide him the earnings that could afford him a night in the Palace without resorting to his scandalous behavior. Until that day, hotel owners throughout the city should be wary of a man calling himself "Horse" and asking for free lodging.' "

Ben grinned. "At least Hoss reached San Francisco safely."

Adam stood and walked to the window. "Newspapers print more lies than truth."

"Perhaps," Ben replied, "but even in the biggest lie there's often a grain of truth." Ben offered the paper to Adam.

Adam took it and tossed it atop the assay reports on his desk. He patted his flat stomach. "I could do with a bite of lunch."

"Just as well," Ben said, standing up and looking disgustedly out the window. He shook his head. "After lunch, I'll go to the telegraph office and see if Davey's sent a message. Otherwise, I'll send him a telegram ending his work for Cartwright Enterprises."

Nodding, Adam grabbed his hat off a hook by the door. "I can't say I don't agree with you, Pa, I'm just surprised at Davey."

As Ben took his hat, footsteps pounded up the stairway. Adam swung open the door to see Little Joe appear, a wide smile lighting his face.

"Our cooking problems are over," Little Joe announced, crossing his arms on his chest.

Adam stared at Little Joe. "If all our chores were so small or so easy, little brother."

Little Joe's arms fell from his chest and he swaggered forward. Then Ben stepped from the office. The swagger melted in Little Joe's step. "Pa," he muttered, "I didn't realize you were here. I figured you'd be at the Washoe Club for lunch."

"We were headed that way," Ben replied.

"Before you go, Pa, I've hired us a cook for the Ponderosa. She's outside. I figure to take her home tomorrow."

"Tomorrow?" Ben questioned, his eyebrow lifting.

"I figured to stay another night in Virginia City," Little Joe said, licking his lips.

"You're returning home with her today," Ben said as he reached the stair landing, Little Joe close behind him.

"But Adam's here all the time. You let him keep a suite in the International Hotel," Little Joe protested.

"Joseph," Ben commanded, "you'll return today."

The Bristlecone's office staff smiled, drawing Little Joe's angry glare and embarrassing him, particularly when he saw Adam's narrow grin.

Ben opened the door and emerged onto the plank walk. He was greeted by a big woman of Hoss's proportions. Ben tipped his hat. "Afternoon, ma'am," he said, taking in her broad shoulders, wide hips, dark eyes and gray hair, her fleshy jowls and flat nose. She had eaten too much of her own cooking over the years, but for a woman of her girth, she was neatly attired in a white blouse and blue skirt half hidden by a big red apron.

"Ja, ja," she answered and lifted her hand. Ben made a move to shake it, but the woman was merely straightening the green scarf entangled with her gray hair.

"Pa," Little Joe said, "this is Frau Kreidt, our new cook."

Ben offered her his hand, and she rubbed hers on her apron before taking his. She had the grip of a blacksmith and a smile of perverse satisfaction as she squeezed Ben's fingers. He was glad to break loose from her hold and wondered if Hoss could take her at arm wrestling. The thought made him smile, his grin drawing a frown, as if she feared he was mocking her. She lowered her head.

"Can you start today?" Ben asked as Adam emerged from the Bristlecone office.

"Ja, ja, ja," she said, pumping her head vigorously. "Gather things, not many, then go," she said, her words overpowered by her strong Germanic accent. "Tiny Joseph can help, ja, ja?"

"Little Joe," interjected Little Joe.

She nodded. "Ja, ja, Tiny Joseph."

Ben grinned widely. "Joseph, help her with her belongings and make the next train. You'll have her to cook supper for you tonight on the Ponderosa."

Little Joe sighed deeply. "Sure, Pa."

"Frau Kreidt," Ben said, "I want you to meet Adam, my oldest son." Adam tipped his hat. "Now, Joseph, we'll see you at the Ponderosa."

Little Joe gave a feeble wave of his arm. "Where are your things?"

"Ja, ja, ja," she answered, grabbing two handfuls of her wide skirt and starting back toward the central section of Virginia City.

Little Joe shrugged and followed.

" 'Bye, Tiny Joseph," Adam called in his wake.

Little Joe grabbed the brim of his hat with both hands and pulled it down tighter over his head as he trailed Frau Kreidt.

Adam laughed. "If Hop Sing returns, we can tell him he'll have to wrestle Frau Kreidt for his job."

"I'm not sure Hoss could whip her," Ben said, slapping Adam on the shoulder as they left for the Washoe Club.

The club stood on C Street down from the International Hotel, where Adam kept a suite to attend to his mining activities. It occupied the second floor of the Crystal, a drinking establishment known throughout Nevada as "the millionaires' saloon." The club was even more exclusive than the saloon, allowing only men with clout in railroading, timbering, and, of course, mining to enjoy its dining room, lounge, bar, card room, and most of all, its exclusivity. The Washoe Club was a retreat of thick carpets, plush chairs, cut-crystal chandeliers, oil paintings, and bronzes.

Thaddeus Bradford met Adam and Ben at the door of the club. Bradford oversaw the club's food and functions, and, as fussy as an old maid, he took his responsibilities seriously. Along with his black tie and cutaway coat, he always wore a somber expression. Getting a smile out of him was harder than squeezing juice from a prune, and on those rare occasions when he did smile, it was less from joy than from the satisfaction of knowing his preserve for the elite would not be violated by someone he did not feel appropriate for such august company. Bradford stared through the sparkling lenses of his wire-rimmed glasses and nodded emotionlessly at Ben and Adam.

"Afternoon, gentlemen," he said. "Two for lunch, or will Joseph and ..." Bradford paused, clearing his throat as if he did not approve of such a common name. "... Hoss be joining you?"

"Not today, Thaddeus," Ben responded.

Bradford's lips parceled out a thin approving smile as Ben and Adam deposited their hats in the cloak room. "Follow me, then," he said, moving from behind his desk and into the dining room. Several men greeted Ben and

Adam as they approached a vacant table with spotless white linen tablecloth, fine bone China, sparkling crystal, and fine silver place settings. The room was perfumed with the aroma of the finest cigars money could buy.

"This will be fine," Ben said when Bradford stopped at a table.

As Ben grabbed the high-back chair to seat himself, he saw Clarence Eppler, the Cartwrights' personal services lawyer in Virginia City, at a corner table with Monville Pyburn, Ben's stockbroker. Eppler looked up from his salad and motioned with his fork for Ben to come over. Eppler was a tall man with slender build and stooped shoulders that made him seem to hover over the table. A middle-aged man, his hair was the color of fine chocolate and was so thick that most thought it a wig. Men who didn't know him laughed at his odd hair, but those men had never faced him in a courtroom. There the laughing stopped, for Eppler had an astute legal mind. Placing his fork on his salad plate, Eppler made a move to get up.

"No, no," Ben said as he reached the table, "keep your seat, Clarence. Monville, how are you?" Ben shook the stockbroker's hand first, then Eppler's.

Pyburn shrugged, scratched his gray muttonchop whiskers and blinked at Ben through thick glasses which made his eyes seem owlish. "I'd be better if you sold Bristlecone stock instead of keeping it all. It'll drain you and the boys before it's all over."

"Adam's got confidence in it and I've confidence in Adam."

"I don't have confidence in either of you, Ben." Pyburn pursed his lips and reached for a decanter of brandy to refill his glass. "Ranching's your strength, Ben, and the railroad stock'll carry you as long as the mines hold out. Then what?"

"That's when I come to you, Monville." Ben laughed as Pyburn shook his head and poured brandy. "Now, Clarence, what did you need?" Ben turned to his Virginia City attorney.

"The timber leases, any word on your bid? I heard

old man Kendall died and his son is handling his clients. Let me know if you need any help."

"I may want to do that, Clarence, once I get a report from Davey Kendall on the situation. He's been a mite slow getting back to me, though he's likely had a lot on his mind since his father's passing." Ben elaborated no further on the leases, instead spending a couple more moments on pleasantries before rejoining Adam.

Ben ordered smoked salmon and vegetables while Adam requested baked teal. Their efforts at conversation were perfunctory, each understanding the other's need for quiet reflection. When they finished, they lingered over a glass of brandy apiece, then departed.

Stepping out onto C Street, Ben turned to Adam. "You head on back to the Bristlecone and I'll join you a bit later."

Adam nodded. He knew that his father was heading to the telegraph office to fire Davey Kendall. "Sure, Pa, I'll see you when you get back."

Ben stuck his hands in his pocket and marched away with more determination than anger in his step. David Thornton Kendall, Jr., had been a good lawyer, a dependable one. His son might be good, but Ben was certain that David Thornton Kendall, III, was not as dependable. Though he felt an obligation to the father and wished he could transfer that allegiance to the son, he had reached the end of his patience. Even so, it was still difficult to end his relationship with the Kendall family.

At the train depot Ben took a pad of paper and a pencil from the counter and sat amid those awaiting the arrival of the next train. After a few false starts, he slowly wrote out his message, several times scratching through words. Finally he copied the finished message on a clean sheet of paper and perused it.

> Receiving no response to previous query, Cartwright Enterprises relieves DTKIII of duties. With DTKII death, all past agreements void.
> B. Cartwright.

Ben stepped to the counter and slid the sheet of paper toward the telegrapher, giving instructions on the recipient's name and address. As the message was sent to San Francisco, Ben wadded up the messy original message and pitched it over the counter toward a trash can. Moments later the telegrapher came back to acknowledge the message had been sent. Ben paid and thanked him, then left the depot and headed back up C Street, stopping at the Crystal and lingering half an hour over a shot of whiskey. Then he walked to Clarence Eppler's office. He had wanted to talk with the lawyer about some legal contacts in San Francisco, but Eppler was out.

Emerging from Eppler's office, Ben wandered down a street teaming with men heading to the saloons after shift change. More than two hours had passed by the time Ben got back to the Bristlecone offices. Climbing the stairs to Adam's office, Ben saw the door ajar, then spotted Adam looking at him.

Adam waved a yellow envelope in his hand. "From San Francisco!"

"Davey or Hoss?"

"Kendall," Adam said.

Ben bounded up the steps, taking the envelop and ripping it open. He read it once, then read it again in disbelief, his jaw clenched in anger. He thrust the message at Adam.

For a moment Adam studied his father's anger, then took the message and read it aloud. "This law practice will handle timber leases or fight you in court. D.T.K. the Third." Adam whistled.

Ben's hand tightened into a fist and pounded his palm. "I'm going to San Francisco and settle this once and for all."

CHAPTER 13

Aldina scurried around the kitchen attending minor chores and periodically checking Hin May in bed upstairs. After Hoss and Hop Sing had returned from the opium den last night, she had insisted they take baths—as if it could wash away the memory of what they had seen. She washed their clothes and ironed them. Now at breakfast, both Hop Sing and Hoss looked better at least.

Hoss downed a cup of coffee and stared across the table. Hop Sing had eaten even less of his breakfast than Hoss, who detected a quiver in Hop Sing's hand as he forked at the food on his plate. Maybe Hop Sing had changed his mind about saving his niece, in spite of the auction that had graphically demonstrated the horrors the girl must be facing. Hoss felt his hands knot into fists as he thought about the abuse. He wanted to find Hop Sing's niece, if for no other reason than to save one more girl from a degrading life, but he was no longer sure Hop Sing felt the same way. He hated himself for feeling he had to ask, but he had to know.

"I've been thinking, Hop Sing," he said. "I still want to find your niece, but I can't do it without your help. It could be dangerous. You still want to find her after what you saw yesterday?"

His lip quivering, Hop Sing nodded slowly. "Hop Sing must find niece."

"I'll help too. Anything to save another girl," Aldina interjected as she refilled Hoss's coffee cup.

Hoss stared at her, admiring the determination in her green eyes and the cut of her fine figure. Her beauty was deeper than just her looks, because she was committed to these girls. The fragile lines at the corners of her eyes must have come from the worry and the tears of knowing she could save so few of those delicate Chinese flowers from prostitution.

"Maybe you better stay and care for Hin May," Hoss said to her.

Aldina tossed her head and sniffed. "I know more about the people and places of Chinatown than either of you."

Hoss sipped his coffee. He didn't like a woman contradicting him, especially when she was right. Studying her as he lowered the coffee cup, he said, "Dad-blame-it, the risks are too great for you to get involved, Aldina."

"Lin Wo Pai, the Chinese doctor," she responded, "he's the next one we see."

"Too dangerous for you," Hoss said, crossing his arms over his chest, trying to focus Aldina on the potential threat.

She folded her two arms over her breast, her eyes narrowing in on his, her chin thrust defiantly forward. "It's safer for me than you two. A couple of men—even a white man—getting killed in Chinatown would not cause near the stir of a white woman, one who's been working with local benevolent organizations to save these girls. Think about it, Hoss. Do you believe I'd know my way around your Nevada ranch as well as you? Certainly not! You don't know Chinatown like I do. It's that simple." She was adamant, but even in her obstinacy there was a soft edge.

Sighing as he considered another gambit, Hoss retreated to his coffee, draining the cup. He shook his head. "You've got to care for Hin May. We can't do that."

Aldina stepped toward Hoss, exasperation in her eyes. "Hin May's not the first I've saved. I couldn't tend or support all the girls I've saved from that hellhole, but I've contacts and supporters who will find her care. It'll take a couple of hours to place her, and besides, you'll not get in to see Lin Wo Pai until late this afternoon, if at all, so I've plenty of time."

Hoss slapped his hand against the table, startling Hop Sing, who listened meekly. "Woman, you're about as obstinate a female as I've ever encountered."

Smiling, Aldina curtsied as if he had complimented her profusely. "We city girls are different from those you're accustomed to in the country, Hoss."

Hoss's face flushed. He stood up from the table and turned away from Aldina, not knowing how to reply.

Realizing that she had embarrassed him, Aldina excused herself. "I must go check on Hin May," she announced as she left.

Now Hoss was really confused. Was she upset? Embarrassed? Or just concerned about Hin May? "Hop Sing," he said, "I just don't understand women." Hoss paced around the table a few minutes until Aldina returned, holding Hin May's hand. The girl looked bashfully up at Hoss, then released Aldina's hand and ran across the room to hug him.

"It's her way of saying thank you," Aldina said. "Her fever's broke, and good food for a while will help her as much as anything."

Hoss squatted beside her and stared down into her dark eyes. "It'll be okay, honey. Nobody'll hurt you now."

Hin May threw her slender arms around Hoss's neck, and pressed her cheek against his. Hoss wrapped his arms around her and took her to the table. She offered him another smile in return.

"She knows a good man when she sees one," Aldina said, embarrassing Hoss again. "Let me fix her breakfast, and then we'll decide how we'll find Hop Sing's niece."

Hoss motioned for Hop Sing to come into the parlor, and Hop Sing followed him all the way to the front door. "I need a dollar," Hoss said.

Hop Sing twisted his head and shrugged.

"You'll get it back when we return home."

"Hop Sing understand," he said, digging his money pouch out of the loose folds of his clean clothes. His fingers untied a leather thong around the pouch and worked its mouth open enough to pull a silver dollar from inside.

Hoss snatched the coin from Hop Sing's fingers. "Thanks, Hop Sing. Tell Aldina I had to go out for a few minutes and not to go anywhere until I return."

Just as Hoss grabbed the doorknob, he heard Aldina's voice coming from the kitchen. Turning around, he looked into her puzzled face.

"Going to the store?"

Hoss nodded. "Dad-blame-it, yes, and don't you leave until I get back."

"You didn't like my cooking?"

"No, no, dad-blame-it," Hoss said, his brow furrowing. "When I get back, I'll explain. Just don't anybody leave before then."

He was a good man, Aldina thought when Hoss left, but he seemed too secretive about this trip for it not to be the result of some shortcoming of her hospitality. Was it her cooking or something else? She shrugged, not knowing what to make of it. Retreating into the kitchen to prepare Hin May's breakfast, she saw the girl resting her head on the table, Hin May's sad, dark eyes peering into nothingness. Aldina placed her hand upon her cheek, gauging its warmth. Hin May was still weak, sitting listlessly at the table, not responding even to her gentle touch. Aldina lingered, stroking the girl's shiny black hair.

Hop Sing returned to the kitchen. "Hop Sing fix Hin May food, plenty rice."

Aldina smiled her approval, then picked up Hin May and carried her into the parlor. Taking a seat in her corner rocking chair, she began to hum to this delicate flower plucked in China and carried halfway around the world for the carnal pleasures of men. Hin May snuggled against Aldina's breast, each breath contented. From the adjacent room, Aldina could hear the sounds of Hop Sing's cooking and singing. The aroma of rice seeped into the parlor and Hin May perked up, her nose wriggling approvingly at the fragrance. Aldina wondered if the smell reminded her of home, if she missed her family, if she would ever see them again. Were she sent back to China—though no one had the money or the will to pay for her way back—would she be accepted by her family? Some families sold their daughters into slavery. Was Hin May the daughter of such a family or was she just one of those stolen by the slave traders, leaving her family in anguish over her fate?

Shortly, Hop Sing appeared in the kitchen door. "Hop Sing cook good meal." He bowed slightly, then backed into the kitchen.

Aldina carried Hin May back, sat her at the table and brushed the black hair from around her face. Hop Sing had found vegetables in a bin and now placed a bowl of rice topped with steamed vegetables and a fork before her. Hin May grabbed the fork awkwardly, her hunger offset by her clumsiness.

"Here, here," Aldina said softly, "let me help." She placed her hand before Hin May, who surrendered the fork, then she fed the girl small bites, allowing Hin May plenty of time to chew and swallow. Hop Sing placed a cup of tea before Hin May, who grabbed it with both hands, cradled it to her lips and drank greedily.

Aldina heard the front door open and glanced back as Hoss entered. He held one arm behind his back, and wore a big smile befitting a big man like him. Aldina cringed when he shut the door too hard, rattling the glass in the bay windows. Hoss's smile disappeared until he entered the kitchen.

"Hin May," he said softly.

The young girl twisted around in her chair, her lips trying desperately to find the energy to answer his smile. Hoss slowly pulled his hand from behind his back and Hin May's eyes widened. He held a doll, made of wool fabric stuffed with cotton and having a painted face. Hin May's own face flooded with a wide smile and she climbed tentatively out of the chair, as if the doll might not be for her. She stood a moment, then rushed to Hoss, grabbing his arm.

Hoss bent over her. "For Hin May," he said, and she

understood. She grabbed the doll from him and held it to her chest, caressing its softness.

Hin May kissed the doll, then slowly returned to her chair.

As Hoss straightened up, he realized Aldina was at his side. Her eyes moist, she stood on her tiptoes and gave him a peck on the cheek.

Embarrassed, Hoss nodded at Aldina. "I figured if you were gonna give her to someone else to keep, I should get her something to remember me by."

A tear ran down Aldina's cheek. "But Hoss, she'll remember you always as the man who saved her life."

"Any decent man would've done the same thing."

"But there are too few decent men around, Hoss, or these things wouldn't be happening in San Francisco." She dabbed at her eyes with the cuff of her sleeve, then turned back to the table, sliding into the chair beside Hin May. Deliberately, she began to feed Hin May again. The girl ate with greater enthusiasm now, while holding the doll tightly and swaying in her chair between bites. "It's hard to hit a moving target," Aldina half laughed, half cried at the contented girl.

Hoss had expected such a reaction from Hin May, but not from Aldina. Though hers were tears of joy, Hoss felt helpless around a crying woman. And a sense of frustration was tugging at his conscience. Hin May was but one girl among the fifteen he had seen sold during a slow day's commerce at the slave market. Aldina was the real hero because she had saved others. Hoss stepped up to Aldina's chair and patted her shoulder.

Aldina placed her free hand upon Hoss's and squeezed it. "There are so many, and we can't save them all," she said. "At least we can save a few and maybe make them as happy as you've made Hin May happy. If only more people cared, Hoss. That's what's so frustrating."

Hoss had no answer. He had seen the police harass Hop Sing as soon as he stepped out of the ferry building. He had seen wagons of Celestials attacked by the hooligans at the docks. He had seen the wagonload of girls taken in cages from the dock to the auction house. He had been refused a room because of Hop Sing at the Palace Hotel. He had seen Chinese men bidding for the girls as if they were heifers at a livestock auction. And he had been able to buy one and walk out of the auction house without fear of prosecution. It seemed Aldina was the only one who cared. Damn if cities didn't have more problems than he could think through!

Aldina finished feeding Hin May, then took her upstairs and dressed her in American clothes before bringing her down to say good-bye to Hoss and Hop Sing. "The church will see she is sheltered and educated and protected from man's evil," Aldina said. "Hop Sing, please tell Hin May that I will take her to another place where she will be safe. She must say good-bye to you and Hoss."

Hop Sing translated the message, and Hin May frowned, then puckered her lips, her eyes watering and overflowing. Hop Sing hugged her and released her. She ran to Hoss, who bent down to pick her up. She grabbed him around the neck, squeezing both him and her doll at the same time. When she released her grip, she held the doll for him to kiss. He obliged, then kissed her on the cheek for the final time.

"Good luck, Hin May," Hoss said, "I hope you find a better life than you started in San Francisco with."

Aldina took Hin May from Hoss and started toward toward the door. "When I return," she said, a hardness in her voice, "we'll see if we can scare Lin Wo Pai into giving up Hop Sing's niece."

CHAPTER 14

L ike everything else in Chinatown, the waiting room was cramped. Hoss fidgeted uncomfortably and impatiently in his seat, as he had for two hours, hat in lap, awaiting a chance to see Dr. Lin Wo Pai. He was alone with the other patients. Aldina was too well known in Chinatown for the doctor not to be suspicious, and Hop Sing was too nervous to press Lin Wo Pai for details about the girl he had purchased last week. Hoss was nervous as well, liking doctor's offices only slightly better than dentist's offices. Aldina had convinced Hoss his only chance of seeing the charlatan was to sit in the waiting room until all the patients had left, then force himself into the doctor's office. Occasionally, when he glanced through the murky window to the street, he could see Aldina or Hop Sing passing like sentries.

It surprised Hoss that most of the patients were white men and women. Of the eight besides him, only two were Celestials. And all, save him, were dressed in clothes that bespoke of a comfortable life if not outright wealth. Aldina had explained that Lin Wo Pai was little different from a snake-oil salesman, except that the rich of San Francisco were taken with his mysterious potions, believing them to cure everything from baldness to arthritis to impotence to flatulence. The root of all evil in the body, according to Lin Wo Pai's strange medical advice, was always the iiver, which, depending on the malady, could only be treated by his bizarre pharmacopoeia of everything from frog skins, tiger teeth, crab eyes, and rattlesnake skins to deer horns, dried shrimp, centipedes, and spiders.

One by one the patients were called into the back room by a voice from behind the black door. Every time the door opened, Hoss craned to spot the Chinese doctor, but Lin Wo Pai remained out of view, hovering like a faceless spirit over the exchange of patients. His services were expensive but his patients were known for their riches and, in Aldina's words, their gullibility, having little better to do with their time than seek sham cures for real or imagined health problems. Aldina had spoken with contempt for Dr. Lin Wo Pai, but she saved her real disgust for the white patients whose time and money were spent on his quackery when they could be better spent on saving the slave girls imported to San Francisco.

"Next," came the accented voice behind the door. A middle-aged woman in the latest fashion stood up, allowing her predecessor, an old man with a crushed felt derby and gold-headed cane, to pass before she entered the doctor's inner sanctum. Occasionally, as the door opened, Hoss would sniff a sweet fragrance emanating from the room. Aldina had instructed Hoss to feign an illness so he could see the doctor and ask questions about Hop Sing's niece.

It was better than any plan Hoss could come up with, but he was still uncomfortable. If only he had Little Joe's skill for making up believable tales. He smiled at the thought of his younger brother, wondering how he was getting along with the cooking and dishwashing at home. Occasionally, outside, Hoss would see Aldina pass, and that gave him a bit of comfort, even if no more confidence. She had warned him it would be a long wait, since Lin Wo Pai worked by appointment only.

It was after six o'clock, Hoss guessed, when the last patient was called into Lin Wo Pai's office. That left Hoss alone. He stood up from his small chair, plopped his hat on his head and walked about the room, stretching his arms, studying the Chinese paintings on the walls and wondering what the odd characters represented. In front of a mirror by the door leading into the doctor's room, he studied himself, surprised at his bloodshot eyes and haggard face. He had lost weight since leaving the Ponderosa. Oh, what he would give to be working cattle on the ranch and coming home each evening to a table of Hop Sing's cooking. He took off his hat and ran his fingers through his brown hair.

As he was looking in the mirror, the door opened and the last patient emerged. Pulling his hat down and watching the satisfied patient pass, Hoss stepped to the door just as it shut in his face. He heard the latch being set, and anger welled inside him. He had waited all afternoon and now the doctor was locking him out. Hoss knocked on the door. "Doctor," he cried out, "I'm next."

"No next today. Doctor tired," replied that same faceless voice that Hoss had heard call each previous patient.

"I need help, Doctor, with back pains." Hoss pounded on the door, harder and harder, rattling the adjacent mirror.

"Leave," came the reply.

Hoss pushed on the door and it budged. He lowered his shoulder and pressed against the door, straining the latch. The door gave more but still didn't break.

He was answered by a string of indecipherable Chinese words.

Stepping back, Hoss lowered his shoulder and plowed into it. The door ripped away from the latch, swinging all the way around on its hinges, banging into the wall with such force it cracked the mirror Hoss had been looking into.

Hoss stumbled into the room, caught his balance and searched for the doctor. In the back corner beside a wall lined from floor to ceiling with shelves stood Dr. Lin Wo Pai, his narrow eyes unblinking, his stance defiant. Hoss checked the room for others, but the doctor was alone. On the wall by the door where a framed certificate had fallen from the wall, he saw a square hole in the wall. Through a piece of dark glass, now cracked, Hoss could see the waiting room. It was a two-way mirror that had allowed the doctor to keep an eye on who entered and left his waiting room.

Angered, Hoss stuck his hand through the hole and shoved the cracked mirror into the waiting room. It crashed to the floor as he stepped toward Lin Wo Pai, who backed deeper into his corner. The doctor stood no more than five feet, four inches tall, and his queue dropped to below his knees. He wore baggy green silk pants and a silk blouse with dragons embroidered upon it. He had a pencil-thin mustache that had been twirled into two dark strands of hair which drooped down over either side of his face, giving him a perpetual frown.

Between Hoss and the doctor stood a barber's chair. Behind the doctor, the wall of shelves was covered with jars of insects, rodents, snakes, and dried plants and roots. On a table by the barber's chair, a container of incense gave off a wisp of smoke that gave the room a sweet, almost sickly smell.

Without taking his eyes off Dr. Lin Wo Pai, Hoss eased over to the barber's chair and took a seat. For a moment the two men stared maliciously at one another. Hoss knew that in a physical encounter he could overpower the doctor, but there was something sinister, something appalling about the doctor, as if he held some supernatural dominion over others. That, combined with his weird medicines, left Hoss uneasy, his palms sweaty, his eyes jittery.

Lin Wo Pai crossed his arms and stared at him.

"My back's been bothering me," Hoss said finally, drawing a wicked smile from the doctor.

Approaching Hoss, Lin Wo Pai lifted his arms, then pulled back his baggy sleeves, exposing his pale arms. At the barber's chair, Lin Wo Pai jerked a lever and the seat reclined. "Doctor check back," he said, moving behind Hoss and placing his hands on Hoss's shoulders. Intermittently, Lin Wo Pai pulled, then jabbed at Hoss. The manipulations were relaxing, except for one instant when the doctor's fingers tightened just a bit around Hoss's neck, then moved back to his shoulder.

"Back hurt now?"

"Some," Hoss lied, nodding for effect.

"When most hurt?"

"Most of time," Hoss replied.

Lin Wo Pai nodded, then pumped the chair lever until Hoss was slightly more elevated, bringing him face to face with the doctor. Hoss stared into his dark, inscrutable eyes.

"Oowww," Hoss moaned as he shifted in the seat. "Another sharp pain in my back," he lied.

Lin Wo Pai clapped his hands three times sharply. Then nodded. "Movement makes pain," the doctor said.

Hoss nodded, pleased that he had fooled this charlatan.

"Problem not back," Lin Wo Pai said, stroking the end of his mustache with one hand. "Liver problem. Evil organ liver is," the doctor announced. He placed the palms and fingers of his hands together in front of his chest and began to circle the barber's chair. "Medicine can cure. Rest easy. Doctor fix medicine. You forget problem with back."

Hoss smiled as the doctor made a final circle around the chair.

Stopping at the lever, the doctor lowered the chair back, and Hoss settled comfortably into the plush cushions of the seat. Hoss took his hat from his head and placed it over his face to block out the light from the oil lamp overhead.

The doctor moved to his shelves of medicine, and Hoss could hear him taking down jars and opening them, pulling out pinches of dried plants and dried animal parts to mix together with mortar and pestle. The noises were soft and unthreatening, except for one brief instant that reminded Hoss of the buzzing of a rattlesnake. Hoss dismissed that as some strange ritual the Chinese used to ensure the success of their medicines. When the doctor returned, Hoss planned to ask if Lin Wo Pai knew where he could buy a fine young China girl. If he could pretend to want to buy the girl, he could demand to inspect her before the purchase. Then he could steal her. If the doctor said no, then Hoss would force the whereabouts of the girl out of him.

The doctor sang or chanted reassuringly at his worktable, and gradually the sound seemed to lose itself somewhere in the back of Hoss's mind. Then all was silent. Had the doctor escaped? Before Hoss could move, he heard the sinister voice of Lin Wo Pai beside the chair.

"Mr. Cartwright," the doctor said.

Hoss flinched as he pulled his hat away from his face. He had not told the doctor his name!

On his chin Hoss felt a drop of something warm as he opened his eyes. Instantly Hoss froze in terror. Not six inches from his nose was the gaping white and pink mouth of a rattlesnake, held firmly in Lin Wo Pai's right hand. A drop of venom grew from one of the snake's fangs, then dropped harmlessly onto Hoss's cheek. Hoss's muscles tightened like an overwound spring and he could feel the breath of the rattlesnake in puffs against his face.

Lin Wo Pai hovered over his face, holding the snake behind its head to force open its ugly jaws. The doctor circled the two fangs carefully over Hoss's eyes, occasionally pushing the snake closer to his nose and laughing madly.

Hoss sank as deep into the plush cushion as he could. He knew he shouldn't risk shoving Lin Wo Pai, for the doctor might drop the snake on his chest. Looking past the snake, Hoss's eyes met Lin Wo Pai's. They had a serpentine quality of their own.

Through gritted teeth and clenched lips, Hoss mumbled, "Get away, Doctor."

Lin Wo Pai laughed crazily. "Back hurt still?" he taunted, then answered his own question. "Back never hurt! Doctor hear of big man after slave girl. Hip Ye Tung tell doctor so, after auction last time." Lin Wo Pai laughed crazily again, his high-pitched voice almost a shriek as he shook his head.

Thinking he saw an opportunity to save himself, Hoss raised his arm toward Lin Wo Pai.

Instantly the laughter died and the doctor shoved the rattlesnake within an inch of Hoss's nose.

Instinctively Hoss rolled his head over, putting a little

extra space between himself and the snake's gaping mouth of deadly poison. As he saw Lin Wo Pai pull the snake back, Hoss let out a deep breath and slowly turned toward the doctor. "I want the girl," Hoss whispered. "When I get her, I'll leave you and Chinatown alone."

Lin Wo Pai sneered. "Doctor bought girl. Girl doctor's."

"How many girls you buy?" Hoss said, his voice rising until Lin Wo Pai lowered the snake.

"Many," he sneered.

Hoss's muscles tightened in anger, his fists clenching by his sides as he so desperately wanted to strike at Lin Wo Pai.

"Doctor buy many girls," Lin Wo Pai said, "use girls, sell girls."

"You're a snake like your friend."

The doctor sneered again. "The woman, Aldina, is snake."

Hoss studied Lin Wo Pai's eyes. "Where's the girl? Here?" he demanded, stalling for time.

Lin Wo Pai shook his head, smiled broadly, jiggling the snake before Hoss's eyes.

Hoss scowled. "Did you use the girl, sleep with her?"

Pursing his lips, Lin Wo Pai spat at Hoss, then shoved the snake right at Hoss's nose. Hoss jerked his head aside. The snake brushed past him, its fangs sinking into the cushion. Lin Wo Pai laughed crazily as he pulled the snake back, its tail buzzing in anger now.

Hoss looked at Lin Wo Pai again. He took a breath, ready to make his move, then heard a noise as someone entered the waiting room.

Lin Wo Pai seemed not to hear over his own laughing.

"Hoss," came Aldina's voice as the front door slammed shut.

Lin Wo Pai glanced over his shoulder.

It was the instant Hoss had been waiting for. He exploded from the chair, throwing his beefy arm against Lin Wo Pai and the rattlesnake. Rolling over the chair's armrest, Hoss threw his shoulder into Lin Wo Pai's chest.

Lin Wo Pai screamed as if he had been bitten. The room was silent for an instant.

Hoss broke away from the doctor, his eyes focused on the doctor's hands. Both were empty! The snake! Where was it? Hoss heard an angry buzzing at his feet.

"Behind you!" screamed Aldina.

Hoss bolted forward, running into Lin Wo Pai, dragging the small doctor across the room as he jumped out of striking distance of the snake. The doctor slipped free and dashed to a cabinet against the wall. Jerking the door open, he pulled a long knife from within.

Aldina screamed as Lin Wo Pai slashed at Hoss.

Hoss dodged the knife, stepping aside rather than back because he still had not seen the rattlesnake. "The snake!" he shouted, "Where's the snake?" Hoss could hear the rattler's angry buzzing, which seemed to come from everywhere in the small room.

Out of the corner of his eye he saw Aldina grab a broom and swat at a spot on the floor near the barber's chair. "Stay on that side of the chair," Aldina shouted, then screamed as the rattler struck at the broom. With a desperate swing, she knocked the snake out of the air in midstrike, then clubbed it over and over with the broom until she was sure it was dead.

Hoss danced around the floor, watching the gleaming knife in Lin Wo Pai's hand. "When I get my hands on you, you skinny runt, I'll wring your neck till you're as dead as that snake."

Lin Wo Pai lunged at Hoss, swinging his knife in a deadly arc, then darted beyond Hoss's reach. Hoss and the doctor circled, gauging each other. Hoss saw Aldina circle behind Lin Wo Pai, raising the broom. Hoss made a feint at Lin Wo Pai, and the doctor took a step back.

Aldina cocked the broom and unloaded a ferocious swing that caught Lin Wo Pai under the ear, staggering him.

Hoss leaped for the knife, firmly grabbing Lin Wo Pai's wrist. Squeezing with all his strength, he loosened Lin Wo Pai's grip and the knife clattered to the floor. Shoving both hands under Lin Wo Pai's armpits, Hoss lifted him off the ground and shook him as easily as a woman would shake a rug. Lin Wo Pai screamed and Hoss dropped him on the floor. The doctor crumpled in a heap where he fell. Lin Wo Pai's eyes focused on the knife beside him, but before his hands could reach for it, Hoss kicked it across the room to Aldina.

"Don't let him get that," he commanded, and Aldina swept it against the far wall.

Hoss bent down over Lin Wo Pai and slapped his face with the back of his hand. "Where's the girl? I want to know where she is."

Lin Wo Pai twisted his head to avoid another blow from Hoss's hand. "No," the doctor shouted defiantly.

Grabbing Lin Wo Pai's loose blouse, Hoss jerked him to his feet and shook him vigorously.

"No!" Lin Wo Pai still called out. "No! No!"

Hoss dropped him again to the floor, then grabbed his queue and jerked him to his feet. Lin Wo Pai's teeth snapped from the jolt. His face was contorted with pain. His fight was gone, but not his defiance. Hoss shoved him down and pinned his head to the floor with his boot.

"Where's the girl?"

Lin Wo Pai struggled against Hoss's boot, then went limp when Hoss increased the weight on that foot.

"I want to know where the girl is," Hoss demanded. The fuse on his anger was growing shorter and shorter. "Your last chance, Doctor," Hoss demanded. "Where's the girl?"

"No," said Lin Wo Pai.

Hoss laughed. "I'll hang onto you like a bulldog until you tell me where she is."

When the doctor didn't respond, Hoss picked him up again, and again dropped him. Lin Wo Pai hit the wooden floor with a thud, his nose beginning to drip blood over his pencil-thin mustache, now misshaped from the fight. Lin Wo Pai rolled over, groaning and stunned, but conscious enough to crawl up on his hands and knees, his long queue sliding from his back and shoulder onto the floor beside his hands.

Hoss had a sudden idea and turned to Aldina. "The knife, the knife, give it to me!"

Aldina's eyes widened in terror as she picked up the knife and stepped tentatively toward Hoss. She paused just out of Hoss's reach, as if fearing a murder should she give him the knife. She mouthed a prayer and reluctantly offered him the weapon.

Hoss's right hand tightened around the knife handle. With his left hand he grabbed at the braids of Lin Wo Pai's queue and jerked the doctor to his feet. With blood dripping from his nose, Lin Wo Pai stood groggily beside Hoss. Hoss twisted the queue until Lin Wo Pai could see it before his eyes. Then Hoss slid the knife under the queue, bringing the blade's razor sharpness against the rope of hair. Lightly he began to saw at the queue. Lin Wo Pai's eyes filled with terror.

"No!" he said.

"Where is she?"

"Don't know," Lin Wo Pai answered as a few strands of hair separated from the queue. He grimaced. "Gamble her away!" he shouted. "No cut hair, no cut hair," he pleaded, his eyes watering.

"Who has her now?" Hoss demanded.

"Chan Tan Tan," the doctor shouted.

"Who?"

"Chan Tan Tan," he yelled, even louder.

"If you're lying, I'll come back to scalp you," Hoss threatened. "Where will I find him?"

Instead of Lin Wo Pai, Aldina answered. "In Stout's Alley."

Hoss shoved Lin Wo Pai away. "How do you know?"

"He's a dangerous man, a gambler and king of the Chinese underworld," she said.

Lin Wo Pai lifted his hand and swiped at the blood dripping from his nose. He pointed a bloody finger at Hoss. "Men know of you, Mr. Cartwright, and of girl you want. Longer you follow her, deeper she fall in Chinatown. She pretty girl, may find rich husband to keep her. She have much value as what called virgin. Seek her more, value fall and she not stay virgin, instead work in cages like ugly girls."

"We'll find her," Hoss answered, shoving Lin Wo Pai's bloody finger away.

"If you live," Lin Wo Pai said, sneering, glancing at Aldina. "Woman pest but no danger to Chinatown." The charlatan turned his gaze to Hoss. "Some fear you, know you come from rich family with power."

"You won't scare us away!" Hoss answered.

"You will be killed unless you leave Chinatown." Lin Wo Pai shook his head, then laughed insanely.

Hoss motioned to the door and followed Aldina out of the doctor's office and onto the teeming streets of Chinatown.

CHAPTER 15

Outside Lin Wo Pai's office, Hop Sing rushed to Aldina and Hoss. Darkness was closing in on San Francisco, and Hoss felt the dampness of his shirt sticking to his skin. He shivered as much from the thought of the rattlesnake over his face as from the gentle breeze at his back.

Hoss had had enough of Chinatown for a day and certainly didn't want to be on these streets. He herded Aldina and Hop Sing along as darkness drew its blanket over the town. When Aldina turned up a street that led deeper into Chinatown, Hoss grabbed her arm.

"It's getting late, where you headed?"

"Stout's Alley," she said matter-of-factly, then stared at him. "You're not giving up, are you, Hoss?"

Hop Sing stepped between them. "Hop Sing not give up! Hop Sing find girl."

"No, no," Hoss said, "I'm not giving up."

"Then why not now?" Aldina asked.

"If it's dangerous for us here in daylight, it'll be worse in the dark. You said this man was a gambler."

Aldina nodded. "So?"

"More men gamble at night. I don't want to approach this man when others are around. Show us this Stout's Alley and we'll come back tomorrow in daylight."

"Every minute we waste threatens the girl's well-being," Aldina replied.

Hoss raised his voice. "We're the only hope she's got, Aldina, don't you understand? Something happens to us, she has no hope."

Before Aldina twisted her head away, Hoss thought he saw hurt in her green eyes. He could not be sure if the pain came from his words or the thought of Hop Sing's niece spending another night in slavery. Determined, Aldina plowed ahead, Hoss and Hop Sing trailing her through the masses flooding the street, chattering in their strange tongue, looking suspiciously at them.

Several times Hoss suspected they were being followed. He glanced over his shoulder and even turned around to check, but the Celestials were dressed so similarly that he could not say with certainty.

After a few minutes on streets teeming with activity and men, Aldina turned onto a quieter street. She stopped halfway down the block at a narrow alley that sliced between two three-story brick buildings. In the gathering darkness, Hoss could make out little except that the alley was narrow and cluttered. He could not believe that a gambler of Chan Tan Tan's supposed success would live off an alley of such squalor. Nothing about the buildings on either side of the street denoted even a modest degree of financial success.

"This is it?" he asked.

Aldina turned to him. "Yes, but don't let it fool you. Chan Tan Tan is one of the richest and most powerful men in Chinatown."

"It ain't Nob Hill," Hoss replied, thinking of the exclusive area where many of San Francisco's moneyed lived. He spun around, convinced he saw a dark figure leap into an alleyway. "Let's get out of here while there's still some light left."

Aldina lingered a moment, staring down the alley with disgust.

Hoss grabbed her arm. "Now," he said. Instinctively, he patted his side where his holster and .44-caliber Russian Model Smith & Wesson would normally be. Then he cursed silently, wishing he had not left it at the Ponderosa. But then, he hadn't expected to wind up in San Francisco, looking for a lost girl he had never met, staying in the home of a woman who had attacked him with her purse, fighting off a charlatan's rattlesnake, eating dog soup and buying a slave girl.

Steering Aldina through the crowd, Hoss glanced occasionally over his shoulder, checking to make sure Hop Sing was nearby. Hop Sing followed faithfully, but Hoss could not shake the strange sensation that someone else was following them. He thought he understood the lay of Chinatown, but at one street he moved left.

Aldina tugged his arm to the right. "This way," she said. "We're going home, aren't we?"

"Yes, ma'am," he replied, glancing around for Hop Sing. He was gone! Hoss felt a rush of panic. He looked at Aldina and started to speak, then sputtered when he saw Hop Sing just ahead of him.

"Something the matter, Hoss?" Aldina asked.

"Thought we'd lost Hop Sing."

"You're jumpy."

"I don't like Chinatown, not in the dark."

"It's not as bad as the Barbary Coast after dark," she replied.

"At least they speak English down there," Hoss answered.

The sky had gone black by the time they cleared the fringes of Chinatown. The gas lamps were taking effect, creating bright circles of light augmenting the trickle of indoor light that seeped through dirty windows onto the street. Traffic on the street had dwindled and pedestrians were heading into the scattered saloons where the gay laughter and music overflowed, punctuated by loud talk and profane words. As they passed saloons, Aldina would cling tightly to Hoss's arm. Though the air was cool against his damp shirt, Hoss enjoyed it, taking deep breaths. There was just a different smell about Chinatown, not necessarily bad, just different, one Hoss was unaccustomed to; he was glad to be beyond it.

Occasionally Hoss looked over his shoulder, but the

farther they got from Chinatown, the less he worried about the ghosts trailing him. Aldina tugged more tightly on his arm and leaned her head against his shoulder. It was a comfortable feeling to have Aldina beside him, Hoss thought, a woman brave enough to kill a rattlesnake with a broom yet still vulnerable to her emotions.

"Why'd you take up this crusade for these girls?" he asked.

"Nobody else cared," she said softly, almost warily, as if she feared where Hoss might be leading.

He detected her reluctance and his curiosity grew. "There are many causes no one else cares for, so why this one?"

Aldina walked silently for half a block, and when she finally spoke, her voice quivered. "I lost a child in birth," she whispered, her voice breaking. "A little girl."

Now Hoss felt awkward. "I'm sorry. I didn't mean to upset you."

Her hand tightened around his arm again. "Doctor said I couldn't have any more children. If I couldn't have another girl, I decided I'd save other girls, little Chinese girls. You've got to lose a child to appreciate how precious they are, no matter what race or color."

Now it was Hoss's turn to walk silently, but he was even more curious than before. "You have a husband, then?"

Aldina laughed softly, not in joy, but in mockery. "Had one. He left me eight years ago, haven't heard from him since. He left me the house, and I've lived on the gifts of the church to do my work."

"I'm sorry about your husband," Hoss said as they turned up Aldina's street and began the climb to her house.

"Don't be sorry about him, be sorry for my daughter who never had a life. My only solace is that in losing one daughter, God led me to save the lives of dozens more. That doesn't replace my baby, but it brings me comfort."

Hoss turned and planted a gentle kiss upon the top of her head, enjoying the softness and fragrance of her hair.

Reaching her home, they walked through the gate and up the step. Releasing her grip on his arm, Aldina took a key from her pocket and inserted it in the lock, opening it with a click. She pushed the door and entered ahead of Hoss and Hop Sing. The house was dark, lit only by a patch of brightness seeping in from a gas lamp at the top of the street.

At the table near the door, Aldina patted around the base of a kerosene lamp for the tin of matches she kept. Hoss closed the door, glad to finally be back within the safe confines of Aldina's home.

"There you are," Aldina said to the match tin, quickly opening it and striking a match.

The light was weak and it took an instant for Hoss's eyes to adjust to the darkness. Looking away from the flame, he spotted a moving shadow in the far corner of the room. Instinctively his hand grabbed for his waist, but he was unarmed. "Watch out," he yelled as his hand came up empty. He saw a glint of something head high and dove for Aldina.

She screamed as Hoss tackled her, the match dying as they fell to the floor. Something thudded into the door overhead.

Hop Sing cried out in Chinese, then dove to the floor, cutting loose with another barrage of angry words.

"Stay down," Hoss commanded, untangling himself from Aldina and scrambling toward the corner. In the darkness his head bumped into the sofa, but he plowed ahead toward the corner, knocking over a chair. Lunging with both arms out, he grabbed a thrashing body. Arms wrapping around his target, Hoss crashed to the floor, squeezing his assailant with the strength of a bear.

The attacker gasped in Hoss's grip, bucking wildly beneath him but quickly losing strength. By the door, Hoss heard Aldina fumbling for the match tin. Finding it, she jerked a match free and struck it. A tiny beacon flared in the room.

Aldina screamed. "Behind you, Hoss! Another one." She jumped to her feet, moving that way, but Hop Sing darted in front of her toward the second assailant. Then the match died and the room fell into darkness again.

Warned of the second assailant, Hoss rolled over on

his back, shielding himself with the man he was crushing between his arms.

Hoss heard a commotion and then Hop Sing's shout as a chair crashed into the floor. Glass shattered. Above him, Hoss could just make out two shadowy figures grappling wildly at one another. They struggled against each other, and Hoss saw an arm uplifted in the air and the shadow of a weapon. A hatchet! Then it came down and Hoss lost sight of it in the darkness as Hop Sing was flung away. Hoss squirmed with his human shield to dodge the blow. The man gasped, then screamed at the same instant Hoss felt the thud of the hatchet in the man's back.

Hoss shoved the human shield away and scrambled to his hands and knees, lunging for the hatchet man's legs. The assassin evaded his grasp with two retreating steps, but stumbled over an upset chair and fell backwards onto the floor. The crash of his body was followed by the clatter of his hatchet striking the floor as well. Hoss struck at a squatting shadow, grabbing an overturned chair in place of the assailant.

"Dammit," he yelled, clambering over the chair and lunging toward a moving shadow this time. He caught a wisp of silk material in his fingers for a second, then lost his tenuous hold as the assailant squirted around him, aiming for the door. Hoss made out a fleeting shadow running, then saw another shadow dive into him. He recognized Hop Sing's shout as the assailant was tackled, his escape cut off.

From around the door, Hoss heard Aldina slap at the floor and shout triumphantly. As he scrambled to his feet, a pinpoint of light appeared in Aldina's hand as she struck another match. Hoss jumped over a chair toward the rolling ball that was Hop Sing and his assailant. Aldina ran to the table and grabbed the kerosene lamp, lifting the glass globe and lighting the wick, the room brightening slowly as she adjusted the flame.

Standing over Hop Sing and the assailant, Hoss grabbed the intruder's arm and ripped him away from Hop Sing, whose face was bloodied. He tossed the assailant over the upset chair, away from Aldina. Like a cat, the assailant hit the floor on his feet and bounded up the stairs.

Hopping over the chair, Hoss charged after him, reaching for the assailant's feet at the head of the stairs and tripping him on the top step. Before Hoss could reel him in, the assailant jumped away and into the front room.

Scrambling after him, Hoss lunged into the bedroom in time to see the assailant bound across the bed and land on his feet, poised to take his charge. The assailant was a small shadow outlined by the dim light coming in through the bay window at his back.

Behind Hoss, Aldina and Hop Sing were climbing the stairs. Suddenly, the upper floor was awash in light; Aldina had brought the lamp with her. "Stay out there, Aldina," Hoss commanded. "Hold the light up, high as you can, so I can see him." But the assailant covered his face with the baggy sleeve of his blouse and stayed in Hoss's shadow by mirroring his movements. By the man's attire and height, Hoss knew he was Chinese, but could tell nothing more.

"You little rat," Hoss called out, rubbing his hands together, "you're trapped now." He stepped around the end of the bed. For a moment the man was fully exposed to the light, then he stepped forward into Hoss's shadow again, like a bug scurrying for cover after a rock was lifted from it.

The assailant took another step toward Hoss, then whirled around and flung himself toward the window. He screamed as he hit, then burst through the window, glass shattering in a thousand pieces, wood splintering. With another cry, he thudded on the ground.

Stunned, Hoss stood petrified for a moment, then rushed to the window, Aldina and Hop Sing behind him. He stuck his head out the broken window in time to see the assailant jump over the fence, then limp down the street, holding his right shoulder and clinging to the shadows.

Hoss spun around, remembering the one downstairs. "The lamp," he said, taking it from Aldina. He headed for the stairs, and upon reaching the bottom floor, looked around the room, noting the overturned chair and table, the shattered vase, the crumpled throw rugs. "Dammit," he cried out.

"What is it?" Aldina called from the top of the stairs.

"This one's gone too," Hoss said, studying a trail of blood that led into the kitchen.

Hoss advanced to the door, carefully looking around the room as the light drove the darkness away from the corners. The droplets of blood made a trail around the stove and out the open back door. He stopped at the back door, holding the lamp outside to see if the attacker might have passed out in the back, but there was no sign of him. Grabbing the door handle, he quickly pulled the door shut and latched it.

"It's safe now, you can come on down," Hoss said, then turned around, startled to see Aldina at the door. As he placed the lamp on the stove, she ran to him and threw her arms around him, her head falling to his chest.

"Nothing like this ever happened before," she sobbed. "Why?"

His brow furrowed as he pressed her head against his. "I don't know, Aldina. Maybe somebody'll lose a lot of money if we get Hop Sing's niece."

She sobbed loudly now, then whispered, "This is a girl these men are selling, not an animal. Can't they see that? Can't they understand that, for God's sake?"

Hop Sing entered, bowing to Hoss and Aldina. "Hop Sing sorry for the trouble. No longer must Mr. Hoss or gentle woman help find her. Mr. Hoss and gentle woman no danger no more."

"No, sir," Aldina answered, her voice firm and controlled now. "We'll get that girl yet. Nothing'll stop us now."

CHAPTER 16

H oss awoke with the cool breeze breathing through the broken bay window. After last night, he dreaded venturing into Stout's Alley. Who knew what surprises awaited there? Chinatown being a world of its own, Hoss knew that he, Hop Sing, and Aldina could all disappear without a clue. And that might be a real possibility if they got too close to the girl.

Shivering in the cool draft as he got out of bed, he dressed quickly and headed downstairs, surprised to find a light coming from the kitchen and pleased to smell hot coffee. Expecting Hop Sing, Hoss instead found Aldina standing over the stove.

"Morning," he said.

She spun around, her hand at her mouth, then caught her breath. "I'm a little jumpy after last night."

"Me too, and colder without that window. I'll board it up later."

Aldina frowned. "I found a couple more spots of blood this morning and cleaned them up. And look what else." She pointed to the front door.

A Chinese hatchet was impaled in the wood. Hoss walked across the room and studied the glistening blade. It was eye level, just the right height to have split his skull open last night when he entered the house. Grabbing the handle, he jerked on the hatchet, but it didn't budge.

"I couldn't get it out," Aldina said.

Hoss grabbed it with both hands and worked it free with three mighty tugs. He twisted the weapon over and inspected its blade, as finely honed as a razor's. "Close call," he said to himself as much as to Aldina.

"Does this change your mind about going to Stout's Alley, Hoss? Hop Sing and you will be in the greatest danger."

"I intend to go."

"Me too," Aldina said.

Hoss was surprised she still had the courage to go after last night. He walked back to the kitchen, putting the weapon on the table as Aldina filled a coffee cup for him. "Maybe you ought to stay out of this one," he cautioned her. "Stay here."

Her face paled. "After last night, I don't want to be here alone. I could be killed in my own home."

Hoss nodded. She was right. He didn't want to take her, but neither did he want to leave her alone.

"We've got to let someone know our plan in case Chan Tan Tan . . ." Hoss paused, struggling for the right word.

"Tries to kill us?"

Shrugging, Hoss felt a sheepish grin work its way across his face. He nodded. "Yep, that's possible." He slid into a chair at the table, taking the coffee cup as she offered it to him and sipping deeply from its strong brew. "This is good strong coffee, the way a man likes it."

Aldina brought the pot over and refilled his cup. "After last night, I figured we could use something a little stronger."

Hoss pursed his lips, thinking she was right and wondering if she had a bottle of whiskey around. He could use a shot of whiskey in the coffee. But he figured he might insult her sensibilities by asking, so he sat quietly through another cup of coffee, considering who he could notify of their planned foray into Stout's Alley.

"I could leave word with some of my church friends," Aldina offered. "Of course, they might try to pre-

vent me from going, and I don't want that. I want to be
there, to see the vermin that does this to young girls."

Studying his coffee cup, Hoss pondered his options.
There was that San Francisco lawyer his father used on
occasion, the lawyer Kendall. He took a long draft on his
coffee, devising a plan. Aldina could deliver the message,
since he preferred to avoid Kendall, just in case the lawyer
had received word from the Ponderosa that he should return to Nevada. He would write a note informing Kendall
that if he had not heard from Aldina by six o'clock this afternoon, the lawyer should notify police to seek them in
Stout's Alley. He outlined his plan for Aldina. "If Kendall
questions my whereabouts, tell him you were paid to deliver this message and know nothing about where I am.
You have pencil and paper?"

Aldina left the kitchen for the parlor and returned in
a moment with a florid pink stationery and a pencil.

Hoss looked at the paper, grimacing as he took it but
saying nothing about the feminine stationery. He penned a
few sentences about the situation and signed his name.
Then he addressed an envelope with Kendall's name. "His
office is across from the courthouse. Come middle of the
morning, you should deliver it to him. We'll go to Stout's
Alley after lunch."

Following a breakfast prepared by Hop Sing, Hoss
spent the morning boarding up the bedroom window.
Aldina worked with Hop Sing on laundry. Those were minor chores, but things that helped all three keep their worries off Stout's Alley.

Just before ten o'clock Aldina took Hoss's note and
left for the courthouse. Like Hoss last night, she kept
glancing over her shoulder, fearing she might be followed
and attacked. But for all her precautions, she saw no one
who seemed in the least interested in her.

Reaching the courthouse, she circled the imposing
building twice before finding the law offices of David
Thornton Kendall, the name painted in faded gold letters
on the window. Through the window she could see a
young man hunched over his desk, reading a stack of papers. The office occupied the ground-floor corner of a

stone building four stories tall. The door leading into Kendall's office was draped in black crepe. A wreath of dried flowers hung from a nail planted in the center of the heavy wooden door.

Aldina walked up the two steps, pushed open the ponderous door and stepped on a worn maroon carpet. Six chairs were scattered about the anteroom, all pointing toward the open door into the office where she had seen the deskbound man. Aldina brushed her hand against her hair, straightened her blouse and stepped to the door, expecting the man to look up from the papers and law books stacked all over his massive cherrywood desk.

She studied his thick blond hair and bushy mustache, thinking him too young for glasses. The man picked up a pipe from the desk and sucked deeply on the stem while she watched the tobacco glow orange. Between the pipe and the legal papers, he seemed content, as if he could sustain himself without food or water.

Aldina cleared her throat. Jerking his pipe from his mouth, the man glanced up over the top of his wire-rimmed glasses. Aldina was struck by his deep blue eyes, which seemed much too sharp to need glasses. Placing the pipe in an overflowing ashtray, he pushed himself up from his desk as if about to make a pronouncement of significance, then tugged the lapel of his unbuttoned frock coat.

"David Thornton Kendall the Third," he said, his voice as crisp as the crackle of new paper money, "attorney at law. And your name?"

Aldina smiled. "That is not important. Not today."

Kendall cocked his head at her, eyeing her suspiciously while tugging at the corner of his bushy mustache. "A woman of mystery? Well, madam, two women have already been here since the death of my father, claiming they were his paramours, a secret they would gladly share with the newspapers unless I paid them a sizable sum of cash. I gave them a reporter's name at the *Chronicle* and suggested they sell it to him, cut me out as the middleman." He put his hands on his hips, spreading his legs apart. "I don't bluff well, madam, so out with your business."

"I've a sealed message I would like you to keep for one of your clients," she said, holding up the envelope. "If I do not come back by six o'clock to reclaim it, you are to open it and notify the police."

The attorney stood akimbo, licking his upper lip, gauging Aldina and her odd request. He made no effort to accept the envelope.

Minutes seemed to pass, and still he said nothing, just studied her with those blue eyes which now seemed as cold as ice. She felt she must explain more. "It's a life and death matter."

"Whose life? Yours?"

Aldina nodded. "Possibly."

"And I don't even know you or your name?"

"And Mr. Cartwright's," Aldina said.

Kendall stepped around the desk. "Mr. Cartwright's sent me a lot of telegrams the last few days, but you're the first woman. I'll tell you what I told him," he said, his voice as edgy now as a barrel full of knives. "If he tries to fire me before my work is done, I'll see him in the courts for years. I'll create so many legal brushfires, he'll be spending more time in the courthouse than in his own house."

Now Aldina shrugged. "All I know is Hoss thought you'd—"

"Hoss," Kendall interrupted, "it's Hoss, not the old man?"

Aldina nodded.

"Madam, Hoss is a fine fellow, a little slow at times, but fine nonetheless, as are his brothers, but there's only one 'Mr. Cartwright,' and that's Ben Cartwright, patriarch of Nevada's Ponderosa empire."

Now Aldina shrugged. "I don't know about any of that. All I know is Hoss and I must go somewhere in Chinatown today. We want someone to know where we're going."

"Why didn't Hoss come here himself?" Kendall crossed his arms over his chest and wrinkled his nose like it was itching. His glasses wiggled on his nose.

Aldina hesitated, not sure she should be answering questions. This had not gone at all as she had expected.

"I'm waiting for an answer," Kendall said. "I'll not take the envelope without an answer, madam."

Her proffered hand slipping to her side, Aldina felt her shoulders sag. What could she do but respond? Once she left, he could open the letter anyway. "Hoss doesn't want anyone to know where he is right now."

Kendall laughed. "Hoss is as honest and open as the bible, madam. This doesn't sound like a scheme he would try."

Aldina strode across the room and looked into Kendall's blue eyes. He seemed to be enjoying this conversation like he would a game of crooked cards. "Take it or leave it," she said, sticking the sealed envelope beneath his nose.

"I could follow you to Hoss."

"I might not be going back to see him," she said, waving the envelope beneath his nose.

He still made no move to take it.

Letting out a sigh, Aldina lowered the letter. She had never dealt with a lawyer before and she hoped she never had occasion to again. She could leave the note with someone from the church, but they might worry too much about her, realize she was getting deeper into Chinatown than was safe and try to stop her. "Thank you, Mr. Kendall," she said, turning away. Before she could take a step, she felt his hand close around her wrist.

"I don't take on this kind of work without a fee, madam. Did Hoss give you money?"

Lawyers! All they were interested in was money, not in helping folks, Aldina thought. "He considered you a family friend. No money."

His hand tight around her wrist, Kendall lifted her arm to his chest and pulled the letter from her fingers. "My fee is the option to open this letter any time I choose."

"If that's what it takes, I'll tell Hoss." She jerked her wrist from his grasp, staring hard into Kendall's eyes, dis-

gusted at his lawyerly ways and angered at his stubborn-
ness. "Good day," she said coldly.

"Madam, it's been a pleasure doing business with
you." He bowed to her and then gestured toward the door.
"Let me see you out."

Aldina sniffed and brusquely stepped out of the office
into the anteroom. "I'll see myself out." Behind her, she
heard Kendall's cynical voice.

"As you please. Good day, madam."

Angered, Aldina jerked open the door and stepped
outside, slamming the door behind her. She strode down
the street, anxious to get back to Hoss and to visit Stout's
Alley. As she turned the corner by Kendall's office, she
saw him standing in the window, holding something up to
the sunlight and reading it.

It was Hoss's note.

CHAPTER 17

E ver since she entered Chinatown on the way to Stout's Alley, Aldina's fear had grown. Hoss could sense it. She glanced over her shoulder repeatedly and often asked Hop Sing what the Chinese pedestrians around them were saying. Hoss reached for her arm to comfort her. At his touch, she jumped, her other hand flying to her mouth to stifle a yelp of surprise. Hoss steered her through a clump of men arguing over something. He could feel the quiver in her arm.

"I've never feared Chinatown before," she apologized, "but everywhere I've gone today I've felt I was being followed."

Hoss shared the feeling but said nothing of it. "Things like last night always shake a person. You'll learn to live with it."

Aldina shook her head. "Maybe, but not for a time." She leaned closer into Hoss. "I've hated Chinatown for what it's done to so many young girls, but I've never feared it before."

"Maybe I should take you back home," Hoss offered.

"No," she answered emphatically. "I'd feel more frightened there, alone."

Hoss paused at a corner to allow several wagons to pass and to get his bearings. He knew Stout's Alley was nearby but could not place where.

Aldina pointed to her left. "A block and a half, opposite side of the street."

"You still with us, Hop Sing?" Hoss said over his shoulder.

"Hop Sing here," he answered, "ready to find girl."

Hoss maneuvered Aldina across the street, weaving through the wagon and pedestrian traffic, then turned left toward Stout's Alley. He was glad Aldina knew her way around Chinatown. At the middle of the block, Hoss, Aldina, and Hop Sing stopped, staring wordlessly at the mouth of Stout's Alley. It appeared as mysterious and dangerous as an abandoned mine shaft. Even though it was early afternoon, the alley was veiled in shadows, screened on either side from the sunlight by three-story buildings. The wash strung from myriad clotheslines blocked still more light.

Hoss looked all around but saw nothing unusual except for two uniformed policemen across the street, conversing freely and watching Stout's Alley. He did not recall seeing policemen in Chinatown before. He sighed. "We'll never get wet unless we wade into the water," he said, stepping toward the alley.

Aldina hesitated, her face pale.

Hoss paused. "Maybe you should wait out here."

"I don't feel safe here, or in there, or anywhere anymore," she answered firmly, but her eyes were wide with fright. "Chan Tan Tan. I've heard his name a thousand times, the man behind so much of what is wrong with Chinatown. I've always wanted to lay my eyes upon him and then lay my hands upon his neck and strangle the life out of him. Very un-Christian, isn't it?"

"A lot about this world is ungodly," Hoss replied.

Taking a deep breath, Aldina plunged into the narrow alley ahead of Hoss. Both men fell quickly in line behind her, Hop Sing bringing up the rear. The alley reeked of the aromas Hoss had come to associate with Chinatown, only here they were more intense, more sinister. Aldina dodged something in the alley, but Hoss felt his boot step in something squishy amidst the refuse thrown into the alley to rot, attracting vermin like iron filings to a magnet.

If Chan Tan Tan really was the kingpin of the Chinese underworld in San Francisco, he had not squandered his profits on a fine dwelling. In the dimness, Hoss could just make out some dozen doors, all modest-looking, none having the grandeur one would expect from a crime king.

At the end of the alley a rectangle of dim light appeared and two Chinese men worked their way out a door, struggling to carry a heavy trunk down the two steps that led to the alley. At the foot of the steps the two Celestials gently lowered the trunk to the ground long enough for one of them to close the door. With a grunt, the two grabbed handles on the trunk and waddled it down the alley, talking excitedly in their Chinese dialect until they realized others were approaching.

When the two men neared Hoss, they grinned politely, their teeth appearing as white crescents in the alley's dimness. A cool breeze coursed suddenly down the alley, snapping the drying clothes on the lines overhead. Hoss flinched, but Aldina, with new resolve, gave no reaction to the noise. As the men reached them, Hoss focused on the one in the rear. There was something peculiar about his right eye; it seemed to be a black hole beside his nose. Then Hoss realized it was an eyepatch. A pucker of pink flesh snaked from his chin, over his right cheek, beneath the eyepatch, and up over his forehead, ending atop his head. He looked as wicked as Satan on a bad day. Hoss averted his gaze from this man to the one in front, whose face was crisscrossed with fresh cuts just recently scabbed over. Hoss wondered for a moment if this might be the man who jumped through Aldina's upstairs window last night. Coincidence perhaps, but he had learned coincidences were few in Chinatown.

Hoss placed his hand upon Aldina's shoulder and she stopped. "Hop Sing," Hoss commanded, "ask them if they know which door is Chan Tan Tan's place."

Hop Sing spoke rapidly. The man with the eyepatch snarled wickedly as the other spoke over his shoulder. At Eyepatch's reply, both men laughed. Then Eyepatch studied Hop Sing and spoke in a low growl, like some sinister animal protecting its kill. Hop Sing bowed to them as they passed and waddled their way toward the brightness that was the street.

"What'd he say, Hop Sing?" Hoss wanted to know.

"Evil man say Chan Tan Tan's door at alley end." Hop Sing, started to speak again, but his mouth merely hung open.

The men carrying the trunk had emerged from Chan Tan Tan's quarters!

"Is that all?" Hoss asked.

Hop Sing shook his head. "Evil man say Chan Tan Tan waiting for us." Hop Sing's voice trembled.

Hoss looked to Aldina. "You don't have to go."

"I'm not backing out now," she said, striding deeper into the alley and the crime underworld of Chinatown.

Hoss felt as if he were approaching the gates of Hell, uncertain what fate awaited him. He moved fast, passing Aldina, marching up the two steps and pounding on the door. "Open up," he called, "we've got business." His shout echoed along the brick alley, but only the reverberation of his voice answered. Hoss pounded again, the door shaking under each blow of his massive fist. And still only his echo answered. Hoss motioned for Hop Sing and Aldina to step back. As they did, he grabbed the door handle and prepared to shoulder his way into Chan Tan Tan's quarters. He twisted the handle and it turned easily in his hand. A trap? He pushed on the door and it swung quietly open, a dim light seeping out and revealing a carpeted stairway that led to the second floor. At the head of the stairs a gas lamp leaked pale yellow light.

"Hello," he called as he stepped inside, startling a cat which darted between his legs. Aldina caught her breath as the cat shot by and into the alley. Because of his size, Hoss had never met a man who had intimidated him, but not knowing what was at the top of those stairs was different. Especially since Chan Tan Tan was expecting them and was doing nothing to resist their intrusion, even leaving the door unlatched. Perhaps this was some diabolical ambush, a cruel way of enticing them deeper into his lair, then closing a trap around them and destroying them in this strange world that was Chinatown. He was glad he had sent the note to lawyer Kendall, even if Kendall had offended Aldina.

Hop Sing and Aldina slipped meekly into the hallway, closing the door behind them. The scent of incense floated delicately in the air. Hoss climbed the stairs. Each step creaked under his weight, as if the whole building were announcing his approach. Aldina, then Hop Sing followed him, one cautious step at a time.

The carpet beneath their feet might once have been expensive, but now it was worn and unraveling in places. The walls were a dingy brown, coated with a film from the smoke of constant incense and, Hoss suspected, opium. With each step, Hoss began to doubt if Chan Tan Tan was really an underworld king, if this was the best he could afford with all his evil profits.

When Hoss reached the top of the stairs, he caught his breath. He could not believe what he saw.

"What is it?" Aldina whispered from behind him.

"See for yourself," Hoss replied softly, almost reverently, as he stepped aside to let Aldina and Hop Sing join him.

The room's walls blossomed with banners and silk emblems, embroidered in Peking. The threadbare carpet on the stairs gave way to a thick rug of Oriental design, flecked with a golden thread that shimmered, even in the soft light that overflowed a golden lamp suspended from the ceiling. In each corner reposed fine mahogany stands holding golden idols with bejeweled eyes staring at the three intruders. Along each wall were two chairs with thick velvet cushions of maroon, gold, purple, and silver. To Hoss's left was a doorway dressed with strands of pearls and diamonds which formed a bead curtain.

Hoss looked at Hop Sing, then at Aldina, his eyes feeling as wide as theirs.

"It's like I would've imagined King Solomon's palace," Aldina whispered.

Hop Sing spoke softly in Chinese, but neither Hoss nor Aldina needed a translation for the awe in his voice.

Hoss motioned for them to follow as he eased over to the bead curtain. The aroma of incense grew stronger, and

Hoss peered through the strands of the regal curtain, making out little in the next room except some furniture and a dark purple carpet. He reached for the jewel strands with his rough hands, pondering whether he should move slowly or burst through the curtain. A voice made his hand flinch, rattling the bejeweled strands.

"Welcome to my home! I've been expecting you." The disembodied voice came from the next room. The voice was without question Chinese, but the accent lacked rough edges. "Come in, please."

Hoss caught his breath and clattered his way through the beaded strands. As he held them apart for Aldina and Hop Sing, he studied the room, this one even more opulent than the anteroom, with a large redwood table inlaid with gold strips, and tall-backed chairs with matching gold veins in them. The curtains of this room sagged under their elegant weight. Oriental tapestries, one taking up the whole back wall, hung like sheets from a clothesline on wash day. Fresh flowers adorned solid gold vases, and gold and silver trinkets rested like cheap toys on corner tables. Four plush sofas faced the large table. As Hop Sing and Aldina entered, Hoss observed a similar beaded opening in the wall across the room. What treasures and surprises could await them there?

"Come in, Mr. Cartwright and friends," came that bodiless voice.

Hoss studied the great Oriental tapestry on the far wall where the voice seemed to originate. He saw nothing for a moment, then a movement as if a layer of the tapestry had been pulled away and a man had appeared. Hoss blinked his eyes. Indeed, a Chinese man stepped away from the wall, and Hoss realized the source of the illusion was the man's robe, which matched perfectly in color and design a portion of the tapestry. By merely standing at the appropriate spot, he melded into a bouquet of flowers woven into the great tapestry.

This man placed his hands palm to palm before his chest and bowed slightly to Hoss. Then with a sweeping motion toward the table, he spoke. "Please, be seated and let's discuss this matter you have come to see me about. I am Chan Tan Tan."

Hop Sing stepped that way, but Hoss grabbed his arm. "We prefer to stand. What about the girl?"

"Mr. Cartwright, you must learn to be patient. It's easier on the soul. We have learned that over our thousand-year history. Your history as a nation is not even a tenth that."

Hoss studied this man. Attired in a robe of silk with hand-embroidered flowers on the front and back, Chan Tan Tan had gentle eyes and delicate hands. His face was soft around the edges and his black queue was perfumed and glistened in the room's light.

Impatient, Hoss moved suddenly toward him, hands outstretched.

"Mr. Cartwright, I shouldn't think you would want to threaten someone who has allowed you to enter his home."

Hoss stopped at the click of a gun behind him.

Chan Tan Tan seated himself at the table. "Mr. Cartwright, please meet my wife."

Twisting slowly around, Hoss looked at the doorway leading into the next room. Silhouetted behind the beaded curtain stood a woman, her delicate hand pointing a revolver through the bejeweled strands.

Hoss's hands dropped to his sides.

The woman entered, tall, slender, elegant and white, the jeweled bead curtain clicking behind her. Her blond hair was long and shiny like her husband's, but her complexion was pale and powdered, making the natural red of her thin lips appear as a crimson gash across her face. Her green eyes were as observant as her gun hand was steady.

Aldina moved beside Hoss, then in front of him, standing between him and the gun.

"Beautiful woman, Maggie," Chan Tan Tan said. "I married her because she's always brought me good luck. Her luck has made me rich. And without her I'd be dead. With her gun, she shot three of four men who tried to assassinate me because they owed me money. Two died, the third lost his arm, and the fourth just disappeared from Chinatown. Please, don't try anything here because I'd hate to clean your blood from my carpet. Now please, be seated."

Aldina turned around and took Hoss's hand, pulling him toward the table. Hop Sing, too, followed, all three of them taking a seat at the opposite end from Chan Tan Tan.

"Thank you, Mr. Cartwright, you and your guests."

Hoss dropped his hat on the table and held up his arm toward Chan Tan Tan. As he leaned forward, his brow furrowed and his eyes narrowed. "Just how is it you know so much about me?"

"Now, Mr. Cartwright, a man your size poking around Chinatown is bound to arouse suspicions. Word gets around fast, and we find the answers to our questions with our contacts, who are paid well. We know who you are, we know what you want. It's a good thing we knew so much or you'd likely be dead, Mr. Cartwright. Several Celestials, as you and other white men often call us, were, shall we say, touched that you wouldn't stay at the Palace without your cook, Hop Sing."

"What about last night?" Aldina blurted out. "Were those assassins your men?"

Chan Tan Tan's soft features hardened for a moment as his wife stepped up to the table, placing the gun against Aldina's temple.

Hoss felt his muscles tighten.

"You are a woman. Don't talk to my husband unless he speaks to you first," Maggie said, then lowered the gun.

The softness returned to Chan Tan Tan's face. "Now, let me continue, Mr. Cartwright."

Hoss nodded, sliding his hand along the table edge and taking Aldina's fingers in his. Her hand trembled.

"The slave merchants went to the opium den, looking for you. They killed everyone there and would have found you the next day had not word gotten out about what you had done at the Palace on behalf of a Celestial. They gave you—what is it you Americans call it?—a reprieve."

Again Hoss nodded.

Chan Tan Tan continued. "The men last night—by the way, you passed the one you threw out the window in the alley—were not mine, but I told them they could scare or kill you if they liked to keep you out of Chinatown. You don't scare easily, nor your woman."

Chan Tan Tan started to speak again, but Hoss waved his words away. "I don't care about all that now. I just want to know where the girl is."

"I will get to that, Mr. Cartwright. Remember, patience is a virtue." Chan Tan Tan smiled. He paused, as if testing Hoss's patience. Finally he spoke. "Yes, I won the girl from Lin Wo Pai. She is a beautiful girl, a fine investment."

Hoss felt Aldina's fingers tighten and he heard the anger in her short breath. Hoss studied Chan Tan Tan. "Did you use her, use her for . . . ?" Hoss couldn't finish the sentence, not with women present.

"Use her for carnal pleasures?" Chan Tan Tan smiled back. "No, I did not. Would you if your wife were as beautiful as mine and as good with a gun?"

Hoss shrugged.

"The girl has not been used by any man. She lacked about a year being at peak value, and then she would have commanded a handsome price from a wealthy man as a wife, not a whore. We were saving her for that. But now, you've made us change our plans, and now the girl will likely be deflowered in a day or two and be kept in a cage the rest of her life."

"What?" Hoss's voice rose, like the anger within him.

"I make too much money gambling to let one girl, no matter how beautiful, ruin it, Mr. Cartwright. I've more than a million dollars in gold in banks throughout California. I might have sold the girl, I might have set her free, but as long as she was with me, I protected her from the kind of men whom you would despise for what they would do to her. Now you three, not I, have ruined her life."

Hoss slammed his fists into the table, then felt the barrel of Maggie's gun against his temple. "You can't blame us. We didn't sell her like cattle or bet her at card games."

Chan Tan Tan waved his wife away. She stood a moment longer with the gun still at Hoss's head, then retreated.

"Now, Mr. Cartwright, the police leave us alone in Chinatown. They and the Irish and most whites harass us in the city, but they don't care what happens to us in Chinatown. As far as they are concerned, it's like animals killing each other. But should a white man—especially one of your prominence—be killed in Chinatown, they'll come in and disrupt the arrangements we've worked out. My gambling brings in thousands a week. You trailed the girl to me, but I couldn't kill you without the police coming in, and I couldn't keep the girl without you coming in. So I had to get rid of her."

Chan Tan Tan pointed to Aldina. "I know your woman friend today went to the law office of David Thornton Kendall and informed him of your visit. Our informants learned that the lawyer notified the police. Two policemen have been watching the alley since. If anything happens to you in here, they will know it and my gambling business is damaged. You are free to search this place if you believe the girl is here, but she is not."

Hoss released Aldina's hand and pointed a finger at Chan Tan Tan. "I'm not leaving here without you telling me where the girl is. And if you won't, I'll tell the police you and your wife tried to kill us."

Calmly, Chan Tan Tan nodded. "But Mr. Cartwright, I would have expected no less from you. And I shall be glad to tell you. Once you are prepared to leave us alone."

Picking up his hat, Hoss rolled its brim between his fingers. "I'm ready," Hoss said to Aldina.

Aldina hit the table with her fist. "But can we trust him?"

"You have no choice." Chan Tan Tan smiled. "And don't forget, I can have you killed easily. Life, like young girls, comes cheap in Chinatown. I just don't want you killed in my place or in any of my gambling houses." Chan Tan Tan stood up and motioned to his guests.

Hoss pulled his hat onto his head. "Why is it you'll tell us where the girl is?"

"You are like cockroaches, the three of you. It's not that you eat that much, it's just that what you fall in you spoil. I want you out of Chinatown before you spoil something of mine."

Maggie leveled the gun at Hoss as he stood up with Aldina and Hop Sing, then eased over to the curtain and held it open, the jewels clinking like fine crystal in her delicate hand.

Chan Tan Tan stuck his hand in a pocket of his robe and pulled out a piece of paper. "This is the address where you will find the girl. You've a night, maybe two, before she starts whoring. I sold her to Chu Sai, who likes to break their spirit by starving them before he turns them over for men to sleep with. Chu Sai's an evil man, with a patch over his eye."

Hoss shot a glance at Aldina, then back at Chan Tan Tan. "Was he here earlier?"

Chan Tan Tan nodded. "The girl was in the trunk."

"Dammit," said Hoss, handing the paper to Aldina.

"I know of this place," she said.

"Don't go there this afternoon or tonight," Chan Tan Tan warned. "They'll be expecting you. Wait until mid-morning. Your chances are better then. They keep the girls in the basement, caged or tied to the wall. Once you get the girl, get outside as quickly as you can. They might kill you inside where there are no witnesses, but outside they would not dare."

Hoss scratched his chin. "Why shouldn't I just go to the police?"

Chan Tan Tan laughed. "Remember to look for those two policemen watching this alley when you leave. A little bribe will buy a lot of information. Chu Sai bribes them too. He'll learn their plans and either kill the girl or move her. There the trail will end and you'll never find her. Your only chance is to do it yourself."

"Why're you doing us this favor?" Hoss asked.

"I want to rid Chinatown of cockroaches."

CHAPTER 18

Ben Cartwright pulled his valise out of the hansom cab and paid the driver, tipping him nicely for the quick ride from the ferry landing to the Palace Hotel. He gazed up at the glass roof over the buggy courtyard, a fine sight any time, but especially in the late afternoon when it glistened like fine crystal. Looking from the roof to the lobby entrance, he strode toward the desk where a half-dozen clerks attended new arrivals. Ben wanted to check into his room, take a quick bath, change clothes, and make it to the office of David Thornton Kendall III before six o'clock, the customary closing time his father had followed for years. The train ride had been pleasant, but tiring nonetheless. The task before him, though, would be unpleasant, severing the Cartwright relationship with the last of the Kendall family.

As he stepped up to the long registration desk, a clerk slid over to greet him. "Welcome, sir, to the Palace Hotel."

Dropping his valise to the floor, he said, "Ben Cartwright. I need a room for an indefinite stay."

The clerk stood ramrod straight in his starched shirt and pressed suit, squinting through his wire-rimmed spectacles at Ben.

Ben awaited an answer, but the clerk continued to stare insolently at him. "Are you assisting someone else?" Ben asked politely.

"No, sir, Mr. Cartwright," the clerk replied, his gaze locked upon Ben for a moment longer. "Just something familiar about you." Finally he moved a couple steps down the counter and pushed the guest register toward Ben. "Please sign," he instructed, embarrassed by the shredded guest register, awkwardly mended along its ripped spine.

After marking the register in a precise, elegant hand, Ben turned the book around and the clerk studied the name. "Ben Cartwright," he said, then scratched his chin. "Oh, yes, I mean no." His eyes widened through the spectacles, bulging out like those of a wild stallion. "You wouldn't be any kin of a man calling himself 'Horse,' would you?"

Ben shook his head. "Don't know a 'Horse.'" Ben didn't have time for explanations.

The clerk stepped away from the counter, checked a file drawer for a couple moments, then pulled a key from the bank of pigeonholes behind the counter and returned to Ben with a smile. Smartly, he slapped the key on the counter. "Your credit's good for as long as you'd like to stay. Thank you, Mr. Cartwright."

Taking the key, Ben nodded, waved off an approaching bellboy, and picked up his valise. He headed for one of the hotel's hydraulic elevators, said to be the first of their kind in California and possibly west of the Mississippi River.

On the eighth floor Ben found his room and quickly let himself in. Soon he was preparing for a bath. The Palace was known for its hot running water, the perfect solvent for the grime of the overland trip on the Central Pacific Railroad.

He quickly bathed and shaved, then dressed for business in a starched white shirt with batwing collar, a string bow tie, three-piece suit, suspenders, and glossy boots. He slipped a gold key-wind pocket watch into his vest pocket and draped the solid gold chain from the watch stem to a buttonhole in his vest, so that the gold nugget charm and key dangled before his flat stomach. Then he slipped his pocketknife into his pants and a pocket revolver into his coat. He had gathered his clothing so quickly for this trip, he had forgotten to bring the black felt hat he wore on business occasions. He considered wearing his white hat with the snakeskin band, but opted to go hatless for his unannounced meeting with Davey Kendall. He studied himself in the mirror. Satisfied, he returned to the lobby. As he passed the registration desk, he saw that his transformation brought an approving nod from the clerk who had registered him.

In the courtyard, he hailed a hansom cab that had just been abandoned by an elegant couple in fashionable attire, then instructed the driver to get him as quickly as possible to Kendall's law office, promising him an extra five dollars if he made it within twelve minutes. Ben jerked his pocket watch from his vest and noted the time. Five-forty. He had little time to spare.

The streets were crowded with people, horses, buggies and wagons, none seeming to be in as big a hurry as he was. In places the traffic was so thick it reminded him of a logjam, and it angered the driver, who was giving it his best to maneuver the cab down back streets and through alleys to avoid the bottlenecks and earn his five-dollar tip. Despite his best effort, the cab didn't pull up before the legal office until two of six o'clock. The cab driver scowled, knowing the clock had defeated him.

Ben emerged from the cab, money in hand. "It wasn't for lack of trying," he said. "Here's your extra five dollars anyway."

A smile reappeared on the driver's face. "Thank ye, sir," he said, taking the silver coins and tucking them in his pocket.

Ben stood at the stoop before the law office, straightening his coat and tie. The door opened and Ben caught a fleeting glimpse of Davey Kendall as a woman with a green skirt and white blouse emerged, patting her brown hair, gathered in a bun. She seemed skittish, looking both ways down the street, then moving cautiously down the walk. Ben smiled and lifted his hand to tip his hat, then felt foolish when he remembered he was hatless. The woman nodded perfunctorily and scurried away.

Adjusting his bow tie a final time, Ben sighed. His

brain told him what needed to be done, but his heart wasn't in firing Davey Kendall. Not because he didn't deserve it, but because his father had been a loyal and honest attorney whom Ben had relied on almost like family. Ben bounded up the steps and grabbed the door handle, taking a final deep breath in anticipation of the difficult moments ahead. He twisted the handle, but it clung fast. He twisted again and pushed the door, but it was locked. Had Davey Kendall seen him when he had let the woman pass? Ben twisted the handle again, then pounded on the door.

"Davey Kendall," he called in disgust. "Davey Kendall."

He stopped when he heard the latch click and felt the doorknob twist in his hand. As he let go, the heavy door cracked open. There, standing before him, was Davey Thornton Kendall, his face awash in a sea of surprise.

"Mr. Cartwright," Kendall said, swinging the door open and allowing Ben to enter. "I wasn't expecting you."

Ben strode past Kendall, through the anteroom and into the office. "I suspect not, Davey," Ben said over his shoulder as he heard the door shut firmly. "Before we get down to business," said Ben, turning to face Kendall as he entered the room, "I regret deeply the loss of your father. He was a good man, a good lawyer, and most of all, a good friend."

Davey stepped around Ben and stood behind his desk as if he wanted a barrier between Ben and what he suspected was coming. Davey adjusted the wire-rimmed glasses on his nose, then plopped back in the leather chair that had been his father's. "Thank you, Mr. Cartwright. He just wore himself down. I appreciate you coming all the way from Nevada just to extend your condolences," Kendall answered with a shrug.

"Actually, there's more, and I think you know it's related to my telegrams," Cartwright said. "I came to give you a message in person that you couldn't understand by wire."

Davey Kendall's face took on a hard look like the one Ben remembered in his father when he was narrowing in on a crucial legal point during a negotiation or a trial. Beneath the son's thick blond mustache, his lips slowly worked into an arrogant smirk. Picking up his pipe from the ashtray on the cluttered desk, Kendall tapped it in the palm of his hand, then emptied the char in the ashtray. "You came to discharge me."

Ben nodded. "That's the plain and simple of it."

Tapping the pipe in the ashtray, Kendall shook his head slowly, like an enraged bull preparing to charge. "Can't let you do that, Mr. Cartwright," he replied, his calm eyes never leaving Ben's.

Ben approached the desk, planting his knotted fists atop it amid the paper debris. "Young man," he said, carefully gauging his words, "those timber leases are vital to the Ponderosa." His voice lifted with each word.

As calm as a preacher in a cemetery, Kendall reached by rote for the tobacco sack by the ashtray, his owl-like stare never straying from Ben's eyes. He stuck the pipe into the pouch and worked tobacco into it. He spoke softly, almost at a whisper, when he responded. "My father knew that. I know that. And I've been busting my tail to work these leases out for you and the Ponderosa. And I intend to see these negotiations through to completion."

"What negotiations, Davey? This was a bidding process, very simple. You should have an answer by now from the government. You're stalling, and I can't get a straight answer from you like I could from your father."

"When I'm done," Kendall said, pulling the pipe from the tobacco pouch and pointing the stem at Ben, "you can fire me, not before." He fished around on his desk for a box of matches. He found the matchbox, jerked out a match and flared its sulfur tip, giving off a flame and a bitter aroma.

"I want answers now," Ben demanded, his knuckles turning white on Davey's desk from the weight of his anger.

The pipe made a whistling sound as Kendall drew hard and the flame took hold of the tobacco, overpowering the match's sulfur smell with the sweet odor of fine tobacco. The pipe bowl flamed like Ben's anger and produced a plume of smoke. Kendall leaned back in his chair and propped his feet up on the corner of his desk.

His insolence stoked Ben's anger. His father, Ben thought, had manners and legal finesse. Davey had neither. With the senior Kendall just days in the grave, times must be hard on Davey. Maybe the insolence was a bluff to hide his grief.

Lifting his hands over his head, Davey interlocked his fingers behind his ears and settled deeper into the leather chair, staring out the window at the courthouse. When he finally spoke, his words came out in neither anger nor defeat, but in determination. "This bid is as important to me as it is to you. Complications arose that I could not put in a telegram. The fewer people who know about these complications, the better."

Ben lifted his hands from the attorney's desk and seated himself opposite Davey.

"Father had been feeling poorly for a year or more, but things really fell apart the last three months for him. He was tired. Couldn't concentrate. Was not the lawyer he had always been. Hard as it is for me to say, it's true. He was giving his clients his best, but he was sickly and his best wasn't what you would've expected from David Thornton Kendall, Jr." Kendall unhooked the wire-rimmed glasses from his ears, then pulled a handkerchief from his coat pocket and wiped both eyes. "I caught several mistakes, covered for him, working late into the evening so he wouldn't know what I was doing. Your bid," he said, replanting the glasses on the bridge of his nose and hooking the earpieces in place, "because it was so important to you, he insisted on doing himself. Your bid was his biggest mistake."

Ben leaned forward in his chair and stroked his chin. "He missed the deadline?"

Kendall sighed. "Wish it were that simple. You recall how much you bid for those timber leases?"

"Without a doubt. Seventy-five thousand dollars." Ben nodded. "A generous bid. It should have been highest."

Kendall snickered. "Oh, it was." He dropped his feet

to the floor and rolled his chair up to the desk, resting his elbows on a stack of papers, drawing heavily on the pipe, his face obscured by smoke as he exhaled. "Father took your bid to the Federal Building himself, and I never got a chance to look it over, or catch any possible mistakes. When Father made out your bid papers, he added an extra zero."

Ben caught his breath.

"At three quarters of a million dollars," Kendall announced, pulling his pipe from his mouth, "your bid was the highest by far."

His shoulders sagging, Ben looked at the carpet between his feet.

"This was not something I would communicate by telegram or by letter, Mr. Cartwright. I would never want anything in writing that would reflect unfavorably upon my father. So I could not apprise you of the true situation."

Ben stared at the floor, regrets flooding his thoughts, regrets for the senior Kendall, for Davey, and for the Ponderosa. Could Cartwright Enterprises afford timber for the Bristlecone mine without cutting Ponderosa timber? Had he, Ben Cartwright, overextended Cartwright resources?

"I wanted to save father's good name and your bid," Davey said.

Nodding, Ben looked up from the floor. Things had gone wrong before and the Ponderosa had survived. This time would be no different. From adversity had always come strength, he thought, remembering the losses of his three wives. "You should have told me you had to withdraw the bid."

Grimacing, Kendall slowly lifted the pipe to his mouth and clenched it between his teeth. Drawing hard on his pipe, he stood and walked to the window. His face was shrouded in a cloud of smoke, making it hard for Ben to gauge his thoughts. The young lawyer ran his fingers through his blond hair and, at length, nodded. "I knew it would come to this if you found out."

Now Ben understood. Kendall hadn't answered his telegrams because he hadn't wanted to acknowledge he had already withdrawn the bid. "Then our business is concluded?"

The pipe stem whistled as another veil of smoke enveloped Kendall's head like storm clouds over the high Sierras. Kendall stepped away from the window and out from the fog of pipe smoke. "No, sir, I haven't withdrawn the bid!"

Shooting up from his chair, Ben threw his hands up in the air, then shook his fist at the young lawyer. "Do you intend to break me, young man?"

Jerking the pipe from his mouth, Kendall shook the stem toward Ben. "No, sir, but you should never have come to San Francisco. You should have left it to me to handle. I know the bid is important to you, important to the Ponderosa, but there are things that are important to me, like saving Father's good name. I'll not have folks laughing at his tenfold mistake."

Ben pointed his finger at Kendall. "But you'll ruin me financially. Your father was sick, it's nothing that will damage his good reputation. It's something that could cost me three quarters of a million dollars."

"No," Kendall said firmly, "it won't cost you more than your original bid. I'll make up any difference."

Ben laughed. "Your father didn't have that kind of money and neither do you. Your father could've raised that kind of money on his own, but you can't. Withdraw the bid or I'll do it myself."

Kendall shoved the pipe back in his mouth and crossed his arms over his chest. "I can't do it."

"Then I will. I'll go to the land office and cancel it now."

"Do that, Mr. Cartwright, and we'll both wind up in jail."

"What?"

Kendall unfolded his arms from across his chest, straightened his suit coat and brushed his tie. He motioned for Ben to take a seat, but Ben hesitated. "Please, Mr. Cartwright. I didn't intend to tell you all of this because I know it goes against your grain. Had you stayed in Nevada, I might have saved you this dilemma."

Ben unwadded his fists and backed toward the chair, sitting stiffly on the edge, straight as a pine on a mountain bluff.

The young attorney circled the desk twice, then settled into the leather swivel chair and slid it up to the desk. He cleared a space and rested his hands on the green felt blotter that had been covered by papers. He took a final drag on the pipe and placed it in the ashtray, studying Ben intently as he exhaled a ribbon of smoke that floated over his desk.

"Should this ever come up in a court of law, I will deny this conversation, and it is best that you do too, Mr. Cartwright."

Ben should have been surprised, but he wasn't. Not anymore. In just the few minutes he had been with Kendall, he had learned, if nothing else, that Kendall approached legal matters differently than his father. Perhaps there was good in that, perhaps not. Kendall seemed to be waiting for a response. "Go on," Ben said, gauging by Kendall's grimace that that was not the response he had wanted.

"The plain and simple of it all is that I've bribed the federal officials."

Ben felt his mouth drop. He sat stunned for a moment, then collected his wits. "I'll pay no bribe."

Kendall held up his arm for silence, his eyes never wavering.

Ben now saw a command of the situation in Kendall's owlish eyes.

"I'm not asking you to, Mr. Cartwright. That's why it'd been best had you stayed in Nevada. You'd never have known. I just needed a day or two more. Then I'd have had an answer without you having to know what I did."

"I can't condone a bribe."

Nodding, Kendall held up his closed hand, extending his index finger. "First, you want the leases badly and your bid as intended would have been the highest by some nineteen thousand dollars." He extended his middle finger. "Second, father's reputation won't be besmirched by me having to withdraw the bid or acknowledge the mistake.

The federals will simply change the document papers." He flicked his ring finger up to join the other two. "Third, some underpaid government officials will get a little extra money." He held up his little finger. "Fourth, you let me handle this, then you're free to change your legal representation to someone else. If the question ever comes up, you can tell them I didn't meet your ethical standards, that I bribed a government official and you got rid of me. That way, you are protected."

Ben shook his head, confounded by Kendall's logic.

"But now, by coming here and having this talk, you've opened yourself to a perjury charge or a prison sentence, should this ever come to court. You've forced yourself to condone it."

Ben took a deep breath. This was digging a hole deeper than he could fill. He could be no party to a bribe. Was there still time to stop the digging? "Has the money been paid, and how much?"

"I shouldn't be telling you this, but yes, five thousand dollars."

Letting out a low whistle, Ben rubbed his hands together.

"Your bid was a generous bid, one that will make the government money. The purchasing officers could have accepted the incorrect bid and tried to force you into it, but they knew a mistake had been made. They were willing to correct it, with a little incentive."

"Five thousand dollars isn't small," Ben said.

"It's worth it to me, Mr. Cartwright. The government gets a good deal. You get your leases, and I protect Father's reputation. Nobody comes out the loser on this."

"Save possibly you, should this get around."

"It's a risk I'm prepared to take so Father's reputation isn't blemished."

"I'll need a night to think on it," Ben said, standing up.

"You can think," Kendall said, "but the damage's been done."

"I'll still think about it and be back," he said, starting for the door.

"I knew you would, but you have no choice now," Kendall replied, then held up his hand. "Before you go, I've information about Hoss."

Ben spun around. "You've seen Hoss?"

"No, but he may be in danger." Kendall stuck his hand in his coat pocket and pulled out an envelope. "A woman came in here just before you arrived. She was carrying this note." Kendall extended it to Ben, who strode back across the room and grabbed it. "I was told not to open it until tomorrow. This woman—I don't know her name—brought another one yesterday, and I sent police to Chinatown to watch out for them. Apparently, the Chinese have spies with the police, because the Celestials knew. I'll leave it to you to decide what to do. My efforts may put them in more danger."

Ben ripped open the pink envelope and read the note in Hoss's handwriting. He spoke the first couple words aloud.

"No," Kendall said, "I don't want to hear it."

Without looking up from the note, Ben nodded. The note was short and simple.

If you have not heard back from me by tomorrow noon, send police to building on northeast corner of Washington and Stockton. We will be there at nine. Do not tell police before then or our lives may be in great danger.

Ben felt a sinking in his stomach. The timber lease bid now seemed minor by comparison.

CHAPTER 19

B en's hand kept patting the pocket of his coat as he walked toward Nob Hill. He had committed the Chinatown address and the time—nine o'clock—to memory, so the note was no longer important in that sense. But it remained his only link to Hoss and Hop Sing. What could have happened to them? And who was this woman courier they were using? Had this really been an incident started by the pranks of Hoss and Little Joe or was there more to it? Ben knew he would have no answers until morning, when he planned to be in Chinatown.

Rarely did he visit San Francisco without contacting Claudia Morris Thomason, the widow of Giles Thomason, one of the first wave of 'forty-niners to reach San Francisco. Arriving in San Francisco with a shovel and a pick, Thomason figured there was more gold in the miners than in the goldfields. Legend had it that he sold the pick and shovel he had brought from Indiana for $150 each and used that money as grubstake for one of San Francisco's most successful mercantile businesses. Ben could not vouch for that part of the Thomason legend, though he did know that by the time Thomason sent for Claudia Morris, his sweetheart back in Indiana, he had built for her one of the first mansions on Nob Hill.

A foggy shroud pulled dusk over San Francisco, and street lamps were being lit as Ben climbed the most prestigious street on Nob Hill. The grand houses on either side looked down upon him like elegant dowagers at a charity ball, bedecked with the jewels of cut-glass windows, garbed in ornate woodwork and rouged with bright paint. There were newer houses in San Francisco, perhaps even prettier houses, but none more stately than these on Nob Hill.

Had Giles Thomason lived, he might have wanted to build her another house in the latest neighborhood of fashion, but Claudia was as devoted to him as a nun to her calling. Especially after his death, when many of her society friends suggested she leave the mansion and his memories behind, Claudia insisted on staying in the home he had built for her. It wasn't the decision of a woman who refused to face reality, but rather the choice of a woman as confident of her future as she was proud of her past. When others had encouraged her to sell her husband's business because it would be so taxing for her to run, she bowed her back like a cornered cat and scratched out a success of her own. Ben admired that in Claudia Morris Thomason, appreciated that strength in her. Her only regret in life was that she and her beloved husband had produced no children from their marriage.

Pushing on the iron gate that swung easily on its well-oiled hinges, Ben followed the stone walk leading to the broad porch and massive redwood door with its intricate carvings of cherubs and gargoyles. He figured it was about dinnertime as he marched up the steps and across the porch. At the door, Ben straightened his tie, then lifted the great brass knocker and dropped it three times. Instantly the door swung open and Ben could hear the gentle music of a piano at leisure.

A black doorman with a bright smile and a dark suit appeared before Ben, who recognized Carlos, her majordomo.

"Evening, sir," he said, blinking his eyes at the dark figure before him. "State your name and business."

"Ben Cartwright, here to see Mrs. Thomason."

"Oh, pardon me, Mr. Cartwright," Carlos apologized, "I didn't recognize you. Please come in." He bowed as

Ben entered, then shut the door. No sooner had he released the door handle than his hand shot for his coat pocket. Jerking out a pair of new wire-rimmed glasses, he tugged them in place. "Mrs. Thomason said I should wear these since she went to the trouble of having me seen about, but it just don't seem natural, now does it, Mr. Cartwright?"

"Not for a man as young as you, Carlos."

The butler laughed. "Sixty-seven last month, as best I can figure my age." Carlos escorted Ben down a wide-carpeted hall, its walls graced with oil paintings from Europe and ivory carvings from the Orient. The music grew louder and more pleasant with each step. The soft piano was now accompanied by a soprano voice as clear and sharp as the clink of fine crystal.

Ben recognized the aria and smiled. Claudia had never lost her fine voice, even if she had given up her ambition to become an opera singer to marry Giles Thomason. Though her husband was gone, her love of opera survived, and Ben knew no one in San Francisco who enjoyed the opera more.

At the end of the hall, Carlos twisted the twin brass handles of a double door and pushed them open. Immediately the piano music stopped. "Mr. Ben Cartwright to see you," he announced.

Claudia glanced up from the grand piano, a wide smile across her face, and arose as elegantly as a butterfly taking to flight. "Benjamin," she said, patting into place, her black hair, streaked with gray, "what a pleasant surprise."

Ben stepped into the music room and Carlos closed the doors behind him. "Urgent business called me here without time to wire."

Stepping away from the piano, Claudia walked across the room, offering her hand to Ben. He moved to meet her, taking her hand in his and lifting it to his lips. Releasing her fingers, he nodded. "Always a pleasure to enjoy your company, not to mention your beauty."

Claudia smiled. "Benjamin Cartwright, you're such a flatterer." She stared at him a moment, long enough for the smile to diminish. "There's something wrong?"

Ben nodded. "Hoss may be in some trouble, something to do with Chinatown. And some government timber leases I bid for are in doubt. It's been a tiring day for me."

She took his hands in hers. "I was dining alone tonight, but your arrival means I can have a fine conversation if you'll join me."

"Certainly. I'd be delighted."

"Come," she said, "and you can tell me about your troubles." She walked beside him to the dining room.

It was a large room, with a long table that could seat a dozen people. Like everything that was Claudia Morris Thomason, the room was understated. The polished redwood walls gleamed in the reflection of a crystal chandelier, the peach drapes were light and airy, the carpet plush, but there were no paintings or artwork to draw attention to the Thomason wealth. She wore wealth as comfortably as she wore the pale blue silk-taffeta dress, its fringed hem rustling softly as it slid along the carpet.

That the table was already prepared for two was testament to Carlos's prescience and efficiency. It was set with two fine gold-edged china plates, sparkling crystal glasses and gleaming silver settings. Pulling the high back of a solid walnut chair, Ben helped Claudia into her seat, then marched around the table and took the place opposite her.

Claudia's smile refreshed Ben and her blue eyes captivated him. After the discomfort of the trip from Virginia City, the burden of meeting with Davey Kendall, and the worry about Hoss's predicament, he was pleased to be in her company.

Carlos brought a bottle of wine, unsealed the cork and filled the glasses. Ben and Claudia held up their glasses for a toast.

"To the most striking woman in all of California," Ben said.

"And to the biggest flatterer in the state of Nevada," Claudia replied.

The lips of their glasses kissed with a clink. Ben and Claudia sipped wine and talked, bringing each other up to date on people and events in their lives since their last meeting. Over turtle soup they discussed the booming business Claudia had maintained, stock prices on Virginia City mines, and prospects for the Bristlecone mine that Cartwright Enterprises was developing. Over trout almondine they discussed the deaths of old-timers who had come with the original rush and prospered, people like David Thornton Kendall, Jr.

"He was a good man," Ben said. "I'll miss him and his legal acumen."

Claudia's blue eyes narrowed into a penetrating gaze that seemed to read every secret Ben held within himself. "The same cannot be said for his son, I take it?"

"Davey is of a different generation."

"All sons are, Benjamin, even yours."

Ben nodded. "But some things must transcend generations, things like honesty and straight dealing."

With a silk napkin in her delicately long fingers, Claudia dabbed at the corner of her mouth. Her blue eyes, staring intently at Ben, reminded him of Lake Tahoe's deep waters. "He has done something that troubles you?"

"Claudia, you are perceptive."

"Honest men are easy for an honest woman to read," she replied, not pressing for the details of the situation. That would be exceeding the bounds of propriety.

Besides Adam, Ben would trust only one other person with the story of the bribe offer, and that person was Claudia Morris Thomason. Carlos deposited a tray of confectionery desserts on the table and departed back into the kitchen. Then Ben told of his meeting with Davey Kendall and the error in the lease bid.

Claudia's eyelids flickered when Ben revealed the magnitude of the error. "Surely you withdrew the bid, Benjamin?" Her fingers moved to the simple gold necklace around her neck.

Ben offered her a confectionery tart, but she shook her head. Using the silver serving piece, he took one and placed it on his dessert plate. "Davey is adamant about not withdrawing it, for fear someone will think the worse of his deceased father."

"Understandable," Claudia said, "and noble, but he has no other legal options."

Grimacing, Ben leaned across the table and whispered the word as if it pained him to loose it from his lips. "Bribery."

Claudia patted her necklace, her brow furrowing for a moment as she thought through the implications. "You want the leases?"

"They're vital to protect the Ponderosa."

"He wants to protect his father's name. Two admirable objectives. Had your bid been correct, would it have been high bid?"

Ben nodded. "Mine was higher than they will likely get from anyone if it is rebid."

"And the bribe is to make certain officials correct the inaccurate bid without making the mistake public?"

"Precisely. Bribery. It appalls me."

Claudia thought it over a moment as Carlos entered the dining room and cleared the table of dishes, including the dessert plate with Ben's uneaten confectionery.

When he left, she asked, "Are you sure it's bribery, Benjamin?"

"What are you getting at, Claudia?"

"Perhaps young Kendall was approached by the public servants. Perhaps it is extortion rather than bribery."

"Both wrong," Ben replied.

"Certainly, both wrong," she said. "But sometimes a wrong can make a right in a delicate situation."

"I'm not sure."

Claudia smiled, knowing how this situation must play on Ben's sense of propriety. "And Hoss, how does he fit into this?"

Ben refilled their wineglasses and explained how Hoss had left the Ponderosa to bring Hop Sing back. Neither had returned. And he knew by a newspaper account of an unfortunate incident at the Palace Hotel that Hoss had tried to stay there. Except for the mysterious note Ben had accepted from Davey Kendall, Ben had not received a word of Hoss's whereabouts. Ben fished the note out of his coat pocket and passed it to Claudia.

She read it twice, then carefully refolded it and returned it to him. "Then I know where you will be tomorrow at nine. Do you have a horse?"

"No."

"I shall have Carlos request the stable boy to have my finest gelding for you when you leave."

Ben reached across the table and took her hand. "As always, you are most gracious."

Claudia seemed pleased. "Now, come tomorrow evening, you will have plenty to celebrate, with your son found and perhaps your timber leases settled. Would you and Hoss consider joining me at the Opera House then?"

"It would be a pleasure," Ben replied, pushing himself up from the table and assisting her.

When Carlos entered, Claudia instructed him to have a horse saddled for Ben. Then they retired to the music room, where Claudia played the piano and sang popular songs for Ben. It was almost midnight before he returned to the Palace Hotel, his spirits lifted and his troubles temporarily forgotten. A good woman was the best medicine for a man's ills.

The gunsmith lowered his chin, eyeing Hoss over the top of his bifocals, then glanced at Hop Sing. A skinny man with thinning gray hair and gaunt cheeks, his spindly fingers rubbed an oiled cloth over the barrel of a disassembled Colt revolver. The gunsmith wore a leather apron that made him look like an emaciated carcass. "I don't sell to no Chinaman," he said in a wheezing voice.

Hoss held a pocket revolver in each palm, lifting and lowering one then the other, his hands moving up and down like the pans on a balance scale. He wasn't returning to Chinatown without a pistol. He had always disliked pocket revolvers because they never fit his huge hand, but he would settle for one now since it would be easier to hide. In his left hand he held a Marston .31-caliber, five-shot revolver. In his right he balanced an odd-looking .31-caliber revolver marked B.J. Hart/Broadway. Hoss had never heard of either, but the gunsmith vouched for their reliability. Though Hoss liked the look of the Marston, his index finger had trouble sliding smoothly through the trigger guard. The other revolver had an enlarged trigger guard which accepted his finger easily, but its spurless hammer gave it an impotent look. Nonetheless, he settled on this revolver because its grip was shaped similar to the

one on his .44-caliber Russian Model Smith & Wesson revolver which he had left back on the Ponderosa.

"This ugly one and a box of shells," Hoss told the
gunsmith, lifting the Hart model.

The gunsmith relieved him of the Marston, placing it
back in the display case as gently as a mother would place
her newborn in a cradle. Then he turned around and
reached for a box of shells on the back shelf, his sleeveless
arm as pale as a tree limb with the bark stripped off. He
plopped the box of ammunition on the wooden counter by
the scattered parts of the disassembled Colt and pulled the
nub of a pencil from behind his ear. He licked the pencil
lead and attacked a scrap of oily paper on the counter,
writing down a couple figures and carefully adding them
together before checking his total a final time. He shoved
the greasy paper at Hoss. "There's what she comes to." He
wheezed.

"A little steep isn't it?" Hoss replied as he tucked the
revolver in his britches and shoved the box of shells in his
pocket.

The gunsmith shrugged.

Hoss told Hop Sing how much he needed.

Nodding, Hop Sing reached beneath his blouse and
pulled out his leather money pouch, pinching silver coins
one by one from the bag.

Placing his hands on his hips, the gunsmith moved
closer to the counter. "I don't sell guns to Chinamen!"

Hoss's face reddened. He leaned over the counter,
slamming his fist onto its oily top, the parts of the dismembered Colt bouncing up and rattling back down on the
wood.

The gunsmith quivered and wheezed.

Hop Sing stepped up to the counter and tapped Hoss
on the arm, offering him the money.

Slowly, Hoss shook his head. "No, sir. He's gonna
take his pay from you, Hop Sing. Give it to him."

Hop Sing moved to place the coins on the counter.

"No, dammit, hold them in your palm and let him
take them from your hand," Hoss said, his words whistling
in anger.

Doing as he was instructed, Hop Sing lifted his hand.

The gunsmith reached tentatively for the money, plucking the coins as quickly from Hop Sing's hand as he would grab biscuits from a fire. He left the bottom coin in Hop Sing's palm, as if he feared leprosy.

"Take it," Hoss commanded, his voice rising, "and when you've been paid, shake his hand."

Grabbing the final coin, the gunsmith looked at Hop Sing's extended hand and flinched.

"Shake it," Hoss commanded.

The gunsmith reluctantly took Hop Sing's hand, limply moving it up and down. When he released his grip, he wiped his hand on the leather apron.

In spite of the insult, Hop Sing bowed meekly to the gunsmith and backed away.

Out of spite, Hoss plucked a tin of matches from the counter and shoved it in his pocket, just waiting for the gunsmith to challenge him on it, but the cadaver of a man said nothing. "Let's get out of here, Hop Sing, before I get really mad," he said, his eyes aiming at the gunsmith. "And you say one bad word about Hop Sing when we leave, I'll take you apart like your pistol there." Hoss spun around and jerked open the door, letting Hop Sing pass first. As Hoss stepped outside, he slammed the door, the windows rattling as if the earth had trembled.

Hoss stood outside the window, intentionally loading the revolver where the gunsmith could see him. One, two, three, four, five bullets he inserted in the chambered cylinder, cursing the gunsmith silently. Then he sighted the barrel of the pistol through the window, a trace of a smile sliding across his lips as the gunsmith dropped out of view.

"Trouble?" Aldina asked.

At the sound of her voice, Hoss was embarrassed. "Just the city. Too many people, too many problems." He tucked the pistol in his britches and felt Aldina's arm slide under his.

"The city's where the future is, Hoss, where opportunity is," she said.

"Like for little Chinese girls, crooked police, store-keepers that overcharge you, and dandified outlaws."

"No, Hoss, opportunity for schools and universities, for opera houses and libraries, for churches and theaters, for hospitals and parks, and most of all for opportunities to expand the minds and the dignity of men and women. It's not perfect, but it can be."

Hoss shrugged and started toward Chinatown. "Perfection? You want perfection, then see the Ponderosa. Stand on the shores of Lake Tahoe and see the most perfect blue God ever created, see mountains more perfect than any sculpture man ever made, or game that has a majesty no man can match. That's perfection, the way God meant it to be. It's just something we could never agree upon," he said, looking down into her green eyes.

"That's what makes life interesting," she replied, squeezing his arm affectionately.

"No," Hoss shot back, "that's what makes life so hard."

Aldina laughed softly. "You're right, we'll never agree on it."

They walked silently a couple blocks, their muscles tightening as they neared then entered Chinatown, Hop Sing always remaining two steps behind them, no matter their pace.

It was morning, and both shared an unstated feeling that today they must find Hop Sing's niece or she might forever be doomed to the life of a prostitute. Aldina pointed at their destination, a building on the northeast corner of Washington and Stockton. It was a stone structure with rusty iron shutters that had stained the masonry like blood. "That's the place," she said. "When they built the Central Pacific Railroad, the Chinese labor was said to have been hired out of that building."

Hoss nodded but didn't focus long on the building a block away. Though Aldina studied it intently, he watched the passing Chinese men, seeking one with an eyepatch and one with a face crisscrossed with cuts and scratches. Every passing face seemed mysterious and sinister, as if each knew Hoss's destination. The smell of Chinatown pricked his nose, and it reminded him of the odor of death, like coming upon a festering animal dead four days on the range.

Aldina squeezed his arm. "You as nervous as me?"

"Can't say for sure about that, but I feel about as conspicuous as a watermelon in a cucumber patch," he replied as he watched the small Celestials walk by, very few of them even near his weight. Hoss stopped at the intersection, allowing the traffic to pass, and studied the building. Its iron shutters gave it the look of an empty fortress, and the passersby seemed to ignore it. A break appeared in the traffic, and he pulled Aldina across the street, Hop Sing following two steps behind.

As Hoss walked warily ahead, he remembered the words of Chan Tan Tan. "I want to rid Chinatown of cockroaches," he had warned. Now, Hoss wondered if this was just another insidious trap set for him and Aldina. Was the girl really there?

When he reached the front of the building, by the rusty iron door, he studied it again. It was a fortress indeed! All the windows were blackened, from the basement windows at sidewalk level to those on the fourth floor. The basement and first-floor windows were barred as well. An old signboard, its paint so chipped and faded as to be indecipherable, had come loose from its rusted mount and hung at an odd angle over the rusty door. A Chinese man with a whiskey bottle partially hidden among the folds of his baggy pants sat on the sidewalk, leaning against the stoop, his head bobbing down as he struggled between keeping his chin up or passing out. Hoss moved to the corner, studying the passing men. A vendor approached him, offering in broken English to show him and his wife an opium den.

Aldina snickered as Hoss waved the man away. "You sure this is the place?" he asked her.

"Yes, Hoss."

He shrugged, then extricated his arm from hers and patted the pistol in his belt. The entrance, he noticed, like the first-floor windows, was barred. A gate reminding Hoss of a jail door stood ajar in front of a rusty iron inner door. That door was shut. "The way they've got this fortified, getting in may be tougher than breaking out of jail."

"I hear of jail breaks all the time," Aldina offered.

"Not many folks try to break in one," he said, striding up the steps and pulling the barred door open. Aldina, then Hop Sing, joined him on the steps.

Hoss twisted the handle of the rusty door and pushed. To his amazement, it swung easily open on well-oiled hinges. "Luck is with us," he said, unaware of the pair of eyes boring in on his back from the opposite corner of the street.

Ben Cartwright smiled to himself. It was good to see Hoss again and know he and Hop Sing were safe. He also recognized the woman—she was the one he had encountered yesterday emerging from Davey Kendall's office. But who was she? Kendall had had no idea, and Ben believed the lawyer on that count, if not on everything else. But what were they doing in Chinatown? Ben's hand slipped into his coat pocket and fingered his pistol as Hoss walked to the corner and looked both ways at the pedestrian traffic. Ben clung to the shadows on the opposite side of the street, glancing from Hoss toward the hitching post where he had tethered the gelding Claudia Morris Thomason had loaned him.

Though he couldn't see Hoss's face, by his care and by his deliberation in front of the building, Ben knew his son was weighing possible dangers of what was before him. Ben was anxious to talk to Hoss and find out exactly what had transpired since he left the Ponderosa, but he knew he must be patient. He would find out all he needed to know eventually; for the time being it was best not to let anyone know that Hoss, Hop Sing, and the woman had an ally in Chinatown.

When the odd trio marched up the steps and the door swung open easily, Ben's muscles tightened. A building so fortified would not be left unlocked except on purpose. It had to be a trap.

Ben jumped from the shadows into the street, a passing wagon blocking his path for a moment. "Wait," he yelled. Too late. Hoss, Hop Sing, and the woman disappeared inside before he could get around the wagon. Ben was in the middle of the street when the door closed behind his son and companions.

Instantly, a man sitting on the walk by the stoop jumped to his feet and darted up the two steps, holding a liquor bottle in one hand and a padlock in the other. Grabbing the iron-bar outer gate, he slammed it with a clank, pulled the latch flap over an iron eye and poked the padlock's shackle into the eye.

Ben reached the walk just as the man snapped the padlock shut. He bounded up the steps, the man spinning around at the sound of his footfall.

"Place closed, place closed," the Celestial yelled, juggling the liquor bottle in his right hand.

Ben grabbed the man's neck and flung him into the barred gate. "Open it! Now!" He scowled, his powerful fingers slowly tightening around the man's neck.

The Celestial nodded and Ben eased his grip, allowing him to take a couple deep breaths. Then the Celestial smiled, his thin lips taunting Ben as he spoke. "No key, no key."

Ben rattled the man against the barred gate, then heard the sound of shattering glass. As the man thrust his arm up in a deadly arc, Ben caught the glint of the broken bottle coming for his gut. Instantly, he shoved the attacker aside and leaped back. The jagged bottleneck caught for a moment in the sleeve of Ben's coat, shredding a strip of cloth.

The attacker, his face bleeding from a scrape along his right cheek, lunged madly at Ben, who adroitly sidestepped the ragged edge of the bottle, then drew back and kicked the man in the stomach. The man's breath came out in a great gasp as Ben's boot plowed into him, then he collapsed, the broken bottle still clasped in his fingers. Ben lifted his boot and stomped the man's fingers. The crackle of the crumbling glass was mixed with the man's agonized moans.

Looking around him, Ben saw a crowd circling the porch, watching silently. The men made no threats, except by their sheer number. Reaching into his pocket, he pulled out his revolver and waved it toward them. All stepped back and many turned down the street, minding their own business once again.

Ben ground his boot atop the man's hand again, before squatting over him. "The key," he growled, "the key."

With his free hand the man slapped at his waist. Ben used the barrel of his gun to lift the folds of the man's baggy blouse. A leather thong came into view, then a dozen keys hanging from it.

Adroitly, Ben untied the thong, quickly removing the keys and rattling them in the man's face. "Which one?" He fanned the keys out between his fingers.

"There, there," the Celestial gasped.

Ben lifted his boot off the man's hand and leaped for the iron gate, inserting the designated key in the padlock and twisting it hard. The lock clicked and the shank snapped open. Behind him, Ben heard the sound of scampering feet. He turned to see his adversary running away, his hand dotting the walk with blood. Turning back to the padlock, Ben slipped it out of the latch and flung the barred gate open. Shoving the padlock and ring of keys into his britches pocket, he grabbed the door handle and twisted. The handle moved easily, but when Ben pushed on the door, he was chagrined to find that it wouldn't budge.

He pushed again, harder, first with one hand, then with both. Nothing. He leaned his shoulder into the door and pushed and grunted, banging on the door with the butt of his revolver.

"Hoss!" he called. "Hoss, let me in!"

There was only silence, and the snickers of the crowd that had reassembled in the street. Ben cursed. The door had apparently been barred from inside. But why would Hoss do that? Or had someone else done it to make sure Hoss would never escape? Ben knew he had little time. He leaped off the step, and the semicircle of observers backed out of his way. Studying the building a moment, he scanned from the barred first-floor windows to the iron shutters of the second floor. Suddenly he jammed the pistol in his pants pocket and ripped off his coat, throwing it on the stoop. Around him the Chinese men laughed as he jerked off his boots.

Ben had an idea.

The door had come open so easily, it gave Hoss and Aldina a false sense of security. Hoss noted the iron bar propped against the doorjamb, and the iron slots bolted into the wall to accommodate the bar and a latch that could make it impossible to remove. That iron bar would make a good club, he figured, if things got rough and they had to make a run for it. He started to pick it up, but decided he would leave it by the door in case he needed it during a frantic escape. He looked deeper into the long narrow hallway that ended in another iron door. The hallway darkened as Hop Sing followed Aldina inside and closed the door behind them.

Hoss stood a moment, allowing his eyes to adjust to the muted light of a single candle in a wall holder halfway down the hallway between two rooms with closed wooden doors. His huge hand pulled the small pocket revolver from his britches. With his other hand he reached into his pants pocket and fished out the box of ammunition, offering it to Aldina. "Whatever you do, hang on to this."

Aldina grasped the box between trembling hands. "Yes, sir."

"If shooting starts, give me bullets five at a time."

"Yes, sir," she whispered.

Even in the dimness, Hoss could see she was pale with fear. "It'll be okay," he said.

"What if we run out of ammunition?"

"Then we might not be okay." Hoss advanced. Slick and white from innumerable footfalls past, the wooden floor creaked and groaned with his weight. He paused to listen for any noise, but all he heard was the sound of Aldina's breathing.

And a commotion outside the front door!

Hoss spun around, nodding at Hop Sing by the door. Maybe it was a diversion to get them to come back outside. There would be no retreat from this hallway without the girl, Hoss decided.

Hop Sing motioned, asking if he should open the door or bar it.

Hoss whispered, "If the door opens up, jump to the side so I can shoot, but leave it unbarred in case we have to escape."

Aldina was trembling, and Hoss felt sorry for her. He understood her terror of the unknown behind the doors along the hallway. He patted her on the shoulder with his giant paw. "We can't turn back now that we've come this far."

She nodded, her eyes conveying her determination to proceed, as well as her fear.

Hoss advanced a couple of steps, and could hear Aldina and Hop Sing mimicking his movements behind him. Two, three, four steps, and the floor seemed to groan louder each time, announcing their approach to anyone who might be listening. There was a creak and a thud behind Hoss, and he wished Hop Sing would be quieter. "Ssshhh," he said without looking back, his eyes focusing on the iron door ahead.

At a loud clap, Hoss jerked and felt a gust of air pass over him strong enough to batter the flame on the candle. He spun around and gasped.

The iron door was barred shut and padlocked!

And worst of all, Hop Sing was gone, like a ghost. Hoss rubbed his eyes in disbelief, and Aldina grabbed his arm. Hop Sing wouldn't have deserted this task, nor could he have barred and padlocked the door behind him had he run outside.

He was surely hallucinating, Hoss thought, for there was loud pounding on the door and a muffled voice that sounded faintly like that of his father. He shook his head.

Nothing was ever normal in Chinatown!

CHAPTER 21

B en patted the pistol in one pants pocket and the padlock in the other, then looked up at the first-floor window and the iron bars that protected it, his gaze continuing up to the second floor, taking in its un-barred windows and its wide masonry windowsills. The windows were so tall that from the top of one he could reach the bottom of the next. All he had to do was climb them. As a sailor, he had climbed masts much taller, masts that were drenched in water or coated with a film of ice, masks that jerked violently in whipped seas. Never once had he fallen. Ben had no fear of heights.

He took a quick step toward the building, jumping at the chest-high ledge of the first-floor window and grab-bing an iron bar with each hand. With his muscled upper torso, he easily pulled himself atop the ledge and stood up. Releasing one bar, he leaned out over the walk and glanced up toward the second-floor window directly above. About three feet of masonry separated the top of the first-floor window and the ledge of the second-floor window. The cornices and the iron shutters would provide adequate hand- and footholds from the first to the second floor, he thought.

He wrapped his legs and arms around one of the iron bars and began to shimmy up the first floor. Twisting his head as he climbed higher, he caught a glimpse of a Chinese thief dashing to the stoop and grabbing his coat and boots, then disappearing back into the crowd. The higher he climbed, the louder grew the murmurs of the excited Chinese men watching him.

The exertion filled Ben with an exhilaration he remembered from his sailing days. Something about heights put a man's senses on edge. Reaching the top of the window, he released one hand from the bar and strained toward the cornice. His hand slipped on the slick stone and he lurched backward a moment, but his free hand caught the iron bar again. Below him, he heard the gasps of the Celestials. He grinned to himself, knowing he had never been in danger. Again he pulled himself up to the top of the window, wrapping one leg around the iron bar and reaching with the other for the adjacent iron shutter. His toes touched the cold metal and worked against the rusted and pitted iron for a solid hold. He wiggled his foot into a slit between a couple of the iron louvers, then pushed at his hold. The shutter held firm.

With one fluid motion, he used his foothold to carry his weight for an instant while his hands grabbed onto the cornice. With the push of his foot and the pull of his strong arms, he jacked his body atop the cornice, then reached for the window ledge up above. His hands took a firm grasp on the wide ledge and he easily pulled himself up, sitting on the windowsill a moment, his legs dangling over the walk as the crowd pointed at him. He could feel his heart pounding, not so much from the exertion— because he was in good shape for a man his age—as from the worry over Hoss and Hop Sing.

He twisted around on the ledge and rose to his knees, grabbing the iron window frame and pulling against it. The window budged a fraction then held. Trying again, the window creaked and groaned then gave with a screech as Ben pried it open a bit. Pulling his revolver from his pants pocket, Ben slid head first through the window and into the room.

The smell of incense surrounded him, and a hundred or more candles burned. On shelves and tables lined up against the side wall, dozens of idols stared sullenly at the door in the opposite wall. This must be a room the Celestials would call a joss house, he thought, a place where they worshiped their gods. Fortunately, only the gods and none of their worshipers were present. Ben took a moment to gather his breath and collect his thoughts.

Now it was time to find Hoss!

Midway down the hall, Hoss plucked the candle holder from its wall mount and studied the door beside it. Waving the gun, he motioned for Aldina to stay back.

She nodded.

Gun in one hand, candle in the other, Hoss shoved the door open with his boot. The door jerked around on its hinges, slamming into the wall behind it. A veil of smoke floated out, Hoss recognizing the oppressive smell of opium. Stepping inside through the haze of smoke, he saw two men sharing the drug. They reclined on plush chairs in the middle of the room, an opium pipe between them. Hoss carried the candle over, holding it before their faces. Both men were oblivious to everything around them, including the candle Hoss waved before their noses. Both were transfixed by something beyond Hoss, something beyond the room. Hoss recognized neither man. In their trances, they would be no threat to him or Aldina.

Backing out of the room, he explained, "Opium den."

Aldina shuddered. "No sign of the girl?"

"Nope," Hoss whispered, "but we've got a lot of building and basement to search." He pointed to the door at the end of the hall. "Maybe that's the stairs, but we gotta check out this other room," he said, pointing to the next door.

Giving Aldina the candle, he raised his booted foot and thrust it at the door, which flew open with a bang. Inside, the room was crammed with bunks along the walls and with trunks and tables in the middle. Except for the furniture and clothes scattered about, the room stood empty and silent. "Must be where the gang sleeps," Hoss said as he motioned for Aldina to enter.

From the dim candlelight, Hoss was able to count thirty bunks, stacked three high along the walls. "Where are all these fellows, and what've they done to Hop Sing?" He spoke to himself as much as to Aldina.

Stepping back in the hallway, he looked to the front door, then at the back door. Something seemed amiss up front. He spun around and saw a board that had worked its way loose suddenly fall back into place. "What?"

"What is it?" Aldina said.

Hoss shook his head, then scratched his chin. "My eyes may be playing tricks on me," he whispered, "but I swear, dad-blame-it, that I saw the floor move."

A look of exasperation washed across Aldina's face. "The opium?" she asked, looking for a logical explanation.

Hoss shook his head, then retreated to the front door, which had been strangely barred at the time of Hop Sing's disappearance. Falling to his hands and knees, he studied the floor carefully, then waved for Aldina.

As she stood over him, he pointed to a narrow crack that made a square on the floor, and held his finger to his lips. "Trapdoor," he whispered.

Aldina nodded at him.

Now it made sense. While Aldina and Hoss had been intently watching the back of the hall, someone had opened the trapdoor, slipped up on Hop Sing, dragged him into the passageway, then barred the outside door before Hoss or Aldina had realized what was happening. Hoss cursed silently, then whispered to Aldina, "Go hide in the bunk room until I call for you."

He backed up against the front door and straddled the trapdoor, waiting. Outside he heard a commotion, something scraping against the building and a lot of Chinese jabbering, but no longer did he hear a voice that reminded him of his father. Chinatown was a bizarre world. Once he found Hop Sing's niece—if she were still in San Francisco—he no longer cared to return to Chinatown.

The trapdoor budged a fraction, then slowly rose, high enough for whoever was beneath it to survey the hallway. The wooden floor panel seemed to hang in air for a moment, then the door swung partway up and a small man slid half out. As he did, Hoss leaned over the trapdoor and grabbed his queue. With a powerful flick of his wrist and arm, he yanked the man's neck. It popped and the Celestial screamed. Hoss jumped forward, jerking him from the partially-open trapdoor. Twisting him to one side with the queue, Hoss caught a glimpse of his face, crisscrossed with cuts and scratches, and recognized the man who had jumped through Aldina's bedroom window, and later had helped carry Hop Sing's niece in a trunk away from Chan Tan Tan's place. Hoss struck him across the jaw with the barrel of the gun, then pointed it at his temple.

Aldina screamed, and Hoss saw the flash of the hatchet coming toward him. Releasing the Celestial's queue, he fell back into the wall with such force it jarred the pistol from his hand. The hatchet missed by an inch, striking the corner of the trapdoor and embedding itself there. The man grabbed at the hatchet to free it, but it was wedged too tightly into the planks. He moved to slide back inside the trapdoor, and Hoss scrambled up and jumped on the edge with all his weight. The man screamed as the door crushed his chest against the floor. Gasping for breath, the Celestial flailed his arms, then began to weaken. Hoss grabbed the man's arm and twisted it until his face was totally distorted in pain.

"Aldina," Hoss called, "come quick."

She darted from the bunk room, staring wide-eyed at Hoss and his victim, her hand flying to her lips.

"My gun," Hoss said, motioning with his head toward the five-shot revolver.

Aldina, holding the box of cartridges and candle in one hand, picked the gun up with her right hand and pointed it at the Celestial.

"If he moves against you or me, shoot him," Hoss commanded.

The gun bobbed with her chin as she nodded.

Hoss rolled off the trapdoor, and the man went as limp as a deflated balloon.

"It's one of them," Aldina said, recognizing him. As Hoss swung open the trapdoor and pulled the assailant all the way out, he heard a clatter below. Looking into the hole, he saw that the ladder the Celestial had been standing on had fallen to the basement floor. Hoss thought he heard a moan and whimpering below. Hop Sing? In the darkness, he could not see beyond the square of light the open door let into the basement.

Hoss jerked the hatchet free with his massive arms. Aldina squatted beside the limp man, holding the gun against his temple with one hand, the candle and box of ammunition still in the other.

Hoss held the hatchet up to the candle, the anger welling in him like unstable dynamite about to explode. With his free hand he grabbed the man's neck and shook his head, the queue flapping with each jerk. "Where's Hop Sing, where's the girl?" he shouted. "Where are they, dammit?"

But the man was unconscious. Hoss released his neck, and he fell against the floor, his head hitting with a thud. Hoss lifted the hatchet above his head, then brought it down hard, slicing through the air. Aldina screamed as the hatchet smacked into the floor beside the unconscious man.

The man's queue fell free, and Hoss grabbed it, twirling it in the air. "Get to heaven now," he said with scorn. He shoved the queue in his pants pocket, yanked the hatchet out of the floor, then stood and took the revolver from Aldina's shaking hand.

"Let's go," he said, pointing to the door at the end of the hallway. "There's got to be a way downstairs from there." He had taken but a step when the door swung open.

It was the Celestial with the eyepatch—the one Chan Tan Tan had called Chu Sai—followed by five other men, each looking as deadly as poison, each carrying a long knife or a hatchet.

Hoss lifted his gun, aiming it straight at Chu Sai's good eye. Except for a slight twitch of the scar that ran up from his cheek, over his eye and into his scalp, there was no emotion in Chu Sai's face. He held up his hand and the others behind him stopped. His sinister smile reminded Hoss of a rabid skunk.

"Where's Hop Sing and the girl?" Hoss asked grimly.

Chu Sai advanced a step. "Below," he answered with a sneer.

"We want them. Then we'll leave."

"You and the woman will die. You much trouble."

Hoss shook his head as Aldina slid behind him. "I'll send you to Hell, like I sent your friend here," Hoss replied, toeing at the downed man. Hoss shoved the hatchet under his arm and pulled the queue from his pants pocket. He waved it at Chu Sai and the others.

They gasped and stepped back.

"You too much trouble," repeated Chu Sai, taking a cautious step forward.

Hoss shoved the queue back in his pocket and grabbed the hatchet from under his arm. "Come on, fellas. You ain't nothing but half-pints." He lifted his gun hand a hair and fired, the bullet going high, as he had intended. "The next one won't miss," he yelled. Then he whispered over his shoulder to Aldina, "If they rush us, jump into the basement."

"I—I'm not sure I can," she said, looking down into the dark hole. "I'm scared to."

Without taking his eyes off the six threatening men, Hoss used his foot to push the queueless man toward the trapdoor. For a moment the limp body tottered precariously on the edge, then fell below with a thud.

The six men charged down the hall. Aldina screamed. Hoss fired. One of the attackers cried out, but all kept coming.

"Jump!" Hoss shouted, and when he glanced over his shoulder, Aldina was gone. Hoss was answered by a hollow yell, then a clatter from below as she collapsed on the unconscious man. Hoss heard her scrambling to lift the ladder.

Hoss fired again, grazing Chu Sai's arm, but still he came. Hoss was down to two bullets without stopping one of the attackers for good. He hoped Aldina had maintained her grasp on the box of cartridges.

Lunging forward, he swung his hatchet at the attackers. The narrow hall, making it impossible for more than one attacker at a time to get at him with knife or hatchet, gave him an advantage. His long arms also gave him the greater reach. Every time he lunged at them, they retreated. He worked them to the back of the hall.

"The ladder's set," he heard Aldina call from the hole.

Instantly he retreated, the others advancing step by step with him, Chu Sai in the lead. Hoss aimed at Chu Sai's heart as he reached the trapdoor. He squeezed the trigger. The gun clicked instead of exploding. It had misfired. Chu Sai laughed and stepped boldly ahead. Hoss squeezed the trigger again and the gun coughed smoke. A crimson spot instantly appeared on Chu Sai's left shoulder. He grimaced, grabbed his shoulder, then lunged forward, his eyes afire with fury.

Hoss half slid, half jumped into the hole, his feet landing roughly on the ladder rungs, then almost sliding off from the impact. The hatchet slid from his hand and clattered to the floor below. Over his head he grabbed the trapdoor and pulled and latched it shut just as the six attackers reached it. "Bullets, Aldina, more bullets," Hoss said as he scrambled down the ladder into the well of darkness.

Hoss could hear her scurrying about on the floor on her hands and knees, patting at the rough wooden planks. At the foot of the ladder, Hoss stepped on the lump of the unconscious man. "Aldina, are you okay?" he called.

"I dropped the cartridges," she said, "and the candle." She was breathless. "We're trapped, aren't we?"

"As long as I've got a breath, Aldina, we ain't trapped." Above, Hoss could hear the six men pounding on the trapdoor, trying to open it, but that didn't concern him. The door had no handle above, so they would never succeed, certainly not with it latched. He patted his pants pocket, remembering the tin of matches he had taken from the gunsmith. He shoved his five-shot revolver in his pants and hurriedly fished the tin from his pocket, then a match from the tin. He scratched its head with his fingernail and match flared into a ball of light that smelled of sulfur.

"I found them," Aldina said, lifting her hand and offering Hoss five bullets.

Hoss nodded, but said, "The candle, let's find the candle first, get some light."

They looked as best they could around the room, but the match had a short life and died on them. Hoss scratched another one to flame, then toed at the unconscious man, kicking him over and finding the candle hidden in the folds of his blouse. Squatting, Hoss quickly grabbed the candle, touched the dying match to the wick and nursed the candle to life. Placing it on the floor, he jerked the revolver from his pants, snapped the cylinder open and twisted it toward the floor. The empty hulls fell onto the wooden planks with a clatter, like icicles breaking from the eaves of a house.

Instantly Aldina was beside him, her quivering hand offering him five cartridges. Quickly he reloaded his revolver. The commotion at the trapdoor had stopped, and Hoss knew the attackers would be coming by another route to the basement. He was startled by a groan, not from the man at his feet, but from behind a couple barrels in a corner of the dark room. Hoss eased that way, Aldina trailing him with the flickering candle.

Hearing the low groan again, he lunged for the spot, shoving the pistol between the barrels, his finger tightening a fraction against the trigger until Aldina and the circle of light reached the barrels.

"Hop Sing!" Hoss shouted. "Boy, am I glad to find you."

Hoss shoved the barrels aside and squatted beside Hop Sing, noting the bruise and swelling on the right side of his forehead. Grabbing his shoulder, Hoss shook Hop Sing, drawing groans from him with each movement.

Instinctively Hop Sing tried to reach for his head, but he was addled and his hands were tied behind his back. Hoss shoved his pistol back in his pants and dropped to one knee, struggling a moment at the knot, his stubby fingers awkward, in spite of their strength.

Placing the candle and cartridge box on the floor, Aldina brushed Hoss's hand away and, with her long fingers, quickly loosened, then untied the knot and unwound the rope, pulling it free and tossing it behind her. She cradled Hop Sing's head in her hands. Grimacing, Hop Sing lifted his right hand to his forehead, groaning at the slight touch of his own fingers.

"Everything's gonna be okay, Hop Sing," Hoss said, picking up the three-foot length of rope and scurrying over to the unconscious Celestial. Hoss rolled him over on his stomach and jerked his arms together behind his back. After looping the rope over the man's elbows, he tightened the rope and pulled the man's arms awkwardly together, knotting it there. Glancing over at Hop Sing, Hoss saw that his feet were bound as well. He crawled beside Aldina and quickly worked the rope free from Hop Sing's ankles.

Retreating to the unconscious Celestial, Hoss tied the ropes as tight as he could around the man's wrists. Then, to make sure he would have trouble getting away when he regained consciousness, Hoss picked him up, carried him over to one of the empty barrels and dumped him inside head first.

Aldina helped Hop Sing turn over on his hands and knees as he tried to stand up. He tottered on his feet until Aldina grabbed him by the arm, steadying him like an elderly parent. Hoss picked up the box of cartridges, shoving it back in his pocket atop the tin of matches. He picked up the razor-sharp hatchet again and motioned for Aldina to grab the candle. He pointed to a door in the far wall, and the three of them moved gingerly in that direction.

With the silence on the floor above, Hoss wondered if the attackers might not be waiting just on the other side of the door before them. He took a deep breath as he flung the unlocked door open. Expecting to be attacked by hatchet and knife, he pointed the gun into the darkness. He could see nothing, but heard noises, human noises, whimpering and sighing. He could feel the fear in the room as he stepped inside, followed by Hop Sing and Aldina, who held the candle. The circle of light illuminated five forms on the floor. Five trembling girls, their eyes wide with fear.

"We've found her," Aldina cried. "We've found her."

"We hope," Hoss added.

Hop Sing stumbled forward, falling at the feet of the nearest girl, jabbering to her in Chinese.

"The poor dears," Aldina cried.

Hoss shook his head in disbelief. Whatever the problems, whatever fears he had encountered to this point, they had been worth it to save these little girls.

But his triumph was short-lived. He heard a commotion upstairs, then gunshots. The Celestials had guns now. It would be tough to fight them all off. There was a clink and the noise of a key in a lock. The noise seemed to come from above. Aldina lifted the candle above her head, and the ball of light went a little deeper into the room, deep enough for Hoss to see the stairway in the back. It led to a door, and behind that door was noise, then silence, then noise again. Hoss glanced to the girls tied to the floor. "We don't have much time," he said. "Free the girls."

Aldina scrambled to untie the knots around their legs, but was nervous. Coming up with a better idea, Hoss brushed her aside and lifted a hatchet over the first girl. She cowered as the hatchet came down, biting through the rope and freeing her leg. Hoss jumped to each one, cutting her free. Hop Sing was hugging the last girl, a particularly beautiful one, tears streaming down his and her cheeks.

Hoss cut her free as well, and all the girls crowded around Hop Sing and Aldina. Up the stairs the door clicked, then began to slowly open. Hoss dropped the hatchet and took aim at the door. Any bastard who would tie girls to the floor deserved to die. A shaft of light and then a shadowy figure, gun in hand, appeared behind the door. Hoss's finger tightened around the trigger.

He was angry enough to kill now.

CHAPTER 22

Shots! From downstairs! Having seen Hoss's Smith & Wesson back on the Ponderosa, Ben wondered if he was too late. Had Hoss acquired a pistol in San Francisco? Ben cocked the hammer on his own revolver and headed out into the empty hallway, sliding in his stocking feet carefully along the wall toward the stairway. Passing three rooms, he glanced in each. One appeared to be an office, another a storage room, and the third a small arsenal—it was filled with knives, hatchets, machetes, swords, some heavy-ended clubs or blackjacks like the ones he had seen men carry during his sailing days, and a few old-style, cap-and-ball pistols and Civil War rifles. Ben stepped inside, making sure no one was hidden behind the door, then took one of the clubs. He might need it if a fight developed.

The hasp on the door reminded Ben of the padlock in his pocket, the padlock he had taken off the iron gate outside. He slipped his hand into his britches and extracted the lock. Pulling the arsenal door closed, he slipped the padlock in place, snapping it shut with a click.

He paused at the stairway, his heart pounding at a commotion downstairs. Another shot! He descended the stairs, which creaked with each step, sending out an alarm as he advanced. He made it to the landing without seeing a soul, then made the turn. At the foot of the stairs he could see a door opening onto the first-floor hallway.

Ben moved cautiously, extending his revolver in one hand, holding the blackjack in the other. He heard another shot, then the sound of men running down the hall. Reaching the bottom stair, he could see through the open door as a half-dozen men darted for the building's entrance, then fell to their knees on the floor.

Glancing to his left quickly, Ben saw that the stairway continued on into the basement. Perhaps that was where Hoss was, and why they were fixed upon the floor by the entrance. Perhaps it was a trapdoor they were trying to get open. A man with an eyepatch rose up from the floor and looked toward the stairway, giving some instructions to one of his companions.

Ben jumped back behind the door and heard the sound of footfalls approaching from down the hallway. Lifting the blackjack, he waited. The man raced into the stairwell. Ben drew back his hand, then sent it down in a powerful arc. The Celestial saw Ben and opened his mouth to cry, but the club plowed into the side of his head. His expression went blank, and a moment of surprise in his eyes was replaced by whiteness as they rolled up. He collapsed on his knees. Ben grabbed him around the chest before he could fall on his face, and dragged him away from the door.

As he did, Ben saw the man with the eyepatch looking at him, stunned for a moment. The sinister one-eyed man gave out a cry, and five men charged down the hallway toward Ben. He slammed the door and rolled the unconscious man against it. That would delay them long enough for him to find the basement.

Ben darted down the stairs as the attackers pounded the door behind him. The stairway ended at a door. Dropping the blackjack, he grabbed the doorknob. It was locked! He shoved his hand into his pocket, pulled out the ring of keys he had taken from the Celestial outside. In the dimness he tried one, then another, a third and then a fourth. None worked. Then a fifth and a sixth. His hand shook as he slipped the seventh key in and turned it. The lock clicked. Jerking the key free, he shoved keys back in his pocket just as he heard the door up above clatter open and the sound of footsteps on the stairs.

Ben took the pistol in his right hand and aimed it for the top of the landing above him. He saw a ball of blue cloth round the corner, then a flash of metal. The attacker dove back around the corner as Ben fired. His bullet thudded into the wall just as he heard something snap and vibrate in the door frame beside him. A knife had missed his head by three inches. He shot again and heard voices around the bend.

Ben grabbed the doorknob and pushed the door open. He stood for a moment, his gun pointing up the stairway, and waited for another charge, but the Chinese were still arguing out a plan. He turned the gun toward the basement and stepped on the landing. He saw the flicker of a candle, but nothing else.

"Hoss. You down here, Hoss?"

"Pa, that you?" Hoss couldn't believe it.

"Yes, son," Ben replied, moving quickly inside and shutting the door behind him. He bounded down the steps to the basement floor.

Hoss lowered his gun. "Pa, what are you doing here?"

Ben grinned. "I could ask you the same thing, but let's save our questions for later. Right now, we've got to get out of here. Is Hop Sing here?"

"Hop Sing here," the cook said weakly from the corner.

"Yeah, Pa, there's eight of us now, not counting you."

"What?" Ben shot back.

"Me, Hop Sing, Aldina, and five little Chinese girls. That's what this has been all about, Pa."

Ben held up his hand. "Quiet!" He pointed to the door. "Trouble coming."

No sooner had he finished his sentence than the door flew open and five men rushed inside. Despite his bullet wounds, Chu Sai dove off the stairs at Ben. Hoss fired at the leaping man but missed. Ben shot wildly as Chu Sai landed on him, knocking him to the planking, Ben's gun sliding toward the corner, where Hop Sing and Aldina protected the girls.

Hoss fired and missed again, then snapped the trigger twice more, the gun misfiring each time. He'd strangle that gunsmith, he thought, as three attackers leaped toward him. Hoss dodged a hatchet and retaliated with a pile-driving punch to the gut, the air gushing out of the assailant's lungs and the hatchet falling from his grasp. Hoss slammed the barrel of the gun into the ear of this attacker, then kicked the hatchet back toward the far corner as another assailant thrust a knife at him. Fortunately for Hoss, he'd tripped and fallen on his back while retreating, the knife missing him. The knife-thrower's momentum carried him foward, and he fell. Hoss struck him on the back of the head with his revolver and the man went limp.

As another knife-wielding assailant rushed him, Hoss lifted his gun and fired, striking the man in the wrist. Hoss pounced up to take the charge, but the assailant dropped the knife and grabbed at his hand, falling to his knees and howling. Hoss drew back his leg and kicked him in the face. The man fell like a rock.

Jumping toward the door, Hoss saw his father pummeling one of the attackers with his fists, then spotted Chu Sai with a hatchet in his bloody hand, circling around behind Ben. Hoss darted for Chu Sai and grabbed his queue. With all his might, he jerked Chu Sai away from his father just as the hatchet started forward. Chu Sai's neck popped and he screamed. The hatchet flew harmlessly across the room. Hoss snapped the queue again and Chu Sai collapsed on the ground.

Hoss jumped on him and slugged him across his scarred face with the barrel of the revolver again and again until Aldina was beside him.

"No, Hoss, don't kill him, much as he deserves it," she said.

He glanced up, looking into her green eyes, wide with fear. The anger in him still raged, but he shoved himself away from Chu Sai and turned to help has father, who had knocked the final attacker unconscious. Straightening up, Hoss shook his shoulders and flexed his arms as he shoved his revolver back in his britches. He looked about the room, his gaze stopping on Hop Sing, who was gingerly tending the spot on his head where he'd been slugged, and the five Chinese girls cowering in the corner. His anger began to grow again, and he stomped around the room, mumbling. Hearing one of the Chinese moan, Hoss strode to him, bent over and shook his fist in the man's nose. "Just try something," he challenged.

"They're all out," Ben said, patting Hoss on the shoulder.

Hoss spun around. "It ain't right, Pa, them treating these girls this way. They need more punishment than this."

Nodding, Ben patted Hoss's shoulder again. "You're right, son, but that's the law's job."

Abruptly, Hoss smiled. "I know what I'll do," he said, bending over and picking up a hatchet. Slowly, he bent over Chu Sai, holding the hatchet high.

As the blade started down, Aldina yelled, "No!" Then the hatchet thudded into the floor, slicing Chu Sai's queue from his scalp.

"What they did to these girls or planned to do, they don't deserve to go to heaven," Hoss said.

One by one each unconscious man in the room had his immortality cut off. As Hoss moved around the room, his smile grew with each queue he added to his collection.

"There's one up the stairs by the door," Ben offered.

Hoss bounded up the basement steps and then up the stairs, disappearing around the turn.

Ben said to Aldina, "You must be a friend of Hoss's. I'm his father, Ben Cartwright." He offered her his hand.

Graciously, she took it. "What a pleasure, Mr. Cartwright. I'm Aldina Cuthbert."

"The pleasure is mine," he said as Hop Sing stepped up and offered Ben his revolver, which he had retrieved from the floor. "We've got a lot to talk about, I'm sure, but we best gather up these girls and get out of here." Ben slipped his revolver back in his pants pocket.

Hoss bounded back into the room, waving the queues like a Comanche would display scalps, then he dug into his shirt and pulled out the one he had taken first, from the man he had caught at the trapdoor. "Seven pigtails. Seven Chinamen'll worry the rest of their lives whether they'll make it to heaven." He shook the queues in triumph. "Serves them right for selling these girls for slaves."

Ben twisted his head around, surprised. "These men were selling these girls as slaves?"

"That's right, Mr. Cartwright," said Aldina. "Planning on using them as prostitutes or selling them."

"It's true, Pa, they sell them like livestock. Hop Sing and I bought one."

Ben shook his head. "You've got a lot of explaining to do, Hoss, starting with how you and Hop Sing got from the Ponderosa to San Francisco and Chinatown."

"And you've gotta tell us how you found us," Hoss said, studying his father from head to foot, "and why you're just wearing socks."

Everyone laughed. Even the girls joined in when they understood these people were their rescuers and they were no longer prisoners. One girl, with wide almond eyes and a striking complexion, clung to Hop Sing's leg. All the girls were cute, but this one was beautiful. No wonder she had been so valuable, Hoss thought, staring at Hop Sing's niece. Then he was angry at himself for thinking of the girl like that, because that was how their captors had thought of her.

"Let's get out of here," he said.

"I'm ready," Aldina replied, and began to herd the girls out of the corner and toward the stairs. The girls' eyes filled with fright as they slipped past the men who had abused them and kept them tied to the basement floor.

"The front door's barred and padlocked," Hoss said.

Ben pulled the ring of keys from his pocket and rattled it. Hop Sing's niece giggled at the pleasant sound. "Something else I'll have to explain," Ben said as he motioned for Aldina and then Hop Sing to go up the stairs.

"Pa," Hoss said, slapping Ben on the shoulders, "I

never was any gladder or any more surprised to see you than when you came in that door."

They marched up the stairs, Hop Sing and his niece leading the way, followed by the other four girls under Aldina's watchful eye, then Ben and Hoss. They passed the unconscious man at the stairway door, then marched down the hall, Ben moving ahead of the pack to the padlock. The third key worked, and he unhooked the padlock, lifted the bar and dropped it on the floor beside the wall. He swung the door open and let the others pass, slapping Hoss on the shoulders as his son went by. Outside, Ben inspected the stoop and the walk for his boots, but they were gone, as he knew they would be, as was his coat. He turned back, grabbed the iron gate and slammed it in place, then he used the padlock he had taken from the inner door, snapping it in the latch. "That'll keep them for a while."

Hoss stepped off the porch, lifting the queues, drawing the stares and pointing fingers of several passing Celestials, who watched, mouths agape. As Ben stepped off the stoop, Hoss laid the queues out in a perfect line, one beside the other, until all seven were in a precise row. Hoss had never seen such horror as that reflected in the eyes of the passing Celestials. He waved his index finger at them. "This is what'll happen to you that buy and sell girls like these." Several men scurried on by.

Ben pointed down a side street. "That's where I tied my horse, if he isn't gone like my boots."

The adults herded the girls toward the horse, moving in a pack. Both Hoss and Ben watched warily for threats from the Celestials, but the crowd gave them a wide berth.

Hoss took a deep breath, and suddenly Chinatown didn't smell so bad. Aldina grabbed his free hand and squeezed it. He looked at her, realizing he had never seen such beauty as Aldina radiated. She was an attractive woman, yes, but hers was an inner beauty that went deeper than flesh, extending all the way to the heart.

"We saved five lives today, Hoss, five girls from a degrading existence. I've never saved more than one at a time before, but there's so many more that must be saved."

Hoss squeezed her hand. "Chinatown may not be safe for you anymore."

"I'm more scared than ever before," she admitted, "but more determined than ever to put a stop to this. Just look at Hop Sing and his niece. Isn't she beautiful?"

Hop Sing seemed to swell with pride at her comment. Then he picked up his niece and turned her around to face Hoss and Aldina. Everyone stopped for a moment, Hoss studying the resemblance between the girl and Hop Sing, the wide eyes and the delicate cheekbones.

Ben looked from Hop Sing and the girls to Hoss and Aldina. "We've much to celebrate, don't we?"

CHAPTER 23

They rode and walked to the Palace Hotel, alternating the little girls with Hop Sing on the horse. Hop Sing was still groggy from the blow to the head, but his spirits had been lifted by finding his niece.

Hoss told his father of following Hop Sing from the Ponderosa, reciting Ben's edict not to return home without him. He told of the confrontation on the train, the unfortunate incident at the Palace registration desk, the fight with the Irish at the docks, the opium den, the slave auction, meeting Aldina, the quack doctor and the rattlesnake, the attack in Aldina's home, the meeting with gambling kingpin Chan Tan Tan, and the rescue of the girls.

Ben spoke of coming to San Francisco to check Davey Kendall on the timber leases and of receiving Hoss's note about the police from the young attorney. And he told how he got into the building.

"You climbed the wall?" Aldina asked in disbelief.

Ben smiled. "Yes, ma'am. I was once a sailor. Climbing masts on rolling decks broke me of a fear of heights long ago."

She looked down at his stocking feet. "You sure you don't want to ride instead of the girls? This walk must be hard on your feet."

"I'm fine. My old callused feet'll make it just fine, thanks, and we're not that far from the Palace."

"Pa," Hoss said, "where you planning on staying the night? The Palace won't accept Chinese for lodging."

"I bet we can convince them otherwise, son. We may have to tear up another register."

Hoss laughed. "That didn't work the first time."

They turned the corner and the Palace loomed ahead. "Miss Cuthbert, would you care to spend the evening in the Palace? It would be my pleasure to treat you to a room. And I think I might just be able to arrange for you to attend the opera tonight."

Aldina touched her hand to her hair. "I don't know. I'd like to, but I don't have anything to wear."

"Way I figure it," Ben replied, "the Cartwrights owe you for a few nights lodging of Hoss and Hop Sing."

"I'll go, if Hoss will escort me," she said.

Hoss grimaced. He took off his hat and rolled the brim in his hand. "Aw, Aldina, I'm not much for the opera."

"Please."

Hoss looked at Ben, scowling. "As long as I don't have to wear no tie, Pa, I'll go this time."

"Excellent," Ben replied. "I'll check with Claudia Morris Thomason, make sure she has an extra seat in her box."

"A box! Claudia Morris Thomason?" Aldina said. "Why, I've read about her, the wealthy philanthropist. You know her, Mr. Cartwright?"

"I am proud to say I do. A fine woman wealth hasn't spoiled."

Hoss laughed. "Pa's sweet on the widow Thomason. She won't give up San Francisco for him and he won't give up the Ponderosa for her."

"The Ponderosa must be a special place," Aldina answered.

"It is," Ben and Hoss said in unison, then both laughed together.

Ben pointed to a shop opposite the Palace. "You can get a suit of clothes—no tie—in there, Hoss. And Aldina, there are dress shops in the Palace you can use. Just tell them Ben Cartwright's handling the payment."

"Thank you, sir, thank you. And Hoss, thank you for agreeing to escort me. I've grown fond of you over the past few days."

Hoss pulled his hat down over his head to cover the flush of his face. "It's been an adventure, but I'll be glad to get away from all these people—and the opera, nothing against you Aldina—and back to the Ponderosa."

Ben led the horse into the grand entryway and gave the reins to an attendant. "Tend him," he said, helping two of the Chinese girls down. They stared in wide-eyed amazement all around them. After seeing cages and basements and dingy slave-auction houses in San Francisco, the Palace was indeed a palace in their eyes, its interior bright, its glass windows and crystal chandeliers glistening in the gaslight.

"Follow me," Ben called out, and everyone fell in line behind him. They marched past the doorman into the lobby and headed straight for the registration desk. Every head in the lobby turned to watch, staring at Ben in his bare feet, Aldina with her mussed hair, Hoss with his massive shoulders, Hop Sing with his shuffling gait, and the five Chinese girls moving meekly through the lobby, oblivious to all of the stares because of their awe of the Palace.

The three clerks behind the desk paused in attending other guests and watched as Ben strode up. Ben slapped the bell a couple times and a fourth attendant emerged from a room behind the pigeonholed wall opposite the counter. For a moment the clerk stood dumbstruck, then he lifted his finger and pointed at Hoss.

"It's him," he said, "Horse."

Hoss's eyes narrowed and he stepped up to the counter. This was the one who had refused Hop Sing a room. The one who had angered Hoss so much that he'd ripped the guest register in half.

The clerk looked from Hoss to the dismembered guest register still awaiting its replacement.

"We need four rooms as near mine as possible," Ben said.

Adjusting the glasses on his nose, the clerk advanced to the counter. "Four rooms? For whom?" he intoned.

"For my guests, whom you see before you, son."

"I'm sorry, sir, we don't allow Chinese in the Palace."

"I believe you do, son, or I'll have a talk with the manager."

The clerk paled, his gaze moving from Ben to Hoss to Aldina and then the girls and finally Hop Sing. The clerk could not tell whether Ben was bluffing or not.

Hoss smirked, seeing the anger mingled with uncertainty in the clerk's eyes. "Do you understand English?" he asked.

Ben slapped his palm against the desk bell. "Either sign us up or get the manager."

The clerk gulped.

Hoss threw out his chest and cocked his head. "We're waiting."

"Yes, sir, Mr. Horse," he replied. "Excuse me one moment." The clerk disappeared through the door behind the counter. In a moment he returned with the manager, a handsome man with a gentle smile, patient eyes, and a rose pinned to his lapel.

"Afternoon, Mr. Cartwright, how may we be of assistance at the Palace?"

The clerk paled at the manager's familiarity with Ben Cartwright. Hoss, enjoying the clerk's discomfort, rocked back on his heels, awaiting the man's humiliation.

"We'd like four more rooms, but your employee doesn't care to provide them," Ben said, leaning over the counter.

Turning to his supervisor, the clerk frowned. "But, sir, we don't rent rooms to Chinese. Hotel policy."

The manager placed both hands on his hips and stared full into the clerk's nervous eyes. "Mr. Cartwright and his son are not Chinese."

"But—But what about the others?" the clerk said, pointing at Hop Sing and the girls.

The manager peered around the clerk, stroked his chin and shook his head. "They look Irish to me."

The clerk's face reddened at Hoss's laughter.

"We treat the Irish with respect in this hotel," the manager lectured, "so grant Mr. Cartwright's request and accommodate him any way you must or we'll find someone who can."

"I want rooms as close to mine as possible," Ben said.

Turning to Ben and Hoss, the manager nodded. "If there's anything else I personally can do for you during your stay, Mr. Cartwright, please contact me. We value your business." The manager glanced over his shoulder at the clerk. "Mr. Cartwright is a man of considerable influence on the Comstock Lode." That said, the manager spun around and strode back into his office.

Meekly, the clerk went to registering the Cartwrights, fumbling with the pen and almost knocking over the ink well. He slid the guest register toward Hoss and offered him the pen. "Please sign the register, Mr. Horse."

Hoss jerked the pen from the clerk's hand. "It's Hoss. H-O-S-S, not Horse. You can call me Mr. Hoss."

"Yes, sir, Mr. Hoss."

Aldina snickered with Hoss, who signed his name, then gave the pen to her. She entered her own name upon the register in a delicate hand.

The clerk leaned over the desk and motioned around Hoss. "You, Mr. Irishman, you want to sign in."

Ben pointed to the register as Aldina turned around and gave Hop Sing the pen. "Sign it, Hop Sing," Ben instructed.

Hop Sing stepped meekly to the counter and worked the pen over one of the blue lines in the register. When he stepped back from the counter, the clerk studied the Chinese mark. "An Irish name if I ever saw one," he said with a bit of a sneer, then twisted around and pulled keys from four adjacent pigeonholes.

Ben pulled his watch from his pocket and glanced at the time. Half past noon. He had to see Davey Kendall at three o'clock, and before then, he had to purchase some footwear and get a message to Claudia Morris Thomason, to see if she had room in her box for Aldina. He took a piece of stationery from the registration desk and quickly wrote a note to Claudia. Folding the paper, he slipped it in an envelope, wrote Claudia's name and address upon it, and gave it to the clerk. "See that this is delivered to Mrs. Thomason's home promptly," he instructed, "and have your messenger await an answer."

"Yes, sir, Mr. Cartwright."

Ben and Hoss herded the girls from the registration desk toward a hydraulic elevator. The girls stepped tentatively inside, then clasped each other when the doors shut. Their eyes widened when the operator pulled the lever and the elevator began its ascent. When the door opened at their floor, Hop Sing had to explain to the girls that an elevator took the place of stairs.

Ben led the crew around the hall to the first of their rooms. "This is yours, Aldina, and I figured the girls should sleep in the room next to yours, there's a door between. Hop Sing and Hoss have separate rooms."

"Thank you, you're so generous," she said as Ben took the key and opened her door, motioning for her and the girls to enter.

Aldina walked inside as wide-eyed as the girls had been in the elevator. The room was a soft pink with lacy curtains and delicate furniture. "It's beautiful," she said, clasping her hands together before her breast. "I'd read about the Palace, but I'd always thought it was exaggeration."

"In the bathroom," Ben said, "you'll find hot running water."

"This is luxury, thank you."

"You're welcome. Now, in thirty minutes, let's meet downstairs for lunch. I've an appointment this afternoon, and I know you and Hoss have some clothes to buy." Ben tossed Hoss and Hop Sing their keys. "See you shortly after I've bought some boots."

"Don't be late, Pa," Hoss warned, "I'm hungry as a bear."

"That's one thing that never changes, Hoss." Ben laughed as he retreated back down the hall.

He went downstairs and bought a new pair of boots, which would serve him until he returned to the Ponderosa and Carson City. He found the tailor the Palace kept on call and had him take measurements for a suit to be delivered that afternoon, so he could wear a new one to the opera with Claudia Morris Thomason. Then he joined Hoss and the others for lunch. As they waited for their food, Hop Sing discussed what he should do with his niece. He did not want to return her to China, for fear she would be stolen again, but he did not feel he could raise her on the Ponderosa. Ben promised to help find a suitable home for her. When the food came, Ben ate quickly, then retired to his room to bathe and dress for his meeting with Davey Kendall.

Now that Hoss was safe, Ben had the timber leases to worry about. He wondered if he was doing the right thing by Davey. Deep in his gut, he felt he should insist on withdrawing the bid, but Davey was so adamant about that, for his late father's sake, that Ben felt he had let emotion rather than his knowledge of right and wrong influence him.

Ben departed the hotel, advising the hotel detective to keep an eye on the rooms with Hop Sing, the girls, and Aldina in case trouble followed them from Chinatown. He walked briskly down the streets, circling one block twice just to kill a bit of time. He would arrive at three o'clock. Precisely.

Reaching the corner by the Kendall office, he looked up at the office window and was surprised to see Davey gazing down upon him. There was a wisp of a smile visible behind the pipe the lawyer had clenched between his teeth.

Davey nodded at Ben, then backed away from the window. By the time Ben reached the door, Davey had opened it and was gesturing for him to come in. After shaking Ben's hand, Davey motioned for him to go on into the office. Closing the outside door, Davey followed Ben inside, closing the office door as well.

"Did you find Hoss?" Davey asked, walking behind his desk and slipping into the overstuffed leather chair.

"Yes, thanks to you," Ben replied, lowering himself

into a chair opposite Kendall. "Hoss would've been in a spot of difficulty if you hadn't given me the note."

"The woman? She ever identify herself?"

"Aldina Cuthbert, a reformer who's out to break the slave trade of young Chinese girls."

"Didn't know we still had slaves in this country."

Ben nodded. "There's a lot we don't know about the Chinese."

"I'm glad Hoss is safe, Mr. Cartwright," Davey said, "but you and I know we're not here to talk about family."

He leaned forward and picked up two envelopes from the desk. He offered them to Ben, who took them and held them in his hand. One was thick and heavy, the other thin.

"Mr. Cartwright, I think you'll find everything you want inside those envelopes.

"The leases went through?"

Davey nodded, a sly smile working its way across his face. "If you'd just been more patient with me, Mr. Cartwright, you'd've known none of the seamier details."

Ben tore off the end of the thick envelope with the government seal affixed to it, then pulled out a clump of legal papers. He perused them quickly and he couldn't help but smile. The lease had been secured.

"All that's required now, Mr. Cartwright, is your signature on the lease papers. That and a draft for $75,000 I can deliver to the federal building tomorrow."

"The money's been deposited with Wells Fargo. That will be no problem. I shall have them handle the monetary arrangements." Ben read the contract carefully.

As he did, Davey Kendall stood up and walked around the room, pausing at the window and watching the traffic on the street. "You'll find it all in order, not a thing for you to worry about," he said over his shoulder.

"I always read a contract before I sign it, Davey."

"Didn't mean for you to think otherwise, Mr. Cartwright, it's just that I gave this one everything. It meant that much to me to keep my father's reputation whole. A lot of people come out of the woodwork after a man's death, like buzzards over carrion, and try to destroy a man's good name. I would not let that happen to Father."

Ben looked up from the contract, staring at Davey profiled before the window. "He was a good man, Davey. A damn good man. When I look, I see a lot of him in you."

"Thank you, Mr. Cartwright. Nothing you could have said would've made me feel prouder."

After going over the contract twice, Ben had to agree that Davey had dotted every *i* and crossed every *t*. He leaned over Davey's desk and took the pen from the adjacent ink well, carefully writing his name on the contract, then blotting the excess ink away.

"There you are, sir. She's signed and ready." Ben picked up the thin envelope still in his lap. "I suppose this is your bill."

"There's no bill on this one, Mr. Cartwright. None."

"You'll not impress me by refusing to take pay that's rightfully yours."

Davey spun around, jerked the pipe from his mouth and pointed the stem at Ben. "I'm not trying to impress anybody, Mr. Cartwright. I tried to save my father's name and now I'm trying to save yours. If you don't pay me anything, then in no way can you be linked to the bribe. It doesn't sit well with me that I paid a bribe, but that's how far I'd go for my father's good name."

Ben nodded. "No offense meant, Davey." He opened the second envelope and pulled from it a single sheet of paper. Ben unfolded and read it silently. It was a gracious letter of resignation as the Cartwright's legal representation in San Francisco.

"Whoever you designate as your attorney for future business will have my full cooperation during any transition period, Mr. Cartwright," Davey said.

Ben shook his head and slowly ripped the letter in half. "When I came here yesterday, I didn't think you had the integrity of your father. I don't fully approve of what you did, but I understand your reasoning. I hope my sons will be as proud of my name when I die. I've misjudged you, Davey Kendall. You've got your father's look and your father's integrity. I'm retaining you."

CHAPTER 24

The carriage arrived precisely at seven-thirty in the grand entry of the Palace Hotel. It was a fine carriage, built of mahogany and trimmed with brass fittings. Between the velvet curtains that covered each window, Ben Cartwright saw the elegant smile of Claudia Morris Thomason. "Here's our carriage," he said as the matching gray horses came to a stop among the other vehicles loading and unloading passengers at the Palace.

Hoss stood in a new suit and a stiff shirt. The only thing that could have made him more uncomfortable was a tie, though he had to admit it was a pleasure to be seen with Aldina. She had selected a frilly dress of gray, trimmed in black lace around the high collar, the cuffs, the hem, and the front pleat. The dress was gathered in front with a lacy bow at the waist. She had taken her brown hair out of a bun and combed it long, adding black ribbons. A strand of pearls graced her neck. She wore a blush of rouge and a hint of lip coloring, all subtle, yet highlighting the gaiety in her green eyes.

"I've never felt so—so wealthy," she told Hoss, squeezing his arm as one of the Palace attendants opened the door of the carriage.

Ben stepped to the door. "Evening, Claudia, punctual as always," he said, offering his arm. She stepped delicately on the step then easily inside. "Aldina Cuthbert, please meet Claudia Morris Thomason."

The two women exchanged greetings as Ben and Hoss climbed inside.

"Evening, Hoss," Claudia said. "I'm delighted you and Miss Cuthbert could join us for the opera. As I recall, Adam has joined Benjamin and myself a time or two at the opera, but never you." She leaned forward, taking Hoss's massive hand and patting it. She spoke sincerely, without condescension. "The opera is always so much more entertaining with good friends and company."

"And without a tie," Hoss answered, running his finger along the stiff collar of his new shirt.

Both Aldina and Claudia laughed.

"We've much to celebrate tonight," Ben said. "Hoss and Aldina saved five girls from Chinatown, and I've secured the government timber leases I was after."

"Then congratulations are in order, Benjamin," Claudia said, "but tell me, Aldina, how you saved five girls in Chinatown."

As the carriage exited the grand entry of the Palace and turned north on Montgomery Street, Aldina related the story of her crusade to stop the abuse of young girls in Chinatown.

"I've never heard of such," Claudia said, looking at Ben as if she could not believe it.

"It's true, ma'am," Hoss interjected. "I even bought a sickly one for sixty-three dollars." Hoss snapped his fingers. "Pa, I got away from the Ponderosa without my gun and any money. I've borrowed plenty from Hop Sing, and we need to repay him."

Ben nodded. "We'll take care of it."

Claudia Morris Thomason shook her head and stared at Hoss in disbelief. "You actually bought a girl?"

Hoss nodded. "Could've done with her what I wanted, but Aldina attacked me with her purse."

Aldina blushed for a moment. "I thought he had bought her to abuse her like the Chinese men do."

"She was sickly," Hoss explained, "the type of girl who would have had a hard life."

"And a short one," Aldina interjected. "There's hundreds of these girls, kidnapped from their homes in China, brought over here and hidden in the alleys and squalid rooms of Chinatown just for the pleasure of men. It's sickening."

Claudia held up her hand. "But tell me, Hoss, what were you doing in Chinatown anyway?"

Hoss explained how he had followed Hop Sing to San Francisco and what he had seen, from girls being driven through the streets in cages to their being sold to the highest bidders.

At times Claudia would lift her gloved hand to her neck and shake her head in disbelief. Occasionally Aldina offered details that Hoss had neglected.

As the carriage approached the opera house, a stately building with light pouring out of all its windows and people pouring in its doors for the evening performance, Hoss suspended his story.

"Tonight," Claudia explained, "the opera company is presenting *Der Freischutz.*"

"It's a romantic opera by the German Carl Maria von Weber," Ben added.

"Sounds exciting," Aldina said. "I've never been to the opera before."

Hoss grimaced. "Pa's dragged me to too many."

The carriage stopped. Instantly, the door was opened and Ben and Hoss climbed out, each waiting to assist his companion. Hoss aided Aldina, then stepped aside as Ben offered his arm to Claudia. Hoss took a deep breath, not particularly relishing the prissy entertainment ahead for the night, but enjoying the squeeze of Aldina's hand around his arm.

As Ben and Claudia started up the steps to the opera house, both Hoss and Aldina were amazed by the number of people who addressed Claudia. She was certainly well-respected and liked by the moneyed of San Francisco. There was nothing phony in the greetings she received or in her response. A surprising number as well greeted Ben, who each time was obliged to introduce Hoss and Aldina. Hoss hated those introductions. He never knew what to say. He didn't have much in common with these city folks anyway, all dandified in their city suits and ties. He wanted to be back on the Ponderosa, where life was simpler.

But Aldina, by contrast, seemed to enjoy the attention, and she stared at the wealthy women in their beautiful dresses and jewels, and the men with their diamond stickpins and silk cravats. It was the type of show that made city life exciting.

Gradually, Claudia and Ben made their way up the marble steps toward the private boxes, and shortly they had escaped the crowd. The box overlooked the right side of the stage and the orchestra pit where the musicians were tuning their instruments amid the noise of the entering crowd. Claudia's box contained two rows of four seats each. "Please be seated," Claudia said. "It will just be the four of us, so we'll have plenty of room." She took Hoss's hand and patted it. "Once we're seated, please finish relating what happened in Chinatown." There was sincere interest in her voice.

All four settled into their chairs, the women beside each other in the middle, Ben and Hoss on either end. Hoss resumed his story, Claudia shaking her head frequently. Aldina added her perspective on Chinatown, speaking of all the work she had done there and of the futility she had experienced in trying to right the wrongs.

Then the lights dimmed and the opera began, a story set in a forest with simple country people as its characters. The orchestra played dramatic music that caught the sounds of nature and of the supernatural forces at work in the play. At one point Aldina leaned over to Hoss and whispered, "At least it's set in the forest instead of in some dirty, crowded city." With a hint of sadness in her voice, she smiled, squeezed his hand and rested her head on his shoulder.

Hoss liked her closeness, the soft touch of her hair, the aroma of her perfume. She was a fine woman, except that she liked the city too much; and an attractive one, the type a man would be proud to have as a ... Hoss didn't complete his thought. He knew it was futile; too many barriers would prevent them from ever marrying. It was a pleasant thought, nonetheless.

Between acts, Hoss and Ben slipped out of the box to stretch for a moment, leaving Aldina alone with Claudia.

"Thank you for the invitation to join you, Mrs. Thomason," Aldina said. "I've never been to the opera before."

"You must come back with me," Claudia replied, taking Aldina's hands in hers. After a moment, she asked, "You like Hoss, don't you?"

"It shows that much?"

"To another woman, yes."

Aldina blushed. "I've grown fond of him the last few days. We've been through a lot together."

"I'm fond of Benjamin," Claudia said, "but I see you and Hoss are the same as us. You are as committed as I am to your work—your calling, if you will. The Cartwright men are as dedicated to their Ponderosa as we are to our work. We can't give up our callings to join them, and they can't leave the Ponderosa long to join us in the city. Hoss is a fine man, in many ways the best of Benjamin's three sons, but sometimes I think each is fearful of committing to a woman after what happened to Benjamin's wives."

"Wives?"

"Benjamin had three, all different, and all dying tragically young, each giving him a son. Ben has not remarried since the death of his third wife. It's as if he felt he was bad luck to any woman he married. Fine men, the father and the sons. All I can advise you is to enjoy Hoss when he's in San Francisco, maybe visit him in Nevada, but don't set your life's course by his." Claudia released Aldina's hands.

Ben and Hoss returned to the box and took their seats as the curtain rose on the next act.

"By the way," Claudia whispered to Aldina, "how is your work with the Chinese girls financed?"

"Mostly by donations from the church and what money I can raise," she replied.

Claudia smiled, then turned her gaze back to the stage

as the music built. The four of them sat enjoying the opera, though Hoss did tend to fidget more than the others. When it was concluded, they stood with the audience, clapping enthusiastically.

"Bravo, bravo," Ben called down from the box as the performers took their bows and the curtain slowly fell. "A good opera does something for the soul."

Hoss laughed. "It doesn't do nearly as much as a good meal."

Aldina nudged him with her elbow, giggling as she did. "Enough culture for one night?"

"Enough for a year," Hoss answered as they stepped toward the door and emerged into a hallway crowded with people in fancy dresses and suits.

As Claudia exited on Ben's arm, Aldina took her hand and shook it gently. "Thank you so much for allowing me to join you. And thank you, Mr. Cartwright, for inviting me."

Claudia smiled. "The pleasure was all mine."

"And most of all," Aldina said, releasing Claudia's hands and turning to her escort, "thank you, Hoss, for helping me save those girls." She stood on her tiptoes and kissed Hoss on the cheek.

Hoss's face reddened, but he smiled. The four of them flowed with the crowd toward the stairway and then down into the entry, where the crowd was even thicker. When they emerged outside, the air was cool and Aldina drew herself closer to Hoss.

Ben spotted the carriage and pointed to the end of the block. "There's our ride," he said, adroitly steering Claudia through the crowd. Hoss and Aldina followed in their wake. Ben and Hoss helped the women into the carriage, then climbed in themselves as the driver shut the door and awaited his instructions.

"Would you care to come to my home for dessert?" Claudia asked.

"Yes, ma'am," Hoss answered immediately.

"Home," Claudia instructed the driver.

It took ten minutes for the carriage to clear the traffic around the opera house, but the time passed quickly in conversation. As the carriage made its way toward Nob Hill, Aldina realized where it was going and shook her head in disbelief. "A room with hot running water in the Palace Hotel, a night at the opera, and now dessert on Nob Hill. Heaven can't be much better than this."

Aldina was truly awed when the carriage pulled up in the drive of Claudia's home. "You live here?"

"Yes, my dear, it's a fine home, though not nearly as extravagant as some of the newer mansions about town. But this one has special memories of my husband. It lacked only children to be the perfect home, as far as I was concerned." There was a poignancy in her voice that was lost in the sounds of the driver opening the carriage door.

As Claudia slipped out, Ben thought he detected a tear glistening in her eye. She always got emotional when she remembered that she could never have children. It was a heavy burden for a woman her age to carry, as if she was incomplete for having never borne a child.

By the time Ben caught up with her at the front door, the tear—if it had ever been there to begin with—had evaporated. Carlos stood at the door. "Evening, madam. Was the opera satisfactory?"

"Excellent," Claudia said.

"Good evening, Mr. Cartwright," Carlos greeted Ben. "Welcome," he said to Hoss and Aldina.

"We'd like dessert in fifteen minutes," Claudia instructed Carlos.

"Yes, ma'am, he replied, shutting the door and heading down the paneled hallway.

Aldina stood in awe of the polished wood paneling, the plush carpet beneath her feet, and the paintings on the wall. "It's beautiful, Mrs. Thomason, just beautiful."

"Thank you, but you must remember it is not nearly as beautiful as the work you do with those Chinese girls."

Aldina was flattered.

"Let me show you the rest of the house," Claudia said to Aldina, "if you men wouldn't mind excusing us for a few minutes."

"Certainly not," Ben replied. "Hoss and I will meet you in the parlor when you are done."

The women disappeared as Ben motioned toward the parlor. "She's a fine woman, Hoss."

"Aldina or Claudia?" Hoss responded.

"Both, but I was referring to Aldina."

"She is a good woman, Pa, but she's a city woman. I couldn't stand the city for long."

Nodding, Ben walked over to a bookcase of leather-bound volumes and pulled a collection of poems from among the books. He thumbed through the pages, glancing periodically at his son. "I know, Hoss, believe me, I know."

Shortly, Aldina returned on Claudia's arm, her eyes as wide as her smile. "It's a beautiful home," she said, "I see why you must love it so."

Claudia nodded. "It has many pleasant memories."

Carlos stepped into the room to announce that dessert and coffee were ready in the dining room, and the four of them moved that way, laughing in the hallway. At the dining room door, the aroma of coffee was tantalizing. Inside, the men helped the women into their chairs, then took seats opposite theirs. When all were in place, Carlos appeared with individual cream tarts, which he placed in front of the ladies and then the men. He returned moments later with a silver service of coffee. As he poured, Claudia turned to Aldina.

"I've been thinking, Miss Cuthbert," she began. "Your work seems so worthwhile. I certainly did not know these types of evil activities were going on in Chinatown."

"Yes, ma'am," Aldina said, leaning toward Claudia, "it's indeed sad. So much that needs to be done, and so few people and little money to help."

Claudia smiled softly. "That's where I can help. I have contacts, women—and men too—who can stir things up, bring attention to these crimes. And I have money, money that needs a useful purpose."

"Oh, Mrs. Thomason, that would be an answer to my prayers. It really would."

"And perhaps an answer to mine. These girls, what happens to them?"

"A few find families who will keep them. We must

find a family for Hop Sing's niece," she said, glancing at Ben, who nodded in agreement. "Many, though, are turned over to the orphanages."

"From one unfortunate existence to another, is that correct, Miss Cuthbert?"

"Basically," Aldina replied.

"Then I should like to take these five girls you rescued, raise them in this house. And provide you money to carry on your work. We can change some things in Chinatown."

"Oh, thank you, Mrs. Thomason. Things can be arranged, I am sure."

Ben smiled. "I've never been to an opera yet where something good didn't follow."

"Like dessert," Hoss said, his mouth half full.

Everyone laughed.

CHAPTER 25

Little Joe swallowed hard as Frau Kreidt approached the table with a bowl of potatoes in her hand. She brandished the spoon like a weapon and stabbed the potatoes as she would an enemy. "Potatoes, ja, Tiny Joseph?" she asked, then plopped a wad on his plate. "Ja!" she said, answering her own question, her voice rising like a challenge. She deposited the bowl on the table like a drunk slamming a mug against the bar and disappeared into the kitchen, returning momentarily with a pot of red beans. She ladled more juice than beans onto Little Joe's plate, soaking the potatoes and flooding the plate, then plunged the ladle back into the pot and jerked it out with another serving.

Little Joe held up his hand. "Plenty, no more," he said without looking up from the beans. All he could think about was Hop Sing's cooking. Always consistent. Always good. And always served without intimidation. Oh, how he missed Hop Sing and his tolerance. Little Joe had made the mistake of criticizing Frau Kreidt's first meal at the Ponderosa, and she had never forgotten. Each meal since had become a test of wills. Little Joe promised himself that if only Hop Sing would return, he would never take Hop Sing for granted again or do anything that might insult him.

Frau Kreidt dropped the pot of beans on the table, rat-

225

tling the dishes. Escaping to the kitchen again, she returned with a platter of sliced roast beef. The outside was crusty with char, the inside still red in places. He could have done as well, Little Joe thought. He swallowed again, then held his breath as Frau Kreidt stabbed a few slices of meat and dropped them on his plate, splattering a bit of bean juice onto the tablecloth. Frau Kreidt slid the platter onto the table and backed away from Little Joe's chair. Crossing her arms across her abundant breast, she stared at Little Joe, daring him to eat, and most of all daring him to criticize her food.

Little Joe grimaced at the unappealing roast beef, an island of meat in a sea of bean juice. He took up his fork and knife, holding them as cautiously as he would instruments of death. He carved a piece of meat and forked it into his mouth. It tasted even worse than it looked. His lips twisted into a frown which he disguised by shoving a forkful of beans and potatoes into his mouth.

"Okay, ja?" Frau Kreidt asked.

"Okay," he said, waving the knife at the corpulent cook, hoping she would retreat into the kitchen. The beans were burnt and the potatoes uncooked in the middle. This meal would rank with every other one Frau Kreidt had prepared at the Ponderosa as among the worst he had ever eaten anywhere.

Frau Kreidt circled the table like a buzzard waiting for a wounded animal to expire. She spoke spurts of German in a low, menacing voice. "Good, ja?" she asked again.

Little Joe nodded, taking a deep breath before sliding another forkful of supper into his mouth. A noise at the front door gave Little Joe hope. Maybe it was Hop Sing, returning. He could only hope, but his wishes were dashed as Adam turned the corner.

"Evening, Tiny Joseph," he said, his eyes mocking his little brother. "Evening, Frau Kreidt." He took off his hat to acknowledge the cook.

"Supper, ja?" she asked, putting a hand on the kitchen door to fetch another plate.

Adam patted his stomach. "No thanks," he said, "I've already eaten."

"Chicken," Little Joe snarled.

"Nein," Frau Kreidt shot back, "roast, beans and potatoes."

Adam dropped his hat on the table, pulling up a chair opposite Little Joe to watch him suffer. Frau Kreidt circled the table still, her eyes fixed on Little Joe. Adam locked his fingers behind his neck and stretched back in the chair. "Telegram from San Francisco came today."

Little Joe's eyes lit with anticipation. "Hop Sing? Is he coming back?"

Frau Kreidt scowled.

Adam licked his lips, then shook his head. "Don't you care about Pa and Hoss?"

"You'd have told me if something bad had happened to them. Now what about Hop Sing?"

"He's not coming back," Adam said with as straight a face as he could muster.

Little Joe's face clouded over as Frau Kreidt passed, a look of triumph upon her face. "No?" he said in defeat.

"No," Adam replied.

His knuckles whitening around his fork, Little Joe managed another bite of bad food, but the disappointment was more bitter. He swallowed, then dropped his fork into the middle of the unfinished food.

"Tiny Joseph no like food," Frau Kreidt huffed. She slammed her fist into the kitchen door and it swung open. No sooner did she get her abundant body inside than the door swung shut behind her.

Adam laughed. "Now you've offended the cook, Tiny Joseph."

Little Joe clenched his fists. "If you call me Tiny Joseph one more time, I intend to—"

He stopped abruptly as Frau Kreidt waddled back into the room, carrying an apple strudel, the aroma enticing. She dropped the pan on the table beside Little Joe. "Maybe you like this, ja?" she said, then disappeared back into the kitchen.

Little Joe shoved his plate aside and grabbed a piece

of the strudel. "Her strudel is delicious," he said, slice in hand.

Adam selected a pastry and bit into the flaky crust, nodding in agreement. "Good indeed." He laughed. "But man cannot live by strudel alone."

Scowling, Little Joe grabbed another slice of strudel and gobbled it down. "It's the only thing I've had since she started here that's been worth eating."

"Well, little brother," Adam said, "since you created this problem, then you best solve it."

"I can't teach her how to cook, you know that."

"Let her go, Little Joe, let her go. Find us another cook, a real cook."

The strudel seemed to turn rancid in Little Joe's mouth as he stopped chewing. "You want me to let her go?"

"You want to keep eating her cooking?"

"Nothing but her strudel," Little Joe said, savoring the bite of apple and pastry still warm in his mouth. "But get rid of her?"

"Sometimes it's the only way. You ought to do it before Pa gets back. It might be easier on you that way."

Little Joe finished the strudel in his hand, then grabbed another piece. "After she finishes the dishes."

Aldina's tears in San Francisco still lingered in Hoss's mind, even though that was yesterday. No woman had ever shed a tear over him before. He had promised to write her, but he knew that would be a hard vow to keep regularly. He just wasn't much of a writer. He would never forget her, and he would visit her the next time he was in San Francisco, though having had his fill of the place over the last week, that might not be for months. Maybe now he understood better than ever before his father's feelings about Claudia Morris Thomason.

His spirits had begun to rise once his rented buggy rolled onto Ponderosa land again. He was in the back with Ben's valise and Hop Sing's two bags of belongings, enjoying the earth as God had intended it, far from cities and their problems and corruption. As they neared the ranch house, he began to feel like himself again.

"Well, Pa," Hoss said, "you told me not to return without Hop Sing, and I didn't."

Ben nodded. "But I never thought it would take you to San Francisco."

"Hop Sing," Hoss said, "come tomorrow I believe I could eat a bear or anything else you want to fix. I ain't gonna complain what it is as long as there's plenty of it."

Ben shook his head. "You know 'ain't' isn't proper English."

"Yes, sir," Hoss nodded, "but neither is Hop Sing!"

"Hop Sing no care. Hop Sing only want to cook for Cartwrights."

"Now, Hop Sing," Ben said, "I'm square with you on the money Hoss borrowed."

Hop Sing nodded as Ben pulled the buggy to a halt beside Adam's hitched mount. They gathered their belongings and entered the house.

The instant they came in, Little Joe exploded from his chair and darted toward them, straight to Hop Sing. Little Joe grabbed his hand and pumped it vigorously. "Hop Sing, I am so glad to see you!"

"Your cook didn't work out, Joseph, is that it?" Ben intoned.

Little Joe grinned sheepishly. "Her cooking's worse than mine, except for her apple strudel." Little Joe flinched at the sound of a pan being dropped at the table.

"Worsen than yours, ja, Tiny Joseph?" called Frau Kreidt. She peeled her apron off and threw it at the table.

Adam laughed as he rose to greet Ben and Hoss.

"Ja, ja, then cook your own food better. I quittin' from your insults." Frau Kreidt stormed out of the dining room and into the kitchen. "I need ride to Virginia City," she called over her back.

Ben crossed his arms and stared at Little Joe. "Now, Joseph, what's brought this all about?"

Adam moved to his father's side. "Bad cooking, Pa. She's not a good cook, and Little Joe should have let her go after her first meal."

"Very well," Ben said. "Little Joe, pay her for what she's done and give her two extra weeks pay. Then give her a ride into Carson City and get her a train ticket into Virginia City. You can return the buggy we rented." Ben grinned.

Little Joe nodded. "Yes, sir, Pa."

Adam greeted Hop Sing, then slapped Hoss on the shoulders. "Glad you're back, big fellow. I want to hear all about it, but first, Pa, tell me about the timber leases."

Ben shoved his hand in his coat pocket and pulled out an envelope bulging with papers. "A long, complicated story," he said, waving the contract in Adam's face. "Suffice it to say that young Thornton did some fancy legal maneuvering to correct a mistake of his father's and get us the leases."

"Then there'll be plenty of timber available for the Bristlecone," Adam said.

"And for the Ponderosa."

"This calls for a celebration," Adam said.

Ben nodded. "Hop Sing, how about getting us a fresh bottle of brandy?"

The Chinese cook nodded and scurried toward the kitchen, drawing the Germanic babbling of Frau Kreidt.

Little Joe shook his head and shrugged. "Worst mistake I ever made, hiring Frau Kreidt."

Hop Sing returned momentarily with the brandy and four snifters. He gave one to each Cartwright. Ben opened the bottle as Hop Sing went back to the kitchen, drawing another string of Germanic insults from Frau Kreidt.

Ben poured a glass for himself and each son. "Here's to Davey Thornton."

They clinked glasses and downed the brandy.

"Now," Adam said, "all we've got to worry about is bringing in the Bristlecone."

"That," said Hoss, "and making sure Little Joe can return Frau Kreidt to town without getting hurt, him being a runt up beside her."

They all laughed.

Except Little Joe.

CAMERON JUDD

THE CANEBRAKE MEN

Following the War of Independence against the British, a band of Tennessee settlers intends to carve out a new state. But they face the opposition of the federal government, as well as bloody resistance from the Chickamauga Indians. In this untamed land Owen Killefer will find within himself a spirit as stout and strong as that of any rough-hewn frontiersman.

From one of America's most poweful and authentic frontier storytellers comes a sweeping new saga capturing the vision, the passion, and the pain that gave rise to a glorious new nation—America. This is the unforgettable story of the bold men and women who led the way into an unexplored land and an unknown future, seeking new challenges.